THE RED CHILDREN

Maggie Gee

The Red Children

or,
Likeness

TELEGRAM

TELEGRAM
An imprint of Saqi Books
26 Westbourne Grove
London W2 5RH
www.telegrambooks.com
www.saqibooks.com

Published 2022 by Telegram

A full CIP record for this book is available from the British Library.

ISBN 978 1 84659 213 3
eISBN 978 1 84659 214 0

Printed and bound by CPI Group (UK) Ltd, Croydon, CR0 4YY

'To be sure, what a town Cranford was for kindness.'
Elizabeth Gaskell, *Cranford*

'If a human life is described with enough particularity, the universal will begin to speak through it.'
Kenjo Yoshino, *Covering*

'Let them be themselves. It's all anyone wants. So long as I can be myself too, which means shouting.'
Monica Ludd

PART ONE

I

The first Red people came over by sea.

Once upon a time, Ramadan Baqri, a seventeen-year-old Sea Cadet, arriving at the harbour early to hoist the colours just after the January sun had risen, found them sitting, damp and large and red and shaking with cold, on the edge of the quay. They looked up in wonder at the rising sun to the east, then turned their heads to peer west, over the bright cross-hatched lines of the masts of the yachts, at Ramsgate.

Now it's called Redsgate, the same small town on the southeast point of England. People started to call us Redsgate as a joke, because of the migrants. But who laughs last, laughs longest.

When the Red people came, I had lived here for fifteen years. The first visit I made was a drunken weekend on the beach with two crazy friends, all of us nineteen or twenty. Through the haze of golden smoke and headache, serpents of sunlight made watered silk of the sea. I left the others and went for a walk in the park on the cliff on my own, my head cleared for a moment, the air was green, birds sang, and I vowed to come back.

Clean sandy beaches, white cliffs striped with black flint, riddled with pigeons' nests, gulls' nests, whistling starlings, crows watching out to steal eggs. Though people say nothing ever changed before the Red people came, the chalk's always falling, the earth's always warming or cooling. Over millennia the cliffs have slowly retreated, thirty yards or so every century.

At low tide you see lines of stumpy white pillars like a forest of teeth, that thousands of years ago were cliffs. These thousands-of-years-old cliff-stumps are decked with seaweed every summer, a vivid green slime that came only twenty years ago from the hulls of Chinese cargo-ships. Then they look like stromatolites, layered bacterial rocks four billion years old.

Four billion years ago was the real beginning of this story. Long before the cliffs and the crows, long before humans, love and hatred. Long before there was sea between us and

Europe. Long before our town was built in a cradle between two cliff tops. Long before the Romans and the Vikings, all of whom landed here and fought and died on our beaches – on this stretch of shore where British history, written history at least, began. Those who stayed turned into us, the children of invaders, the British.

Fast forward to our town a dozen or two dozen years ago, before this all started. It had 'heritage' fishing boats, trips to see the seals, its Pugin cliff (Catholic) and its Montefiore cliff (Jewish), arched quayside cafes and local historians and an eager, newly bronzed contingent of Londoners.

As Britain warmed up in the twenty-first century, cities were like ovens, while chilly coastal resorts gained weeks of sunshine. Now only February and March were cold. More city-dwellers moved down, then the waves of virus sent even more, people who could work from home and wanted to escape the hot, germy cages of London. People with cash to flash, who put a quick shine on facades of houses and restaurants and a hopeful look on the faces of people with services to sell. So there were cutting-edge chefs and foragers, writers and whelk-potters, jazz bands and brass bands, actors and bakers, atheists, Hindus and Muslims, builders and binmen, line-dancers and lindy hoppers, smoke-voiced silver influencers in super-sized sunglasses and blue-bereted Sea Cadets passing each other, calling, smiling, many different tribes making friends in the summer streets and cafes. Oh, and ghosts. New ghosts and old ghosts. Ghosts of young men and old friends, ghosts of the invaders, Belgians, Romans, Norsemen, though you have to listen. And paragliding gulls and green parakeets, their shadows crossing and re-crossing us.

It's heaven on earth, but not heaven. The seagulls fight for the roof-ridges with the crows. Someone homeless roars on the beach. Beneath the new money lie decades-old layers of unemployment: a cohort of youth who might never have jobs and whose parents grew old without jobs. Plus the new unemployed who lost jobs when the virus came. There are still a few boarded-up shops and cafes, patches of simmering anger that can be diverted into hatred of others, 'Put Britain First!', a table of PBF orators drinking in a pub.

But wait, they've gone quiet of late, and there's a new wreath at St George's Church on Remembrance Day, a large, bright one, for a man not buried here. A thin blonde woman with a tight face, a teacher from these parts, not a Red person, always leads the mourners. Most years, two ravens attend.

When the Red people came, Ramsgate was rather short of men, for reasons I'll later explain. Like Cranford, that small, lost paradise, we were largely 'possessed by women' – not that we'd chosen that state. As to what part I play in this story, you will decide. An attendant lady can watch and eavesdrop and write things down.

But all kinds of people, and birds, and beasts, and the cliffs, and the wind, at night, the whispering aspens in King George VI Park, the invisible fungi feeding the roots of the trees that hold Ramsgate's East Cliff together, told the story to me. And the ravens, of course. They spoke to me as they flew over.

It was ravens, not Romans, who gave our town its first name, Hraefnesgate, 'Ravensgate', later slurred into Ramsgate … Now Redsgate. Ravens. Black hammer-beaked, ruff-necked birds who were *roarking* and *arking* from over the heavy-browed cliffs long before the Romans, wings flared like strong black fingers. Ravens are messengers, omens who perched on the shoulders of old Norse gods and pointed to past and future.

Ravens, the birds who remember.

Whenever I walk towards Pegwell with my daughter we look for the ravens, and if we see them, she laughs and talks to them, but I listen.

Roark. Aark.

Once upon a time, the ravens noticed something new.

3

Strangers, incomers, migrants.

'They were all touching,' Ramadan Bakri told his girlfriend Sandra Birch. 'And pointing at the masts. And their clothes were wrong.'

Their clothes were a gift from Mrs Jackee West not ten minutes earlier. On her way to open up the Sailors' Church, she was shocked to see four naked people with their arms round each other sitting on the ground, red in the first rays of the sun.

'Oh dear. Oh dear oh dear oh dear,' she clucked at them. 'Too drunk to go home? And lost your clothes?'

But she realised after a second or two they were talking in a language she didn't understand. They hadn't grasped a word she said. One had a draggle of seaweed on his shoulder. Not quite right in the head, maybe? 'Love ye therefore the stranger,' she remembered, from the Bible, and blushed with shame as she went home to fetch some clothes she was saving for a church sale.

'New kind of Youmans,' craa-ahed Roland the Raven, who was watching from the rigging of a large barge, to his mate, Princess Ra. 'Bigger heads than usual, don't you think?'

'Well they've certainly got bigger heads than you,' the Princess said sharply. The wind was cold, and he hadn't provided a nice dead lizard in ages, nor brought sticks to help her patch up their nest.

'Proportionate to my body, I have a very large head.' Which was true: all ravens do. He turned so the wind fluffed up his feathers and gave him a crest of great dignity.

'Youmen do have foolish heads,' she agreed, to placate him, but correcting his grammar very slightly, for she was well educated from her childhood in the Tower of London, growing up surrounded by Youmen, very near the Crown Jewels. She could even read, though this was a sore point with Roland, who didn't believe in human language – 'It's a series of noises, at most.'

When Jackee West came back with her bag of clothes, the weird creatures lit up by the rose-red morning sunlight didn't seem to know how to put them on. One youth pushed his arms into the legs of a pair of trousers. And then they just looked at each other and laughed, then wrapped themselves up any old how in whatever was nearest.

Jackee had brought a pen and paper to help them communicate. But they didn't.

One of them rubbed his hands together to get warm, then took the paper with a growing smile, rested it on the quay and started drawing. Jackee expected them to write foreign words, or to draw what they needed, bread, or a bed. What slowly emerged was a grid of straight lines, intersecting. He was drawing the masts – not all of them, not the actual yachts, just the masts and the way the crossway spars intersected with them like a scaffold for noughts and crosses.

Then he showed it, not to Jackee but the others, who crowed with delight. They pointed at the masts and then his paper as if he had done a portrait of their oldest friend.

Later we got used to them laughing, but Jackee West felt faintly offended. Maybe they were drunk after all?

Liam Birch and his younger brother Joe were taking a detour on their way to the Grammar School for a smoke, and saw skimpily dressed figures loom into view behind Jackee.

'Who are they?' said Joe.

'Mongs,' muttered Liam. 'She's probably shagging them ... Hallo Jackee!'

'Oh Liam,' said Jackee. 'We still miss you at church. Lovely to see you.'

'Yeah and you Jackee.'

As soon as they'd gone a few metres away Liam hissed, 'Fugly. Looked like migrants.'

'What have they done to you?' said Joe. '*You're* a mong.'

Liam punched him, feebly, but winded Joe, who gave a yell of indignation that made Jackee turn round.

'All right, boys?' she said. 'Remember Cain and Abel.' She meant it as a joke, but no-one ever laughed at Jackee's jokes.

'No problem, Jackee,' said Liam, then after she and the shambling figures had vanished into the red-brick church, 'See, she fancies you as well.'

Soon the ambulance Jackee had called turned up, but not the police, and the newcomers were taken away, then released.

A version of what had happened earlier that morning got passed around the town. 'Illegals turned up. Half-a-dozen of them. Bold as brass. And not wearing clothes!'

A little group of lost teenagers who had never been anywhere but Ramsgate met up on the quay after school with an old man with white hair and a purple face, waving a stick, and shouted a protest against whatever had happened, in case, like everything else in life, it was unfair.

Roland flew back in late afternoon to keep an eye on things. The young Youmans were waggling their ugly little arms and hands in temper, which he did not like to see. Most ravens think arms and especially hands obscene, weird unfledged lumps that stick out of people's sides where wings should be. Ruder, rougher ravens call them 'stumpies', but Roland and the Princess only did that in private.

'Put Britain FIRST!' a few of them were shouting in ragged chorus.

Roland had heard those noises before. 'Put Britain FIRST,' he mimicked with his usual uncanny accuracy from the mast of the barge, so the rabble looked around, disturbed – was some tosser mocking them? 'Put Britain FIRST!' sounded from above again, but there was no-one, just a large bird. Roland reported on the scene later as he and the Princess took the last moment of sunlight on the railings by the Lookout café. 'They were all getting mad and flapping their stumpies.'

'Roland!' The Princess thought it her business to keep standards high. She picked up a piece of dried worm from the tarmac, delicately, as was her wont, and flew off to the blue, gnarled Scots pine on top of West Cliff, beyond the end of the promenade, which had been their home for two decades.

Ten minutes later, because of the cold, and their epic journey, and being fussed over and talked at, the newcomers fell dead asleep in their temporary billet in the Sailors' Church, where Jackee West had put them, and forgot the instructions a tall man with bright red hair had given them before they set off. 'Remember to thank the sea when you arrive. Whatever you do, don't forget.'

There was an item on *BBC Southeast Today*. Then the whole thing was almost forgotten by the people of Ramsgate until, a week later, two adolescents in ill-fitting clothes, tall, heavy, holding hands, appeared at the school gates.

Perched on a turret of the Victorian-Gothic house opposite the school, Roland stopped dead, looked very carefully with his shiny black eyes, took off, shot upward just for fun, planed for a moment on his great black wings then folded them and rolled over in a headlong dive, righting himself six feet above the children's heads, landed on the wall of the school playground, jumped sideways to get closer, jump-jump-scratchety-scratchety on the brick, peered carefully across, said 'Hi!', a nearly perfectly human noise, just to make the strange Youmans turn round so he got a better look at them, squawked in alarm and took off at top speed to report what he'd seen to the Princess.

'More of those different Youmans. *Youmen.* Things are going to change.'

4

The School Secretary, Nina Sharon, remembered the story on *BBC Southeast* about the naked 'Red People' on the quay, and called the Acting Head. 'Two Red children have arrived.'

'Red children?'

'It was on TV, Winston. They turned up in the harbour.'

'Oh yes. Really? Here? Have we had the MF20s?'

'No.'

'Documentation of application for refugee status?'

'No.'

'C386?'

'No.'

'Oh dear. I suppose I can talk to the parents and explain we're selective –'

'The parents aren't here.'

'Oh *dear*.'

A long, liberal sigh.

'We're supposed to be a grammar school,' Winston said. 'Why did they choose us?'

'First school they came to, probably,' the Secretary said.

'We are selective. They have to pass the exam.'

After a moment of thought Nina spoke. 'Well, we've had enough stick for that, in the past. There was an awful telly piece two years ago that said we were all white and bright and should lose our charitable status.'

Winston, whose father was black, frowned slightly at that.

'So maybe we ought to do something for these kids.' She hesitated. 'On a temporary basis. Windmills is overcrowded, they can't go there. Get some positive coverage. I met the new woman on *Kent Central*. She wants upbeat stories.'

'You should be in PR, Nina.'

'Don't I know it,' she said. 'But I like Ramsgate.'

'Yes.' Winston Edwards, twenty-eight years old, and only Acting Head because his boss, Neil, had had a breakdown, was a very recent arrival, but he liked it, too. Not that he'd got the measure of it yet. For example, he didn't know his appointment had been aided by the simple fact of his name 'Winston', which had always felt horribly dated, to him – but the oldest governor had commented, 'Male, that's a good thing, and patriotic family, excellent.'

By lunchtime the 'Red children' were both in class. The same class, because although they were different sizes and ages, they refused to be separated. Refused without words, for they spoke no English.

Nina and someone from student counselling tried to lead them in different directions. When tears began to mass on the older child's eyeballs, they were allowed to stay together, holding hands.

The woman on *Kent Central* was off sick, but when she came back, left Nina a message to contact her any time 'specially if there's a feel-good element'.

5

Who were they?

'Red children' is what Nina repeated, in the hearing of the kids of Year 10, when she led the two newcomers through the door. The back row, who were playing on their phones, nudged each other. 'Red people. Like the ones on the news. Shit!'

'Hello,' the two children both said, in turn.

'What's your name?' The teacher, kind Ms Potter, asked the taller one. He just said 'Hello' again, so she asked the second, smaller one, probably a girl, who had red-brown matted dreads. She heard hissing from the back of the room, 'Weirdos.'

'Quiet,' said Ms Potter, who had been thinking the same thing herself. It wasn't that they looked foreign, she was used to that since her mother's side of the family was from Barbados – but they didn't look quite human. Everything was slightly shifted, as if in a drawing.

Finally, the child stopped hiding her face in her thick, shaggy hair. 'Hello,' she said, again, then something else Ms Potter managed to make out when she had repeated it three times. She wrote it on the whiteboard: 'Jebble Tarek? Oh, or Tariq. Is that right?' She gestured at the small one. 'Jebble Tariq. Is that your name?'

The small figure looked at the writing with pleasure, then pointed to her chest. 'Jebble Tariq,' she repeated, and carried two fingers from her lips towards the writing on the board. 'Jebble Tariq?'

When the teacher nodded, the girl laughed, pointed at the writing and said something rapid to her older companion.

'Jebble Tariq,' they said together louder, index fingers stretched towards the board, then each other, laughing. When they finally stopped laughing, they said 'Hello. Thank you!'

Maybe they're brother and sister, the teacher thought. Jebble Tariq might be the family name. 'Divs,' said a boy in the back row. His friend agreed.

'Pakistani,' said Belinda Birch, Head of Year 11, to her daughter Sandra, once she was back home and safely out of hearing of the staffroom. 'They don't look like Pakis but apparently they're called Tariq. Why did they have to come here?'

'Well it's only two children,' said Sandra, who was used to her mum. She wasn't really racist, Sandra thought, for her mum had grown fond of Ramadan, her Sea-Cadet boyfriend, who worked in the phone-shop at weekends and had been the very first person to see the new people on the quay. 'Nice manners,' Mum had said after meeting him, 'unlike some.' Also, Sandra's brother Joe's father was Turkish, which surely proved it. Her mum was just down on everyone when she was in a bad mood.

'You'll see. This is just the beginning.'

Belinda was right. By the end of the week, there were four of them. At the end of the month, there were eight, and they couldn't all be fitted into the same class. But they spent every break time together and, when the bell went for lessons again, they followed each other in a long untidy conga, shouting with laughter as they tried to cram themselves onto three or four vacant chairs.

The children of Ramsgate were interested.

Who were they? Where did they come from? With only a few words in common, they couldn't ask them. They did peculiar things but seemed happy and said, 'Thank you' and

'Hello.' Their laughter was catching. One of the newcomers was challenged to a fight and turned out to be strong and heavy and silent, and won by patience and weight. But they looked so ... different. And they had no phones. How did they get by? Why weren't they bored? It was unnatural.

'Where are they living?' asked one of the mothers when her daughter Jude came home and talked about the newcomers. 'Is it hygienic?' She didn't want to freak out her daughter by mentioning the risk of infection.

'Dunno. Sailors' Church, I think,' said the girl, which silenced her mother, since it was religious.

In fact, after two weeks in the Sailors' Church (where once again, they forgot to say thank you to the sea, though they certainly had a chance) they were sleeping in the Old Fire Station.

Would they be liked? It hung in the balance.

6

At first, the Red children, speaking only a few words of English, were a lot of extra work for the teachers. True, they understood more than they spoke, and one small boy in Year 9, nicknamed 'Little Bighead', was learning at a hundred miles an hour. He was heard swearing in cockney (the accent of Ramsgate, since most people's ancestors came from London), and laughing. What he had found was that some words made people laugh or stop in their tracks, frowning: those words had power. *Fug, Cud*. He had not yet learned when to use them. Little Bighead got into trouble.

Soon he was in worse trouble for imitating to perfection Francis, a boy in his class with special needs and a speech defect, who greeted everyone with 'Yawwight?', which made people laugh. So Little Bighead started squeaking 'Yawwight?' all the time to everyone too, till the class teacher heard and everyone got told off, especially Little Bighead.

In the staffroom, there was unrest.

One Friday at the beginning of the lunch-hour Winston emerged from the door of his office to be faced by a delegation of fiery-faced teachers. Most of them were older than he was. They started talking before they had even got over his threshold.

'We're not racist, obviously –'

'– *obviously* we're not –' (this was embarrassing to state but, they thought, essential, given that Winston himself was mixed race)

'– but our teaching practice is being severely affected.'

'They hardly speak English –'

He knew at once who they meant.

'No, to be fair, that one boy does –'

'– but most of them don't speak at all –'

'– they just keep on laughing –'

'I don't want to be personal but they do smell, you know, some of them smell.'

'One of them brought in a bag of dead birds and expected me to be pleased. Pigeons!'

'There's fungus in pigeon droppings, you can breathe it in. Health and safety issue.'

'Slow down, everyone,' said Winston. 'Come in and sit down.' But there weren't enough chairs. Most of them thronged round his desk, instead.

More complaints, self-righteous, excited: the Red children were always touching or hanging on to each other. 'It raises, you know, issues. Our kids will be doing it too.'

'I've suggested,' said Winston, 'we avoid saying things like "our kids", if possible.'

The Red children wouldn't sit still. Were they even making an effort?

The Red children sang in lessons which had nothing to do with music.

The Red children laughed more than usual in Religious Education.

The Red children were always tipping their chairs back and falling over.

The Red children kept drawing what looked like the criss-cross trellises for games of noughts and crosses on blackboards and indeed any surface they could find, 'although they never fill them in.'

Some of the Red children had started pulling earpieces out of the Ramsgate children's ears when they were listening to music and seemed astonished when they got cross. Red children were also attempting to replace earpieces with feathers, which they collected for reasons that no-one could understand.

'As I said earlier, feathers can cause disease,' said Belinda Birch, crossly, but Ms Potter, who had come along out of curiosity, said, 'Well it's really caught on, now lots of them are wearing feathers or flowers in their hair, and frankly it disturbs their learning less than their mobiles.'

'They shouldn't have mobiles in lessons!'

'No, but they do, Belinda, as you know.'

'Not in my lessons, thank you.'

'Shall we try not to get stuck on this issue?' Winston asked gently.

'I don't want to mention this, but whenever a Red child does you know what –'

'What?'

'– makes, you know, a *smell* –'

'Oh, farts –'

'– which is often, they have no inhibitions, all the others laugh a lot and run around flapping their hands and pulling faces, which makes all the other kids laugh as well.'

'If you can't beat them, join them,' said Winston with a smile, but no, all the teachers stared back at him stony-faced. None of them had ever found farting funny or farted themselves.

'I hear you,' said Winston, with his shy, intelligent, winning smile, pushing his halo of dark curly hair back from his forehead and looking them one by one in the eyes. Each of them suddenly believed the Acting Head thought only of their best interests. 'I know your overriding concern is the children's welfare. Indeed, I know you love all your children. I am not overstating it, am I?'

And they felt less angry, more hopeful. Some started nodding, because who could say 'No' to Winston? Who was rumoured to be so sympathetic to others because he himself had a tragic family history – a twin brother who died, someone said, but 'His uncle was murdered. By a racist. Famous case,' someone else claimed. Tragedy gave him the depth that youth might have otherwise denied him. 'I know you will give our new children a chance. I believe in your patience, your generous spirits.' (He was shepherding them, gently but firmly, out of the door.) 'I want to see you next week, same time, back here. I know you will bring me your suggestions for making the life of these children better.'

As he closed the door behind them, he drew a deep breath.

7

But Belinda Birch hadn't left. She stood there behind an armchair in the corner of Winston's office, pulling at her bleached blonde hair which she daily tortured into a thin tight ponytail, the style she had worn twenty years ago when, with her neat, pointy features and tiny waist, she had won Margate Festival Princess.

Head of Year and Head of Maths, senior teacher and single parent of three good-looking and well-dressed kids, two of them a year and one nine months apart, you'd have thought she was doing well at life. But she didn't like her subject, and men, she thought, had let her down. All her children had different fathers and her two sons disliked each other.

I knew Liam, her eldest, by sight, because he ran on the East Cliff, his pale hair flying behind him. Liam, nineteen, pink skin and long fine nose reddened by wind or drinking too much, someone said, used to sprint in phenomenal short bursts towards the Park and back again. I got to know the younger, darker son, Joe, a bit later, when I taught a few lessons for his year group. Her daughter Sandra was amiable and pretty.

'Winston, we need concrete help,' Belinda said. She was a practical woman, hard to charm. 'Language support, for example. At the moment, I can't teach our own kids – sorry – I can't teach the rest of the class.'

'I'm on it,' said Winston. He knew she was one of his best teachers, clever and focused, with good discipline, almost too good. 'Belinda, you're right.' His best smile. 'Trouble is, we don't know what their language is. We know it's a mixture – a few words of Arabic, bits of Spanish and English, even Italian – but it's not like anything we know.'

Belinda said, 'With respect, you'll have to find out.' She was aware of possibly losing points with Winston, so in order to gain some back, she said, 'We should be aware of their heritage.'

Winston did not quite manage to hide his amusement.

Belinda flushed and said, 'Identity is very important ...' But again, a glint of scepticism on his handsome face. Exasperated, she burst out, 'You'll soon learn, Winston, we're on our own down here. It's not like London. Last ten years we got zero help from anyone else, so we just have to keep up standards.'

Winston summoned a serious expression and said, 'Indeed. I've asked the Head of Languages and the Head of History to look into it. You know I count on you, Belinda.'

His eyes were a marvellous caramel brown with big dark pupils. Everyone knew Winston was unavailable, said to be deeply in love with his young wife Ella, who was either an artist or maybe a writer, and either bipolar, or recovering from a breakdown, but Belinda had a sudden sense that her new winter jumper was too hot. 'Thanks Winston. It's just that I'm committed, you know. To the school. To it being ... a grammar school. We've got an identity too.' Her voice was apologetic, for her, and soft, but she knew what she said was the nub of it all.

'Then I'd like you to know this first.' Winston picked up a pile of paper from his desk. 'I haven't had a chance to look at these properly yet. I'll be telling all the staff once I have. But to pre-empt any questions about standards, I've let the new children sit the Telltale Culture-Fair Ability Test. Doesn't penalise them for not knowing English, etc. Most of them came out right at the top of the scale.'

She reddened again. 'Is that fair?'

'Is the Culture-Fair Ability Test fair?' Winston raised an eyebrow.

'Is it fair to the others? I mean, the others who had to do the … you know, the not-fair test, the eleven plus.' Belinda tried to laugh. 'That sounds silly, I know. Never mind, forget it. I'm glad if they're bright.'

He softly closed his door behind her, then gazed out of the window.

Identity. She thought I would yield as soon as she used the word. But what's your identity, Belinda? he thought to himself. Nina had told him Belinda once belonged to the local Put Britain First group. The idea could be used in the wrong way, by the wrong people. As a way of saying, 'You're not like us,' or more pointedly, 'I'm not like *you.*'

Shirley, his mother, had taught him to think about love, and likeness. 'You're as good as anyone else, remember. We're all just human in the end. Your granddad was all for identity – white identity. I couldn't stand it. And your poor, crazy Uncle Dirk. Then I hear the same thing coming at me from the other side. The council's making me say I'm white on forms, even if I don't care what colour I am, even though I'm married to your dad, and I'm your mum. Where is it going to end, Winston? You just remember: you're a good boy, you're a good human being.' As a boy he had thought her out of date, but now he wondered if she had a point, all the same.

And the Red children's arrival – what was he to do about that? He should still be a Deputy, really, at most, at his age, he knew, but Neil Purseglove had not returned to duty. So the whole problem of the Red people had fallen on him.

He tried to think 'One love.' And tried not to think 'Just as long as no more of them arrive.'

8

Something strange happened, very early one morning in Gibraltar, over a thousand kilometres away from Ramsgate as the raven flies, before anyone, even the cleaners, were up. A big group of people, mostly male, large-headed, broad, maybe a dozen of them fully grown, the others still adolescent, walked along the Sir Herbert Miles Road on the eastern side of a steep, rocky promontory in southern Europe. There were two sturdy girls, who held hands. Even before sunrise, it was hot. A vermilion line on the horizon turned into the sun and climbed steadily out of the black and scarlet sea. Most of them stopped and stared at it, awed, then laughed.

But their leader, a massive man with red hair, called them to go on.

The road bears right, with the sea and grey railings on the left, towards the mouth of a tunnel, which is tall and high, big enough for heavy lorries. After a moment's hesitation and what sounded like a prayer for their journey – '*Wafaqna Allah rihlatan aminatan*' – the travellers disappeared, like the road, into the tunnel. Except for the gulls and gannets, everything was silent again.

9

Something strange happened not so very much later on Ramsgate's West Cliff. A thirty-four-year-old Afghan called Arash, hunched in jumpers, setting up by the beach-side railings to catch whiting on his day off, happened to be watching.

The tunnel mouth in the cliffs, far below the pine-tree where the ravens live, is tall and high, big enough for heavy lorries. The road towards it bears right, with the sea and grey railings on the left, then disappears into the tunnel.

It's a long way west of Ramsgate's harbour and the Lifeboat station, beyond and below the Pugin house and the grand but neglected Georgian terraces (five storeys high) that face south to the sunshine, beyond the 1920's marina with its pale balustrades, and the bowling green, and the low lines of humps that look like a golf course but are really grassed-over air-raid shelters. The tunnel swallows the old ferry road which, after the demise of the ferry, still runs, mostly empty, just above sea-level and flat rocks black with mussels. To the landward side of the tunnel there's pampas grass, succulents, palms. To the seaward side of the road is a narrowing pavement, grey steel rails, grey sea, and over the waves, low on the horizon, Europe.

A group of figures walked out of the black into January sunshine, five abreast, their faces bright with hope as the light hit their faces, shouting *'To bien ... Alhamdulillah!'* (Meaning 'Thank God,' Arash knew, because Arabic was one of the languages he had learned as a boy in the *madrassa*, before his mother snatched him and his brother away.)

A bright frieze of men and children were coming towards

him in a blaze of gold. *Malaikah*, angels, Arash thought, suddenly a child again remembering his lessons, they are angels of light, fresh released from darkness. The figure in the middle was taller than his companions, and behind that group, there were others, vanishing into the shadows. The tall one had flaming red-gold hair. He stretched his arms up to the sky, like wings, then the others copied.

Angels? Arash frowned them into clarity. They were quite solid, he saw. Oddly big heads. The tallest one was dressed old-fashioned-English, jacket, even tie – though they couldn't be English, they were putting their arms round each other and laughing, now, but talking in another language, one he'd never heard. Then something happened that made him want to laugh as well: one of them, a dark-haired lad in a bright red tee-shirt, ran a few steps, then suddenly turned into a flashing succession of arms and legs Arash realised were cartwheels, coming back to his feet and strolling nonchalantly onwards, and the others clapped and cheered. Then the tall one held his spread hands up to heaven again.

Malaikah, Arash thought once more. Angels from elsewhere. The tall one was walking towards him.

After long loneliness – even in the great betrayal, few Afghans had ever come here – Arash was ready to make friends.

There had to be a meaning and a pattern, the Professor thought, as they emerged from the mouth of the tunnel into daylight. Just for a second he turned and looked back: as the photos on the internet had shown, it was identical, in all but a few tiny particulars, to the mouth of the tunnel at home. 'Like moves to like: likeness in difference makes love.' Just as he had written in his notebooks (when the universe spoke, he wrote it down).

He took a deep breath of chilly air, *milagroso*, miraculous, *muejazaten*, and raised his hands to the English heavens. '*Alhamdulilla!*' And thanked the earth which had released them.

Glory to God, glory to the universe, glory to the echoes and likenesses that bind the world together. Glory to the great net of mirrors which reaches out to the constellations, from the dark scuttling scorpions in sand to the far pale Scorpion of stars. Glory to the Twins who hide their white flame behind the blue sky of Ramsgate and the blanker blue sky of home; glory to the feelings all living things tremble with, similar, similar, he's smiling and throwing out his arms, his hands, his long musical fingers, the antennae of his light-rinsed nerves.

They will like us, I think

and look,

glory to

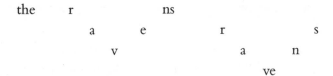

(and he bows to these brothers of the ravens over the mountain ridge of his home)

Glory to light. To the intricate wonders of golden string which hold the world together. To the sun, which gives life and burns it away.

But not yet, the Professor prays.

We are safe arrived, like the others. Let me live.

So far that morning Winston had managed to adapt two assembly plans, one on global warming and one on recycling. They were dull, but at least they were done. So back to budgets. Rolling up his sleeves with a purposeful grunt and a heavy heart, he opened up his spreadsheet.

A knock on his door.

Anna Segovia, Head of Languages. 'Winston, just a thought.'

'It's not really the moment –'

'It won't take a second. "Jebble Tariq", right? What the first Red girl said?'

Winston went on frowning at his computer.

'I think something like that was an early name for Gibraltar,' she went on, louder. 'Gibraltar? Are you listening, Winston?'

After several seconds staring at the screen, her boss returned from the land of debt, holding a single word in his head. 'Gibraltar. You said Gibraltar?' he asked. 'Extraordinary. Ella was talking about it this morning. She wants us to go on holiday there … I'm not keen. Look, can we talk about holidays later? If I don't sort out this spreadsheet we'll get no budget at all next year.'

Anna walked away, frustrated.

In any case, the name was most probably a coincidence. She thought no more about it, but a tiny part of Winston's brain recorded 'Gibraltar' for later.

'Idiot,' Arash's wife told him. 'Angels! Illegals, more like. Must have been Red people.'

'Who?'

'Why don't you ever know what's going on? Red people. Everyone's talking about them. They're sneaking in on boats. Maybe they came from Pegwell? It'll make it harder for people like us who've been here ages. Better tell the police.'

'One of them was a professor.'

'Don't make it sound as though you're on their side!'

Ramsgate had long ago lost its police station, but Arash reported what he'd seen on the non-emergency police phone line. Nobody from the police ever got back to him, but later that day a reporter from *Kent Central*, a young woman in a tight pink jacket with a girlfriend in the police force, tracked him down in the Hovelling Boat Inn, where he should not have been drinking.

'They were laughing,' Arash said. He'd changed his story somewhat after speaking to his wife. Besides, he would say nothing about angels to this beautiful woman, he didn't want to seem like an ignorant foreign believer (he wasn't sure if he believed anything at all, though he took his sons to the mosque in Margate.) 'Very odd. The Professor asked me about fish.'

'There was a Professor? He asked you about fish?'

'Yes, I was fishing. *Qal 'iinah 'ustadh.* He said, "I'm Professor Something." I didn't hear the name. Then he asked what fish I was catching. He sounded as English as you.'

'My mother is Dutch,' the young woman said, 'but go on.'

'I told him, "It's winter, so if I'm lucky, whiting. If not, dogfish. But no-one likes dogfish, just my Mum." "Where can we eat?" he asked me. They'd come from very far away, he said. They were hungry.'

The young reporter in the tight pink jacket kept nodding and smiling, and Arash, whose own wife was rather forbidding, thought he was falling in love — surely he could tell her *everything*, his mother's long, hard journey to the UK, their shortage of money, the way only one of his children had made good friends, how both his sons missed their cousins, his British-born wife who no longer respected him as she should, and in winter, the cold — although one week last summer had been hotter than Spain, so hot the tar on his garage roof had melted, making him hope that at last, Ramsgate was going to get warmer.

'"Sunrise Fish and Chips," I told him. "Big portions there." Then he asked, "Where are the caves?" So I told him about the ones between Ramsgate and Pegwell. But the tide was very high, so they couldn't —'

'How did you know they were Red people?' she cut in. Most people in Canterbury thought the so-called Red people must be Iranians or Syrians.

Alcohol sang in his blood. 'I thought they weren't real at first. Like, ghosts. Or angels? But they looked funny. Heavy eyebrows. Big head.'

'Were they, actually, red?'

'Must have been.' He was uneasy — he hadn't really noticed. But there had to be a reason for the name. Looking back on it, they became red. 'The Professor had red hair. And he bowed to some birds. Big crows.'

'You mean ravens. They're supposed to be magic. Something

funny's going on,' said Sam, who was a little drunk by now and had shed her jacket. 'Maybe they *are,* like, ghosts or angels. There's lots of ghosts round here. Vikings. Romans. It's a mystery how they came to be here.' (She knew no history.) 'Lucky I don't have really to go into stuff like that. My editor just wants a story about illegals.'

Did they ever explain how they came to be here? At any rate, we soon knew. At first it was just one word, once the Red people learned it, repeated over and over, with a gesture across the sea to where they had come from, as they shivered in our icy English January.

Heat. They were running away from the heat.

Once they had enough English, some of the Red children told their classmates that they'd lived underground until heat drove them up to the surface. But they didn't like being questioned, even when their English improved. Questions made them laugh and walk away. There were always mysteries that fell through the tunnels of language, questions blocked by invisible doors. The tale that they'd lived underground was hard to believe. When a few schoolchildren took it home, their parents dismissed it.

To be fair, since the virus and global warming, everything was hard to believe. 'The world's gone mad,' people said in the streets. Could whole species, really, go extinct? If so, could we? What had happened to our young men? What were young women supposed to do? – though some of my friends were quite happy loving each other. In the third and fourth waves, we'd lost so many men. Maybe I myself would have met someone else if that weren't the case – I who moved here for many reasons, but mainly to escape the lees of a long love affair, the sadness of the sweaty city. As soon as I got here I could breathe again, though the men were all older, or ten years too young. 'I want grandkids,' hard-faced blonde women with all-year-round tans complained, drinking prosecco as they shivered and smoked outside the pubs.

The Red people, at first, seemed like a rumour, because most people had never seen one. And then, among those so inclined, they became a focus for discontent.

Winston had other problems as well. He was slowly getting to know his staff, though no-one, he felt, was really getting to know him. On the whole the staff liked him; they were mostly women, for reasons I've just explained, and he was a man. It was good for the boys to have a male role model, someone in charge, they said to each other, forgetting that for decades in the previous century there'd been nothing but men in charge. Winston sensed how even in their rebellion, his maleness took the edge off their anger. But being new in his job, and young, he had to impersonate someone grown-up, softly spoken, and moderate, part female priest, part cautious librarian like his white Uncle Thomas, part policeman. He had found allies: Anna Segovia, Mr Muggeridge the caretaker. He also knew who to look out for: Mr Phelpham the history teacher, a polymath but rumoured to belong to a cult, had never looked him in the eye; Eileen Killarney in the office, who had taken against him god knows why, though he always assumed, and told himself not to assume, it was because he was black, and Belinda of course.

But the teacher who had made the biggest impression on Winston so far wasn't one of the rebels who came to his office en masse.

Monica Ludd was a maverick. Many people feared or disliked her, though she was a local hero, the woman who had single-handedly knocked out the terrorist who killed three staff at Windmills, her previous school. My neighbours said that the children there, where she specialised in kids with problems, loved her.

The first time I myself ran across her, or rather she ran across me, was in a queue at a café. The wrong café – I hadn't lived here long. 'Flat white,' I said. 'Half-shot. Skinny. Decaf.' The girl serving bent forward towards me as if she didn't speak English and frowned. Behind me there was a strange hiccupping noise. I repeated my order. The barista slowly screwed up her eyes as if peering into the distance. Then with startling force a large figure with a mane of coarse black hair and a big-toothed grin projected her shoulder and massive back between me and the counter and said in a deafening whisper 'Wants a *lah-tay*, Tracey, weak as puke, skim milk if you've got it which you haven't and forget the decaffeinated bit, people never know the difference.' Once the assistant was busy with the roaring machine at the other end of the counter Monica turned to me and said in a normal voice, 'I used to teach her – dim but quite nice. In general, go to *L'Archivio* on the harbour. You're from London, I'm Monica, cheers.'

Winston had been warned about Monica by Neil Purseglove, the head teacher he had come to work under, that melancholy, nervous man with his nasal voice. In his initial briefing Winston had asked a question about the school's Social, Personal, Behavioural and Academic Counselling Unit. Neil handed him a file. 'This name looks familiar,' Winston said, leafing through it. 'Monica Ludd?'

'Oh God Monica. Monica!' Neil's voice was semi-hysterical with dislike. 'Yes, she was famous for a bit. A terrorist got into school. I was on hand to call for help.'

'You don't sound keen,' Winston observed.

'She's following me,' Neil said.

'Round the school?' asked Winston, puzzled.

'No. From my last school to this one.'

'Isn't that a compliment?' Winston inquired.

'Not in the case of Monica Ludd.'

'What does she hope to gain, then?'

'She wants to kill me.'

Winston laughed, then saw Neil had beads of sweat on his forehead.

One week later, Neil went off sick and Winston, to his astonishment, had become Acting Head of the school, aged only twenty-eight.

Only two hours into Winston's first day in Neil's office, feet thundered on the wooden boards outside the door.

'Knock knock, Monica's here.'

God help me. 'Come in and sit down,' he said.

She was a lot bigger than he had imagined, maybe too big for a normal-sized school. The floor squeaked as she bounded across the room. She did not sit down. 'You the new Head?' She loomed over him, looking like a giant horse with – he wouldn't look at those.

'Acting Head. But yes.'

'Have you actually left school yourself?' Monica inquired. She seemed to have a big piece of chewing gum in her mouth, and was chomping on it with vigour.

'I'm twenty-eight,' said Winston.

'I'm forty-three,' Monica told him, jutting out her impressive jaw. 'I could be your mother.'

He suddenly picked up that she was on the verge of laughter. Some anarchic streak in him shot back, 'Only if you started having sex at fifteen, which is illegal.'

Monica regarded him with friendly interest. 'Let's talk about the Red children,' she said.

14

The Professor led his cohort of followers, smiling and laughing and shaking with cold and blinking at the light, down the sweeping curves of road into the town, admiring the fine red brick arches that ran alongside.

Sunrise Fish and Chips, as recommended by Arash, turned out to be a winner. The Professor ordered wonderful fresh fish like they ate at home (though he informed them sadly that there was no shark, barracuda, or octopus) with thick-cut, ungreasy chips. And the people who ran it were friendly and only glanced briefly at the slightly different appearance of these hungry customers – what was it? – something about their skulls, or the way their heads sat on their thick, broad shoulders, or how the people who couldn't fit in the dining room rollicked and laughed on the pavement outside, very noisy and happy compared to the quiet locals. Difference was nothing to Sunrise, who were Turkish. A few local people had harried them when they first arrived, asking them where they came from and how long they were staying, so they were never going to bother anyone else.

The Professor waited till everyone was happily eating, paid, and then said, 'I'm off to do something important.' He was clutching a piece of paper in his pocket. He had one address in the whole of England, one name, of a woman he'd met twenty-odd years ago when he was very young, on a cruise-ship, Holly Palermo.

Soon he was ringing at the elegant Gothic door of a big house overlooking the harbour. He waited. Swift feet on stairs.

'Yes? No it can't be … it *IS*! Darling Juan! Professor! May I call you that?' Long pause while they stared at each other. 'I can't believe it! Your hair is still red! Oh come in, come in!'

15

Holly Palermo, and somehow exactly the same, large blue eyes alight with amazement as she stood gazing at him in the hall. When she turned and laughed, head tipped back, on the stairs, she was still the tall radiant girl on the sunlit deck. On the landing the light was fierce and he saw that her long thick hair was grey. Thirty years had passed. But her jumper was covered with stars! The same, the same.

And so to her balcony. They sat and looked out over the harbour. Cold fresh beauty.

'Are you warm enough?' she asked.

'I've been too hot,' he said, with feeling, then when she looked puzzled, made a split-second decision to keep it light. 'Fish and chips, I expect. Very warming.'

Now she pours him an ice-cold gin in a crystal glass and they look back across the bright midday waters of the Channel to youth and Europe. Some intimate knot in the pattern of fate is blissfully loosening, weaving itself again.

'Yes please, more gin.'

'Our letters,' she said, as she poured it. 'They've been marvellous. You're a man, but you wrote letters! We've lived each other's lives, in letters.'

'True. But still wonderful to see you in the flesh. Your letters were better than mine.'

'Not true.' She smiled her beautiful smile. 'We know everything about one another.'

'Nor everything, I think,' he said.

When they first met he'd been a steward on *The Golden*

Fleece, a 1990's cruise ship which laid the foundations of his courteous manners, his sheaf of languages, his general knowledge. He used to slip in at the back of the on-board guest lectures, on everything from 'Phrygian pottery' to 'Latin for Leisure: Roam with the Romans' and 'Evolution Explained'. On the latter he took careful notes and later engaged in earnest, shy debate with the lecturer, till the chief steward tapped him repressively on the shoulder. Still, he attended the follow-up, 'Ancient Man: How He Learned to Walk Upright', which had made him laugh, as he pushed trolleys loaded with ice-buckets and bottles across the deck, for a week. In which time he was quietly choosing a new name, 'Juan Der Tal', and in his next posting, used it.

But Holly, in those days, only knew him as 'Juan'.

'You came on a six-week cruise,' he says.

'I did.'

How beautiful she was. Big eyes and a high, soft laugh. Juan first saw her float down the stairs in a long white dress, on the arm of her husband, to dinner, one of those tall, wealthy couples 'from a life I could only imagine', he tells her now, and she pats his arm.

'You were so kind,' he tells her.

'And you were so shy!'

'I was just a boy.'

'You looked like a docker! As strong as an ox! But handsome, with flaming red hair!'

'I had a tremendous, painful crush.'

'I may have been aware.'

She smiles at him, unguarded, and their eyes meet. New sunlit avenues open, just out of sight. A lifetime of knowing and not knowing each other slips into the background, winding through decades, back to the sea.

They were two of the youngest adults on the ship, so they noticed each other. He had almost run to beat other staff to her side to offer her a damp flannel to rinse her hands after shellfish, or an umbrella against sun. One day she left behind her book, *The Voyage Out*.

'I was so happy! I ran after you with it.'

'And I asked you your name.'

One day her husband, twenty years older, was laid low, seasick, as they crossed the Bay of Biscay. The band played madly, the winds blew harder.

'That evening! I'll never forget it,' they both agree, and their glasses chink, and the sun strikes a diamond flare.

When everyone else had left, Juan found courage to ask her to dance, and they flew from one side of the deck to the other, laughing and shrieking. After a while, though, she'd said 'We must stop. You'll get into trouble, Juan' – since he wasn't one of the men with varnished nails who were paid to dance.

'You remembered my name!' he says to her now, still with wonder, staring at another stretch of ocean, three decades later. 'That was the marvel, you remembered the name of a steward!'

'And I gave you my card.' A white bird of hope.

'And we always wrote,' they agree, and smile across the table with mutual approval, travellers clasped at last, once again, in one time and space.

'It's miraculous. I have all your letters, every one,' Holly says.

Letters tell stories, small windows through which each has seen bright intimate patches of truth, what the Professor does in the morning, how Holly likes to lay down her head at night, but as yet only a shadowy outline of the rest.

Now, in this moment, magical connection. Closeness. Her

friend in the flesh, whole and mysterious.

Juan has kept none of her letters. He fears possessions – what you have you can lose – yet his great head and remarkable memory store every word. So he knows she became a craftswoman, a jeweller, lived in Egypt and Rome, and since the death of her second husband, has lived by the sea in England, making beautiful things out of metal.

'I wrote to you with all my successes,' he says now. 'Trying to impress!' How he moved to the onboard entertainments team, then led it; went to England to university, and gained one degree, then two, then a third at Cambridge.

'Did you tell me that?' she asks.

'Surely I did …? Though it was quite dull.'

'Then the letter never arrived. Of course, I was far away,' Holly sighs, 'in Rome, with a jealous husband.'

'I was earning my keep as "Monsieur Shuffleur"! Singing in French while doing card tricks. £100 an evening! Good money in those days.'

'In *Cambridge*?' She's a little surprised, and he stares at his glass.

'Oh … London. Caught the last train back.'

'If only I'd seen you,' says Holly, after a pause. 'It's chilly, I'll get you a scarf.'

So at last he 'became a professor', and made his name, and a life, and completed the long journey back to his people at intervals, helping, advising, paying. Few details of that. He has never had a chance to tell her, in fact, who his people are. She senses he's deeply tired and doesn't ask questions. 'We'll have time, I hope.'

Besides, she herself has so much news! Births and deaths, including two husbands'. Art she has made, gold jewellery

44

inspired by the Romans ('Who landed here, as you know'), crowns of fragile gold ivy leaves, emperors' rings with glowing red tourmalines, awards for her work, her happiness here. 'I still have so many clients in London, though, darling, my favourite is Lottie Lucas, so naughty, and always in the news! You haven't heard of her? Juan, you are falling asleep.'

He listens in a comfortable daze, his half-urban heart relieved to be back among *sapiens* comforts. But after a while he stirs. There's a rabble below on the quayside. Oh dear, it's his party, suddenly unkempt to his eyes, as Holly's laughter (at his gentle snore) rings out over the harbour, a run of plucked harp-strings.

The large, heavy heads turn and look up. The Professor with a strange woman! They're starting to feel hungry again, as if some massive quantum of energy has been drained from them since they left home. 'Professor!' *'Ustadh!'*

'Dear lady, I'll have to leave.'

'But *darling,* who *are* these people? Is there something wrong with them? Never mind. If you must go, you must. And where are you going to stay? – but with me, of course. Borrow this coat, it was Rex's, I couldn't quite bear to throw it away. Dior, which is silly, but warm. Wool and silk, and wonderful epaulettes.'

The Professor disappeared for the rest of the day.

16

And came back in the evening, as she told me later, her beautiful large eyes looking down in mock-modesty then up, glinting with mischief.

'Where are your cases?' she said as she let him in.

'I have no cases.'

Pause. 'None?'

'It's a long story.'

'Oh I hope so, darling, I hope so.'

He wouldn't have tea. Nor coffee. No drink.

'Sorry, I just want to go to bed.'

Now suddenly both are self-conscious, though Holly quickly recovers and leads him upstairs. 'Your bathroom. Your bedroom ... but –' She turns in the doorway and almost walks into him.

'But?'

They look at each other. For a moment which extends. And then laugh. And she sits in the armchair and watches as he runs his bath, removes his jacket.

'Darling,' she says. Just that. It's enough, but he's not quite sure.

'Should I be shy?' he asks her before he unbuttons his shirt.

'We're too old for that. You're so ... solid!' she says. 'Your shoulders! You could lift me with one hand. You're more like a wrestler than a Professor.'

'Do you like it?' he says, very humbly, not looking at her, as he removes the last of his clothes. 'I know I'm a monster.'

But sees she does not agree, for she is neatly removing hers.

That night, in her enormous bed, after sleeping like children they wake and talk. Briefly, he explains. 'When the crisis came, back home, the whole world was already on the move, fleeing from war or warming. We had to get out, but where to?'

And he'd asked himself, where was there a place that was cooler and wetter, with fewer people? A country that did not, so far as one knew, actually kill migrants?

Ideally, a place a bit like their home. With caves, and tunnels, and tropical palms, and fish, and sun, and high winds, and wildflowers, but especially tunnels and caves? 'And do you remember, you'd written to me about your palms. And sent a picture of your garden which showed them in flower. Huge white spires.'

'My dear old Cabbage Palms, love.'

A town, preferably, far enough from that country's capital to have a thousand things going on that never showed on the national radar. ('You'd written that people felt neglected by London. You said the one police station had been closed down, that the welfare state barely functioned, but the locals were kind, and there was a shortage of labour, a shortage of men.')

Where had Holly, 'my dearest friend, and my one real friend in England', moved to?

Ramsgate.

It was sunny, but the annual average temperature was ten to fifteen degrees cooler than where he was, the internet told him. Were there caves?

He did research. There were caves.

Ramsgate had everything they needed. And more: Ramsgate was in Kent, where his people had come long ago, before history started, before Britain and Europe were separated by sea, making the long, gradual shift across Doggerland, as the world warmed, strong feet treading the spine of the North Downs. Then it had cooled. Once more their range drifted south. South. And now it was warming again. 'Half the world's on fire,' he said. 'Have you felt it, even here?'

'You sound tired, darling,' she said. 'I know, America, Canada, Australia and so on, the fires, appalling, but what can we do? We're not on fire here ... If you mean to stay long, I'll give you a key.'

'Hard to know.' She can't see his face in the night. 'We might need to go home.'

She doesn't ask where. Instead, 'Will they be all right, your companions?'

'I think so.'

'If they're not,' (but here she is more hesitant) 'I could help out.'

'That's marvellous.'

'Though alas, I'm always busy,' she adds swiftly, but his smile in the innocence of darkness remains undimmed.

Leafing through the local paper late next morning, on the sunny balcony with her scrambled eggs and smoked salmon, Holly read the headline aloud. 'TUNNEL MYSTERY AS MORE RED PEOPLE ARRIVE.'

'Darling,' she called back inside to the Professor, who had only just got up from their bed.

('I adore you, I always did and always will,' he had muttered, full of emotion to wake beside her at last, her hair loose, her cheek soft, comfort and peace. 'Of course,' she had said, with absolute conviction and calm. The shadow of a big bird, her raven friend, was just folding its wings on the blind.)

'Could you bring out the jug of orange juice, Juan? Freshly squeezed, of course. Come and have breakfast. I think these headlines must be about you. Do you want to explain?'

'First I must eat. And then introduce myself to the local school.'

'Which one?'

'Whichever school has recently had a fresh intake of refugees. More are coming. I hope they won't mind. I hope *you* won't mind.'

'Darling, I'm a gypsy, like you,' said Holly, though she wasn't much like a gypsy, and in other moods took a dim view of the travellers who sometimes brought their caravans down from Ireland to the sea for a holiday, and ran noisy generators in the car park by the sea, and left litter. 'Try the Grammar School.'

Fortunately, Winston and the Professor hit it off almost from the start.

Winston, sitting hunched over a spreadsheet in his office, was startled by a loud, confident knock. A strange man opened the door, without waiting for an answer, filling the entire doorway. Winston brushed past the Professor without looking him in the eye and called out in what was for him an exasperated voice, 'Eileen, I can't possibly see any parents at the moment, I'm doing the accounts.'

But the instant before, Eileen Killarney, who worked two days a week when kindly Nina was volunteering at the hospice, had left the premises at high speed for a smoke.

'I'm not a parent, Mr Purseglove,' the tall stranger said in flawless middle-class English. 'I'm a Professor.'

Winston gave the man his attention. Tortoiseshell spectacles, tie and sports jacket. How could he have thought this was a parent? Parents wore tracksuits and t-shirts.

'Sorry,' he said automatically. Then tried to recover. Hard to remember, at his age, that he was in charge. 'I'm not Mr Purseglove, ignore the name on the door. I'm the Acting Head, Winston Edwards ... Are you a visiting speaker? I haven't seen this term's programme – too busy with accounts, I'm afraid. Would you like to take a seat?

'Very kind of you,' said the Professor, who had already sat down. 'As it happens, I'm not a visiting speaker. I believe this school has some children only recently arrived in Ramsgate.'

'Yes,' said Winston in a different tone of voice, and sat up straight. The school, he knew, had merely been firefighting the problem of the Red children, with a total disregard for procedure, a thing Neil would have abhorred. Oh God, was this smooth type someone from the Government – the Department of Education? Worse, Immigration? Both departments were so starved of funding that since the first flurries of conflicting measures, pro-active management had practically ceased. All the same, there was something worryingly confident, almost commanding, about the strange man.

Once in Winston's school, all children were *his* children, and Winston made ready to defend them.

But the big man just smiled. 'Good, good, I'm in the right place. I have come to help,' he said.

'Tell me more,' said Winston.

The card the Professor presented drew attention to the fact that his degrees were from Cambridge. Winston did not notice that the institution where the Professor held his current post was absent; the string of letters after his name was far longer than Winston's own. He clutched the card in his hand for reassurance as the two men began to talk.

By the time Eileen, wired by her ten-minute dose of nicotine, knocked on the door with a query, they were deep in conversation. Winston hardly raised his head as he said, 'Real coffee, please, Eileen?'

'*Real* coffee?' Eileen repeated. It was for visiting governors only.

'Real coffee,' Winston said again, with a meaning look. 'More of the – new children – will be arriving shortly,' he added, and over Eileen's gasp of alarm, 'the Professor here is volunteering to help us.'

Eileen dragged out the cafetiere from the back of Nina's

cupboard, making the maximum noise. Then she got on the phone to her mum. 'There's more of the weird kids coming, Head's letting them in,' she complained. 'Walking all over us, these people are. And I'm to make real coffee for one of them!'

Though not well educated she was a bright, sharp girl who noticed a lot, particularly faults. What she had deduced was something that other people, misled by his expensive clothes and educated voice usually failed to take in: the Professor, under his spectacles and tweed, was just another of the strange incomers, another Red person, another bloody migrant with big bones and a strange, big head.

PART TWO

19

Many things had changed since the recent virus strains that preferentially killed young men. Some had grown rash about precautions, to show they weren't afraid; but even though they were young and strong and liked parties, they died at a faster rate than women. Parties there were, in the later, mutated waves all over the country, with twenty young heroes drinking and leaping around to the music. At midnight they flung their arms round each other to shout with the love young men feel for their cohort, 'See you later, mate', but some never saw each other again. Mothers hugged their surviving sons closer, and told them to be careful. Thinking back, it was part of the reason I and many others did not have children in our twenties. 'In any case, the world's such a mess,' we said at the time, to explain what was not, in fact, our decision.

The world was a mess, all the same. It was over 0.2 degrees hotter in a decade, which sounds like nothing, but that is an average, and averages meant little to the Red people or to others fleeing the heat. In the Marshall Islands, a series of 'king tides' twenty-foot high flooded the capital, Majuro, and left salt in the drinking water. In Paris flash fires killed thousands in the packed *banlieue*; in Siberia, millions of acres of tundra blazed, while in Chersky, the home-built 'freezers' residents had dug into the frozen ground melted, and basements collapsed. Brisbane's beloved Eagle Street finally had to be abandoned to the sea. In Brazil, drought meant the Apinaje Indians' corn didn't swell and their manioc failed to grow. In Canada, walls of fire roared across from the pines into the towns. In the

Mediterranean, strange creatures from the tropics strained the nets; trawlers sank under the weight of giant jellyfish, rabbit-fish browsed the algal forests to barren rock. For us the threat seemed far off, and yet there were years in England when spring, that gentle, transitional season, my favourite, just burned away.

In our first experience of lockdown, which now seems long ago, spring came here with slow perfection, keeping pace with the virus slowly perfecting itself in people's bodies. Because we all stayed inside, the cherry-tree in my front garden became slow-motion theatre. I went outside in my coat first thing every day when no-one was about, peering across at the closed curtains of my neighbours' houses, listening for coughs but only hearing a small dog despairingly barking. Then I looked up through the cherry branches, longing for spring. All I could see of the future was tiny black points on the hard straight lines of the twigs. Then stems pushed out frail as hairs, waving little red balls.

One morning just before Easter the sun hit the tree with its hundreds of paired garnets, and one had split open overnight, perfect in sunlight: one fabulous luminous pompom floating against the dark bark. A few days later the whole tree was a layered wedding-dress of light. I looked up through clusters of almost-white blossom at white and blue sky and remembered Japan – yes, the existence of elsewhere! And even in that year of death all over the world, rejoiced. Days later I read that Japanese parks where thousands of people congregate in April to look up through blossom in the sacred *Hanami* ritual, had also closed.

The Red people's first spring in Ramsgate was very different. There was no logic to the weather that year: January bright and clear and not cold for the season, February freezing, dank and dark, the warmest April on record predicted. The year's first two local cases were reported in the local care home in the middle of dark grey February, unfortunately only weeks after the main party of Red people walked out of the cliff with the Professor – and the rumour was that the Red people came from abroad, like the virus, and liked touching and hugging and laughing into the air.

Enter the local PBF, who claim to 'Put Britain First'. We knew them by sight, there were only half a dozen of them, usually, at any one time, and no-one took them seriously. But maybe we should have done. Not all of them met at that noisy corner table in the pub where at least their beliefs could be aired and sea breezes and sunlight could blow them away. Some of them, lonelier and sadder, watched far-right propaganda lost on their own in their bedrooms, lost in the arms of imaginary soldiers massing in the deep web, lost to their mothers and fathers, who thought they were gamers; unhappy, overweight youths too full of hatred and hormones to realise the virus didn't arrive complete with people to blame but was simply part of biology, like them, randomly evolving in dark close corners of the world human beings had made.

'Stay home,' people said to each other once again. Once again I, a two-day-a-week supply teacher, stayed home and taught stare-y lessons online, and all teens, even sane ones, grew slightly madder. But the Red people had no home to stay in.

On a temporary basis, the Victorian red brick Sailors' Church on the quay had installed a dozen mattresses, but there were far more than a dozen Red people by now. Where were the others sleeping, a few people asked? 'On the beach,' someone said, which seemed likely, after raw fish, seaweed and samphire started turning up in corners of the church.

The congregation, who had welcomed them at first, began to complain. 'That young chap laughed at me when I tried to give him a Bible,' one of the church-goers said, 'it's disrespectful.' Jackee West, who'd given them clothes that first day and become fond of them, disagreed. 'He wasn't laughing at you, he was just laughing. You got to get used to them,' she said. 'I didn't like it at first myself, but laughing's better than crying, at the end of the day.' But then the news of the deaths of the two people with the virus in Ramsgate got out. 'Hygiene,' one of the lay readers said. 'We must have hygiene in the House of God.' Jackee West got cross. 'It was the money-lenders that Jesus threw out, not children who have no money at all.' The raw fish began to smell, however, and Jackee lost.

Monica it was who made sure the Red people were not, as February turned into March, on the streets. Monica's strange, saturnine husband, Ginger, a senior detective inspector in the Margate branch who blindly adored his wife, could open every door. The doors Monica told him to open were the doors of the handsome red brick Fire Station, closed for twenty years. Sighing, Ginger leaned on all his contacts to get electricians to fix wiring, glaziers to mend windows, charity-shops to give furniture, cleaning firms to clean. Monica meanwhile was leaning very hard on her colleagues at school and even some of the students. 'Of course they will return your sleeping-bags,' she told the ones from sporty, middle-class families. 'And if they can't, you'll have done the right thing. Which is always the thing I, Monica, tell you to do, right? Hahaha.'

So for a few weeks, all was well. The virus cases were traced to a single visitor (not a Red person), to a single care home, and contained. Everything re-opened. The rumours had nothing to feed on. Yes, new arrivals had been noticed, but they had not brought plague to Ramsgate. The Grammar School was the smallest of the area's schools and odd things often happened, like pupils getting into university or learning a language.

So the school-age Red children went to school and the young Red men mostly stayed in the warm, dark basement of the old Fire Station, where they kept taking showers. Each evening they huddled, laughing, near the motley army of ancient storage heaters, electric fans, and paraffin stoves Monica and Ginger had gathered. We didn't understand until later why they wanted to live in the basement, but they slept there like Dickensian orphans in their sleeping-bags, side by side underground, and out of sight was out of mind.

Then Belinda got wind of where they were, and alerted someone she knew at the Council who worked in Health and Safety. The innocent Red people let the three visitors in high-viz tabards in, and three days later, the day in fact, coincidentally, before the outbreak of fire, the Notice to Vacate the Premises was served.

They vacated, with nowhere to go. They were around. They were seen.

20

'When I said, "Of course you must stay here, darling",' says Holly one morning not long after the Professor arrived, 'I did mean *you*.'

'Excellent.' The Professor is sitting with Holly at the large, circular table eating breakfast. He is busy reading Caesar's account of landing in Thanet and is very content, though perhaps there isn't quite as much breakfast as usual.

That morning, someone had been snoring in the bath in Holly's en suite bathroom below a mural of sunset Venice, giving her a most disagreeable shock. Outside on the landing, a large body lies sleeping. Two more are muttering in their dreams.

It felt too warm, with so many people there, Holly thinks, even though the January sun had just risen above the ocean. 'My house is large. I know I'm fortunate. All the same. With so many people staying, and wanting to stay so close to us, and each other, it feels small.'

'Who?' he asks, lifting his head for a millisecond from the page where he is at Pegwell, two thousand years ago.

'I don't like my house to feel small. They're in our bathroom. On the landing. So far not in our bedroom, but it's only a matter of time.'

'Not in our bedroom? Good.' He must fit in some reading before he begins his long school day. 'Caesar says the Britons used to share wives, seven women to one man,' he says, raising his eyes from his book.

'Five at last count. It's absurd.'

'No, seven,' he says. 'According to him the Britons were "rich in milk and meat."'

'Six guests, if I include you. One poor hostess. No loaves and fishes left.'

'And probably Caesar had no evidence at all of polygamy. Little Eagle told me one of his classmates asked him if the Red people were cannibals. Same sort of rubbish.' (Little Eagle was the real name of the child dubbed 'Little Bighead', for his brains.)

'Juan! You're not listening.'

Soon he has to, because Holly removes his book and his breakfast in one scented, soft-fingered swoop and walks the Professor round the flat, making him count the bodies on the floor. 'No problem at all, I'll tell them to leave, my people are used to roughing it,' he says.

'What's wrong with hotels?' Holly asks. 'Ramsgate has a couple of first-class hotels.'

Not for the first time, the Professor contemplates the gulf between Ramsgate, 'rich in milk and meat', and Jebel Tarek.

'I'd be delighted to help, of course,' she adds, reading his face.

'No, no, it's not right. We'll think of something else.'

21

'Meeting to Talk about Hosting New Arrivals: Grammar School Hall, 12.30,' said the notice. 'All welcome.'

Posters were pasted round the town. Hank Stitch's mate Dirk White (from the Broadstairs section of the PBF) then went around scrawling 'Red "People"!!!?!' in red capital letters on the posters. (White-haired Graham, from the Ramsgate branch, approved of the plain speech but deplored the grammar.) What Dirk had done accidentally turned out to be helpful to the school, since the phrase 'New Arrivals', 'the only acceptable option' according to Winston's admin team, meant nothing at all to the people of Ramsgate. But a meeting about Red people! That was different. The town turned out agog, and in force.

The meeting started well with free chocolate cakes baked in Food Tech GCSE and offered mostly by amiable, large-boned Red children as people filed in. There followed Winston's smiling welcome to 'parents and wonderful, community-minded citizens' ('Expect the best and the worst may not happen,' he thought). He was looking enviably dapper in a suit, open-necked pale green shirt and matching handkerchief in jacket pocket, with a specially close haircut and shave from Ali Barber's. ('You look like an egg,' his wife had said, and laughed rather too long.)

After the smiles, Winston grew grave: 'I have to appeal to this town because my staff have informed me that children enrolled at this school are sleeping outside all night without shelter or blankets, coming into school hungry and falling asleep at their desks.'

Whispers of pity ran round the room, together with a mutinous undertow of something else. Belinda, in the row behind me, hissed to Eileen, 'At least the kids keep *still* when they're asleep.' Before the rumbling could grow louder, Winston introduced another appealingly respectable figure in sports jacket and tie, the Professor.

'We are very lucky to have with us Professor Juan der Tal, a very senior academic with several higher degrees from Cambridge and a distinguished history of research and publication.' ('Research and publication!' Sally Dunston echoed to her deaf mother in her nineties, thrilled, though neither of them had much idea what either thing was.) 'He will be helping *all* the children in Ramsgate. The Professor has known the new arrivals for years and understands their way of life.'

'I don't just understand their way of life,' said the Professor. 'I have lived it. I am proud of being one of the newcomers you know as the Red people. Some would argue my modest success proves what these children can achieve with encouragement and help, and how much we have to offer ...' Then he used all the skills he had gained as a shipboard entertainer to reel in his audience with 'our story': suffering and endurance, losses and courage, hard-earned success.

Afterwards, as they filed away from the hall, the audience was surprised to realise that he hadn't revealed many details. Except the most recent part, the upturned ants' nest that had unjustly been made of the Red people's homes, and the happy ending, as he described it, glad emergence into sunlight on the West Cliff. The joy and relief. And the welcome! Offered first – the first town to do so on the whole South Coast! – by generous, beautiful Ramsgate! Before Eastbourne, Hastings,

Brighton! (His audience wondered, had they failed to recognise how desirable their home town was?)

The first question, pre-arranged, was from Joan Westering, who had actually suggested this meeting to Winston after she and Anna Segovia had found two big children slumped on their step one morning.

'We want to host two, please,' said Joan. 'It'll be great! Tell us how it will work?'

Winston and the Professor answered questions together, smoothing ruffled feathers, turning some questions to the Red children themselves, who answered with their usual simplicity and laughter.

Though was what the children said really simple at all? It was short, often in inverse proportion to the length of the question, but sometimes it was almost – brilliant.

Did the children like special things, different things from British children? 'We like playing.'

Did the children eat special things, things that might be difficult to prepare, cooked in special ways, *special* things? an anxious woman insisted. 'We eat food', a big boy said.

'Could they share a room with a child from, a child from, a different … different … culture?' a nervous father asked.

Little Bighead, Little Eagle as the Professor called him, answered that one. Maybe he alone among the newcomers could understand what 'culture' was, and could guess at some of the silences it hid, in this room, in this town: that it meant everything and nothing, and covered a multitude of much more awkward thoughts. 'We don't have culture when we sleep,' said Little Eagle. His laughter rippled outwards through the crowd.

It was going well! Then at the very last moment, as the Professor demurred 'Perhaps just one last question?,' Belinda put her hand up, and Eileen alongside her gave a small, conspiratorial smile and looked at her lap.

'It's very good of Ms Westering and Ms Segovia,' said Belinda, buzzing the 'Ms' slightly, as usual, 'to say they'll take two children into their home. They have a very beautiful home,' and her smile, which was honeyed, managed to convey what only some of the audience knew, that Joan and Anna had a large house, beautifully restored, in the best part of town. 'Admirable. But do they know, does anyone know, when the children will be moving on?'

She was going to follow up with a sharper broadside, 'When are you going home?', aimed straight at the Professor. Then she glimpsed Winston's kind, troubled eyes. A frown had instantly creased his forehead and mouth into a different shape. She felt stricken – in her whole life, only Winston, and maybe, occasionally, some of the children she taught, had made her feel she might be a really good person. She found she had one palm raised to stop the Professor answering. 'That came out wrong, sorry,' she said. 'I meant, course you are welcome to stay till it's safe for you to go home. I just wondered ...' trailing away. But what came out of her mouth was even worse: 'I wondered because – I'm thinking of hosting a, you know, child, myself.'

Winston's forehead magically uncreased, his handsome, newly shorn head lifted again.

'Thank you so much, Belinda,' he said. 'Which brings us to the last part of this evening. Could I have a show of hands of likely volunteers?'

A tense moment.

Belinda's hand slowly, slowly, started to swim up, of its own accord, and she watched it: *alien*, she thought. *That's not mine.* But the alien hand floated clear in the air above her shoulder, all alone. Around her, the room seemed frozen. Minute scrapings of uncomfortable chairs. In the silence, a cawing, croaking sound outside the open window, getting louder. Ravens.

The Professor said one more thing, into the pause which might bring everything, or nothing. 'A humble postscript.' He did not sound humble at all, he sounded, suddenly, proud. 'You see us now standing before you needing your help. But travellers, seafarers – those who dare their all to cross huge spaces … It's through travel that human beings have survived. I am from a very old people, a simple people, perhaps. Among us, voyagers are seen as the ones who take risks to save the others. Not people who flee and take refuge, but the bravest. Among your ancestors, I am sure there were many great travellers.'

Astonishingly, old Mr Phelpham, Head of History, though thought 'weird' and 'a Plymouth Brother, or worse' (in fact, raised in a cult, with great pain and determination he had got his whole family out), thin as a stick and said to be mad as a hare, stood up, poker straight, and announced, 'You know me as Head of History, but I also teach Special Maths to a few Year 13s for Belinda. I run the school's Maths Club, as it happens, as well as the History Club.' Winston stiffened. Phelpham was old, and white, and dried up, and worked with Belinda. But the thin voice continued, 'These children are bright. Two of them grasped Complex Probability in a matter of minutes. Not just that, they explained it to others …'

Then like pale daisies appearing in a blink between one day and the next till there was a whole daisy-covered cliff-top, hands went up, first three, then a dozen, then twenty, then more.

'… they will actually be an addition to our school,' Mr Phelpham concluded, 'they are our equals.'

Outside the window where Roland eavesdropped, these syllables triggered a memory of the two new strings of meaningless human sounds he had recently learned: 'The yah illegals, *Alhamdulillah*,' he called, and was pleased when a few startled people looked up.

'We will take names and addresses at the door,' Winston said.

'You've gone mad,' Eileen said, indignant, to Belinda on the pavement outside.

22

Belinda Birch's two boys had come through the waves of the virus unscathed, for which she is grateful beyond measure. Sons! Young men! Too busy to give them much time, she loves them with a fierce, protective pride. Yet she feels she has failed as a mother because, though both make a pet of their sister Sandra (whose father is never spoken about), they don't get on.

Liam, the eldest, is the son of an American geophysicist, Brad. She had already dumped Brad for being hopeless when she found she was pregnant. Now Brad sends money erratically, nags Liam to do better at school once a year, but is a terrifying hero to his son, who follows his every move on Facebook and brags about his father's glamorous girlfriends, since he has none of his own.

Liam was mostly famous in his year as a sprinter who represented Kent at the English Schools' championships, just failing to get to the final, though tipped to win. He was a thin, blond, dreamy boy who everyone knew was bright and expected to do better in exams. Very good at Latin and French, he had specialised in science and maths. Unlike his brother, he had few friends. He'd gone through a religious phase, which made him happy. He had a beautiful soprano voice, and had sung every year at school concerts until it broke, becoming a merely passable tenor at secondary school. The vicar of the Sailors' Church was sure he was a future star, but then aged fifteen he had suddenly stopped going to church.

Belinda noticed when Liam no longer left the house in a hurry every Sunday morning. She'd gone into his bedroom one morning: fierce adolescent aftershave and socks.

'Liam? You're not going to the Sailors' anymore?'

'Looks like it.'

'You all right, then? Why not?'

'You don't care.'

'Liam!' she said, impatient, and turned to go out, but his bony neck and shoulders were twisted in such despair that she lingered a second in the doorway and he suddenly burst out, 'I don't belong there anymore.'

'Why not?'

He let her put her awkward hand on his shoulder. 'I don't belong anywhere.'

'It's just your age,' she said kindly. 'You're the boy with everything, Liam. What did we always say? You can run and you can think. You're the Golden Boy.' As she heard herself say it she wondered: was that a pressure?

As he'd grown older, sometimes even his busy and distracted mother could see Liam had something hangdog about him, something shifty and disappointed. Not just the running, where he'd been such a star but flopped when it counted on his big day at the national championships, but A-levels, when he had just failed to get the grades he needed. Belinda had a conversation with Anna Segovia in a corridor; both were in a rush. 'Sorry about Liam's grades,' said Anna, Head of Languages. 'He's clever, we all know that. I can't help thinking, if only he'd gone the other way – his French was good, and his Latin. I still remember an essay he wrote about Achilles.'

'I wish you'd said that earlier,' Belinda snapped.

'I did, actually,' said Anna brightly over her shoulder. 'When he made his A-level choices. But you said he wanted to do Physics and Maths like his father.'

Belinda gave the news to Brad across the Atlantic, who'd exploded, but she cut him short. 'Brad, this means he'll be living at home another year, that costs money.'

'My break-up with Cindy's left me broke.'

'You are his father.'

'With results like that, it's hard to believe.'

Liam's trying again, now, applying again, doing retakes, with time on his hands, failing to keep the bar work it's easy for him to get (as a tall young male) because he drinks too much.

Joe, Belinda's younger boy, could not look less like Liam, though if you sat watching them long enough, sometimes, on the sofa where they occasionally use their devices side by side, there's something about their foreheads and brows, the way they both suddenly sharpen their eyes in a moment of startled interest, that tells you they're brothers. And sometimes, if rarely, now, one nudges the other to get his attention and their shoulders touch and they laugh at the same things. Liam secretly loves it when Joe asks him for help with his schoolwork, but that happens less and less.

Joe is muscular, curly-haired, and a swimmer. He's the son of a Turkish English teacher and small-time entrepreneur who, eighteen years before this story began, picked up Belinda walking bare-headed and blonde and pretty through the old quarter of Istanbul, glancing between the map on her phone and her gold-sandaled feet so she didn't trip on the cracks in the pavement, pushing her pram. 'Let me assist you, Miss,' said Sayeed, and they went on from there.

Quick-witted and relaxed, Joe is loved by his year group despite having Belinda, a teacher, as his parent, because everyone knows Joe won't tell. Yet Joe has his moments of explosive temper. If things aren't fair; if someone is bullied.

So once when Belinda picked him up from nursery, the teacher told her he'd pushed a boy called Anton over on purpose. 'Must have been an accident,' said Belinda. 'Joe, what happened?' Joe sat mute, but on the way home, explained. 'Anton took Jude's chair. Jude cried. Jude's my friend. So I pushed him. Really really hard. An' I'm strong. He fell over.'

'You're not allowed to be violent, Joe,' said his mother, pulling him roughly along the pavement because she had to get back to Liam, who was home with asthma. Joe's rare fits of temper might come from his mother, who spends her life in a low-level state of irritation that her life isn't better, but are more likely to come from his father Sayeed, a gentle, lovely man who once broke a door when Belinda made him jealous.

Sayeed comes to stay once a year, bringing Turkish delight and cheap jewellery for Belinda and Sandra and excellent linen shirts for both boys, whom he loves. Liam loves him back, but in secret fury that Joe is the biological son.

The day after the Grammar School meeting about the Red people, Joe and Liam were arguing once again.

'You like my dad, right?' Joe asks.

'Why are you asking? Course. He's my dad too. He likes me as much as you.' (But Liam secretly doesn't believe that anyone likes him as much as they like Joe.)

'Right. Well he's Turkish, isn't he.'

'Why ask me THAT, twat?' Liam says.

'Because you're always going on about not liking foreigners.'

'He isn't a foreigner, he's just … Dad. He speaks English.'

'Right, that proves it. So do the Red people! They've learned it, in just a few weeks! They're all right too. Like my dad.'

That second 'my dad' cuts Liam to the quick, but he ignores it. 'They're not even human.'

'Bollocks.'

'I hate them. Some of them are actually getting jobs round the Harbour.'

'What's that got to do with it?'

'It's not fair. They're morons.' Liam doesn't want to admit he just failed to get a job at the same bar after they took up his last reference, which mentioned him being 'unreliable with stock'. 'And some of them are, like, homeless!' he adds. 'So they're dirty as well.'

'How do you know?'

'Hank Stitch saw them using the open-air shower by the pier early in the morning.'

'That actually proves they're clean, idiot,' Joe says, and frustrated, tells him the one thing Belinda had specifically asked him not to, wanting to tell Liam herself. 'Any case you'll soon know who's right, one's coming to live with us.'

Liam laughed in his face. 'Expect me to believe that?'

'It's true. At the meeting last night. Mum offered. And they accepted.'

'You're a liar.'

'Go on then, ask her.'

'Liar!'

'I even know his name. It's Molo.'

23

The Professor was so busy he had forgotten to ask where Molo was placed.

Holly was wonderful, marvellous, but not undemanding, because her life had to be beautiful. 'I am so lucky, so fortunate,' she often said, but in fact, she designed life that way. The Professor was lucky, too, to have found her again, and so willing to love him, but being in a beautiful life took up time.

She needed her Lapsang in bed in an eggshell-thin, eau-de-nil porcelain cup at seven every morning except Sunday – to be fair, she made breakfast later – and always fresh flowers (from her garden, from York Street Flowers, or even from the loud, cheap flower market Ramsgate had every Friday, but they must be in the 'right' vase, *just* the right one for the blooms). She liked conversation, when she wasn't 'far too busy working, darling, to talk'. Most of all she liked company in the evenings.

This required the Professor to sit on the balcony, once the weather warmed up, and drink chilled Laurent-Perrier as the harbour lights came on. That part he loved. Strange and blissful to let all his worries about his people drift out of sight as the last yachts slipped back into the marina and the red and green harbour access lights began flashing, hypnotic on the dark as the gemstones glowing from velvet next door in her workshop. Happy. At rest.

Being with Holly assuaged some long loneliness in him, her smell in the night, Egyptian attar of roses, the look of her hair on the pillow, his traveller's longing for ease.

Yet their worlds were so different. Not just because he'd

been a lowly steward and she was a lady, a creature of air, while he grew up in the earth, underground. His world was blazing with urgency; hers had to be calm. It could be taxing living with someone who believed so fervently in looking on the bright side. Often, she simply dismissed a worry he had about the Grammar School: 'Oh I have no time for people like that,' 'Oh honestly, Juan, that's not worth thinking about,' or 'Well really, darling, how *foolish*. You'll see, everyone will realise, it'll be all right.'

When the Red people were newly arrived and the PBF put it about that the first two cases of virus must have come with them, she laughed and stretched her arms wide in the air and said 'How ridiculous, darling, but people will be silly, won't they, we can't stop them. It'll all die down.' She was almost right, for the rumour was forgotten by everyone except the hardliners in the party – which unfortunately included the local leader, Benedito Barolo, whose mother was one of the only two people who had died in Ramsgate that February, alone in the home where he had put her.

At school the Professor was very busy, at first teaching English, which Red children and others learned eagerly. Some understood for the first time the difference between a verb – 'doing! Acting! All verve and motion! *verb*!' and a noun – 'the name of a thing, an idea or a feeling, which has in itself no actor, no action, *non*-active, *noun*' – and apostrophes, those devilish little midges, transformed in a single session into floating butterflies that knew their place and aided meaning (no-one guessed the Professor's expertise in these matters had come in the first place from his covert attendance, standing behind a pillar, tray in hand, at a shipboard course with the passenger-facing name, 'Curiosities of English Grammar: Have Fun with

Words.') So of course he just smiled when some of the regular staff sat in, near the back of the room, on his sessions.

As the children's (and teachers') English improved, his task became supporting, advising, consoling, encouraging, teaching other subjects. He did an assembly which raised a few eyebrows, though the children loved it. (Ms Potter had a word with Winston. 'I mean, he's such a nice man, and inspiring, I agree, but can we tell the children the universe gives us messages? Isn't it superstitious?' 'Oh, it was a metaphor, I think,' said Winston, who'd guessed it wasn't, 'and I loved the part about finding likeness in difference.' 'Oh yes,' she nodded, 'very good.') Despite the Professor's failure to win over Eileen Killarney, at the end of March Nina, the School Secretary, gave him her highest accolade, a key to the stationery cupboard.

He was busy making friends with Winston. Winston saw the Professor as the older mentor he, as a very young acting head, needed, and confided in Juan, over a beer after work, about his troubled young wife. The Professor responded so kindly, not trying to help or advise but just being with Winston as he talked, nodding sorrowfully, sometimes, or laughing if Winston laughed. In the silence that followed, he told the young head about a lover he himself once had who suffered from depression but at other times was brilliant and delightful – Winston sat nodding with such fervour that the Professor held back from the rest of the story, where in a final depression Miranda crunched up her pills in a slurry of whisky, and – that was the end.

When he recounted his conversation with Winston to Holly and got to this part, she took a long draught of the column of bubbles in which the lights of the harbour danced and said, 'What a catastrophe, darling. And so … *unnecessary*!' And refilled his glass.

'Rhymes with "apostrophe",' he said to himself, watching the level climb. 'And true of the apostrophe, too, in some ways.'

'What did you say, my love?' she asked.

'Oh, nothing.'

The Professor let the bubbles float into him and float him upwards: delighted, after a long day of being 'All verve and motion, *verb*!' he could at last be at rest, irresponsible, not guilty, '*non*, a *noun*.' The moment: the beautiful moment, the window of golden light before the sun went down. A single bright point on which thousands of lines converged that ran back three hundred millennia into obscurity, the deep past. This place was perfect; temperate; what had driven him here was blissfully easy to forget. There in the evening light he was suspended, buoyed up by bubbles, dancing with another frail being on the head of a pin, Forget, forget, forget the wave of darkness and heat pressing northwards behind him. Still, he heard himself speak a thought he'd hardly formulated yet: 'One day I fear I'll have to go home.'

Did she hear him? Her beautiful smile remained exactly the same.

24

Thanks partly to the Professor's great efforts, things started to go better for the Red children. They turned up early and keen for school from their new billets. When they met they spent minutes embracing, despite all we had explained about the virus. Many of our children were fascinated and attracted – they had brought difference, like salt and pepper, into our lives.

Was their appearance changing for the better? The redness we noticed when they first arrived, making them look raw and awkward with their big limbs and sore red friendly heads, like people who had never before been exposed to wind or sun, now looked like a light gold tan. They picked up English as easily as the shells they were seen picking up on the beach.

'You must study a lot in the evening,' Anna Segovia said to one boy, but he laughed and replied,

'No, we just teach it to our friends.'

'Your friends?'

'Our friends who are too old to come to school.'

There were other lessons they shone at: art, maths (especially geometry), design and technology. At first, they loved the 3D printers, but the objects they produced made them laugh. 'Not real,' they kept repeating, and lost interest. In other subjects, like history and geography, they actually panted with interest, though they didn't always understand all the words, even obvious things like 'king' or 'court', and occasionally one or other of them would simply say, 'That's wrong,' and laugh. They asked lots of questions, which the English kids did not. They had ideas – strange ones, some of which turned out to be good; others made us uncomfortable.

Sometimes the Red children just seemed what one girl indignantly called 'subhuman' (Winston gave her a detention), farting or laughing or taking off their shirts, which was against school rules, and two boys their trousers, on a freak February day of hot sun.

Despite what Mr Phelpham said at the meeting, the story that the first Red people were found by the harbour, naked, laughing, putting their clothes on back to front and upside down, stuck in Ramsgate's consciousness. The kinder children knew it was wrong, dreadful, to call them subhuman. All the same – were they, could they be, a bit simple? At first their classmates watched them with suppressed, or not very well-suppressed, laughter.

But the Red children were large, remember.

And they didn't often get upset, which took the fun out of teasing them.

As their knowledge of English grew better, of course we all communicated more. But the assumption behind the 'Welcome Sessions' that were held at school and around the town was that *they* were trying to understand *us*. What kind of people we were. What kind of world they were trying to enter. 'We' were always the focus of attention.

(I suppose I noticed that because I myself have always avoided attention – maybe partly because of the name I was given, Mary Smith, which no-one remembers.)

We weren't finding out about them. We adults, at least, were nervous of asking questions, because all of us had been taught it was rude to make someone feel different – and especially taboo to ask where someone came from. Though isn't that the most interesting question of all, and the most profound, if you really want to know the answer? Meaning 'Who are you? What is your history?' We were a bit afraid of the young men, I suppose – afraid of offending them? – although I wasn't the only woman who found them attractive. Genial-looking but shy, big and strong, they hung out together and slept who knows where. I wish, now, I'd just gone and talked to them.

Some of our children, though, were asking direct questions. Partly through paucity of teaching, Ramsgate's children found learning foreign languages difficult, and did it badly. Foreign languages had been clinging on by their fingernails in secondary schools since a particularly idiotic government had declared, 'They shouldn't be compulsory. English is the world language.'

Now only Anna Segovia survived, nominal Head of Languages, yes, but in fact heading a department of one, herself, teaching Spanish from Year 7 to Year 10, because 'the parents remember when they used to go to Spain on package holidays', Latin at the Classics Club Liam had once belonged to, and French to Years 7 and 8 because, as she said to Winston, 'I simply refuse to accept that they can't speak the language of the country nearest to them, even if they're not quick learners. Are we re-entering the Dark Ages?'

One day, two months after the first Red children arrived and the Professor and Anna started special English classes for them, Twainelle, the most popular and stylish girl in Year 10, shouted out near the end of her English Literature class, 'Miss, Miss, I want to ask you something.'

'Put your hand up, Twainelle. I'm always telling you.'

'If I'm already saying it, do I still have to put my hand up?'

'Yes. No. Oh get on with it, Twainelle.' Ms Potter likes Twainelle, but she specialises in quandaries unrelated to the subject being taught – misplaced intelligence, Ms Potter thinks; one day, perhaps too late, she'll realise she is very bright, and apply herself.

'Miss, I'm not very good at French.'

'This is not a French lesson.'

'No, but I'm not.'

'We shouldn't be discussing this now, but it's probably not your fault. When I was at school it was compulsory, five hours a week.'

'But the Red children –'

'Yes?' At once Ms Potter is wary. After all, there are Red children in this class, including Little Eagle, listening, and she won't put up with bullying.

'Why do they learn so quick? They came here, they didn't speak much English, did they, just, like, something weird, not weird, I don't mean that, but like, they spoke their own weird language –'

'Twainelle –' Ms Potter's tone is warning, but Twainelle presses on.

'And now they understand almost everything we say and they can say it too. So are they – is it possible – I mean I don't want to say nothing bad about us, but could they – actually – be more brainy than us? Or not?'

Now Little Eagle and the other Red children in the class are laughing, but more of the children in the class are looking annoyed, and muttering.

'Interesting question, but one I can't answer,' says Ms Potter. 'How do we measure it?'

As the girl's luxuriantly black-curled head bobs past five minutes later on her dancing way out of the classroom, though, Ms Potter gives her a big smile.

'What?' said Twainelle, but smiling back.

'Well done for thinking.'

'I'm always thinking,' said Twainelle. 'Just cos I might sometimes be on my phone, I'm still thinking. By the way, please Miss can I have my phone back now please?' She had had it taken away after three warnings not to use it in class.

'Soon,' says Ms Potter. 'What I meant was, well done for thinking outside the box, Twainelle.'

'I don't even care that much about my phone,' says Twainelle in a rush. 'Like he says,' (indicating Little Eagle who stands quietly waiting by the window), 'phones are quite boring.'

Little Eagle's status rose rapidly within the school when it was remarked that he and Twainelle were hanging out, although both denied that they were dating.

25

The Red children had problems sitting still. Most generalisations didn't fit all of them – this one did. They didn't understand why they couldn't get up in the middle of the lesson and walk around the classroom, smile at the teacher, stare longingly out of the window, then sit down again. This happened three or four times each lesson, so if there were two or more Red children in a class, the whole day was semi-perpetual motion. (Only Monica, who forbade it, asked what they were looking for. Roosha, one of the first two children to arrive, said, 'Home. I miss home. Where I grew.' 'Sorry … Still, lucky you,' said Monica, after a pause. 'Where I grew up was hell.' That silenced the class.)

An informal conference in the staffroom on 'Restlessness' took place.

There were three options, Belinda insisted. 'One, we give them sanctions. Keep them in after school –'

Ms Potter interrupted. 'But – if they can't keep still in lessons, how can they keep still after school?'

Belinda pressed on regardless. 'Two, we exclude them. I know we would all regret that' (she was lying) 'but we are a particular kind of school, an academic school, we've all made an effort but it's not our fault if they don't fit in. There must be a school which is more suitable for their needs – for movement and so on.'

'What would that be, a circus school?' said Monica.

Belinda, unlike others, didn't laugh. She stared fiercely at her before continuing.

'Three, we place them all with Monica's – special group of children.'

'Fuck off, Belinda, but okay,' said Monica. 'Doesn't bother me.'

'Swearing,' said Belinda, wagging her finger at her, pink-faced.

Winston was laughing inside but he said, 'Really, this is unacceptable –'

'Swearing? Jesus wept, Winston,' Monica cut in before remembering kind Ms Potter was a Christian, her mother having come from Barbados (Monica, indifferent to taboos, had asked her).

'Not the swearing,' said Winston. 'We're all grown-ups, though Monica, this *is* a staff meeting. The idea that all migrants have special needs is unacceptable.'

'Well they do,' said Belinda. Round the room, there was a shaking of heads. 'Okay then,' she pressed on, her sharp little nose pecking forward like a bird, 'it's sanctions or exclusion. I favour the latter. So does everyone else, they just don't want to say so. Now sorry, I for one have to get on with my work.'

Monica grinned and showed her big teeth. 'That work ethic, Belinda! Wowzer! But no. This is what we're going to do. Carrot not stick. We'll say that everyone has a right to get up once and once only in each lesson, though as a matter of fact, they almost never do it in mine, everyone's scared of me, because I shout. Hahahaha. If they keep still, they win the right to come on a big walk, we'll call it an "introductory walk" cos it's just for the Red children, it can be a nature walk, or a history walk, or a fucking natural history walk, sorry for swearing, it just popped out, once a week for the last two hours of Friday afternoon, until they get bored, or I do.'

'But the weather,' said Winston. 'It's cold. All kids complain if they have to go out in the cold.'

'This lot don't complain about anything. Little Eagle told me they're on the run from the heat.'

'It's your free period,' said Winston. 'Double free period, in fact. But they'll miss lessons. They'll get behind.'

'Well some of them are ahead at the moment,' said Monica. 'We might as well try it. The other ideas were crap. Let them be themselves. It's all anyone wants. So long as I can be myself too, which means shouting a bit. Everyone happy?'

Yes! The others were relieved, and Belinda had left in a temper as soon as Monica laughed at her work ethic.

This was the origin of the Introductory Nature Walks (as they appeared on the timetable) which did indeed introduce the Red children to the walk along to Pegwell Bay at sea-level, past the line of caves with their long white shawls of broken chalk and shells and seaweed, past the sentry-post of the ravens, at the top of the blue-green pine, past the mussels and the whelks and the curlews. Which changed many things, and the children came back before dark, in that cold February, chilled but mysteriously happy, wildly excited because they had met – had been licked by, played with by, followed for miles by – a most beautiful pale-furred dog called Koda, walking on the beach, who seemed to know them, ran up to Molo, jumped up and started licking his face. Boy and dog stood in rapt contemplation of each other, then Molo and he started talking and growling and playfighting. It was Wayne, his owner, who told the Professor the dog was Inuit, and Juan nodded, gravely, and buried his big hands in the dog's thick fur, telling Molo, 'Inuit people and animals will always be our brothers and our friends.' They had to say goodbye at last, but the walk was a success, their eyes, shaded by strong brow-ridges, were brighter than before, and their pockets bulged with fresh supplies of chalk and shells.

If Monica hadn't come up with an imaginative solution, the Red children might have been excluded from the school, sent on like an unwanted parcel somewhere else, and might well have forgotten what they saw on their very first day in England, when Arash the fisherman pointed them towards it: the Pegwell caves, and the stretch of untouched coast-line, half-covered by the tides, where so much of Ramsgate's history had played out in secret; smuggling, invasion, lovers' meetings, writers and artists, fights, drownings, and deaths.

The Professor only came on one of her walks, but that day Monica showed him his future.

26

Molo had many good points, or he would not have been among the picked band who accompanied the Professor on his great journey. He was extraordinarily deft, for a Red child, which disproved the idea that the Red people's heavy bones necessarily made them clumsy. He was the quickest to understand everything digital, and the one whose handwriting first conformed to the Grammar School's norms. His memory was phenomenal; he was in fact the only one of the Reds (apart from the Professor) who knew by heart the exact latitudes and longitudes of Ramsgate and Jebel Tarek, and the hours, minutes and seconds of the rising and setting of the sun in both locations, and could therefore find the rare dates and days when the distance between the places magically telescoped to nothing, when the beauty of simultaneity linked them, and you could simply slip through that brief golden gateway, and be, for a fraction of a second, both here and there; upside down and right way up; both sides of the mirror, which became as clear as glass.

And he was good-looking: as Belinda, and especially Sandra, noticed.

But Molo was also a damaged child sent into a house where at least one other damaged child was living.

The Professor liked Molo partly because Molo's parents, like his own a generation earlier, had died underground in an outbreak of virus. Most of the tiny orphans were absorbed by other families, but Molo, because he cried so loudly and hit people so hard, was not. He was late to talk, as well, so could not explain his great anger, which was perfectly simple – he had lost his father and mother. But aged eight, he had suddenly learned how to speak and stopped crying, hitting, and fighting. When the Professor came back on one of his visits, Molo had stared at him a long time from the back of the underground chamber, then went to him and took him by the hand. He led the big man to see his secret collection of shells laid out on a damp shelf in the rock, all graded with unnerving accuracy from red to gold. A constant dribble of water kept the colours bright. 'Why do you collect these?' the Professor had asked. Molo looked puzzled.

'For me. Something for me. I like them. They're all different. But they're all the same. There are exactly one thousand. So I've stopped.' The Professor gravely nodded, and later, when Molo got into trouble for stealing and hiding the watch of one of the elders, defended him. 'He's a curious child. Of course he doesn't know right from wrong. Who was there to teach him? We send him out to forage food – he thinks it's his job to collect things.' The Professor gave Molo his own watch.

Now Molo was seventeen and accepted as an oddity by his people. In other societies he might have been called autistic. He hardly talked, even in their own language, and was now resistant to English. He was shorter and squatter than most of his fellows and had long dark beautiful lashes, heavy brows and thick, lustrous, raven-black hair.

Molo could walk on his hands: his strong arms had made that his calling-card ever since he had learned to do it, on the secret singed-grass space that opened up high above the Jebel Tarek tunnels where the Red people drank up the sunlight they needed for their bones.

Molo had been in Belinda's house for a week and both of Belinda's sons were outraged. Liam and Joe had been made to share a room, which both hated, while Belinda turned the junk room into a space for Molo. Maternal crime! They had not been consulted! They were as one: Molo, the intruder, must be turfed out, and their mother, the oppressor, vanquished. They nicknamed him 'Molly'. They agreed he was stealing their illicit fags (though in fact, he didn't smoke – sharing a room, they were accidentally stealing each other's).

On the other hand, Molo was taking food from the fridge. A strange smell from his room gave Belinda the answer to the mystery of the vanished blue cheese. Beside it, neatly stored in the wardrobe, were stale bread and biscuits. She talked to him seriously: 'The food in the fridge is for everyone, the others will go hungry if you do that.' He looked crestfallen, but next day Sandra came down puzzled in the evening. 'Why have you put cheese in my bedroom, Mum? I don't like cheese.'

'I didn't … oh god, it's that boy.' This time Molo had put little caches of food in everyone's bedroom, including Belinda's. She felt pity, and sat him down in the kitchen. 'Listen very carefully. In this house I do the food. I'm the food person. Leave it to me and no-one will go hungry. Fridge: NO.' After that, no more trouble with food.

And Belinda's cat could not stop rubbing herself against Molo's legs and begging him to stroke her head then, rolling on her back, her tummy, which slowly endeared the boy to Belinda, since everyone else in the house thought the cat was old and smelled of piss. She noticed how he liked to go into their garden, lie flat on his belly and stare into the eyes of Taughtus, the fifteen-year-old tortoise that had been Sandra's since she was a toddler. When Liam reported to his mother that Molo was talking to the tortoise she just laughed and said, 'He's foreign, but I'm warming to him.'

'Yeah? Well it's Sandra's pet, he shouldn't muck about with it. And I need my own bedroom back, Mum.'

Joe, on the other hand, was basically a cheerful boy who couldn't keep up a quarrel for long, because he'd forget why he was angry, unlike Liam, who had never quite forgiven his brother for wrecking his life by being born.

Ten days after the intruder arrived, Joe got up early to go to the gym and, as he waited for the kettle to boil, glimpsed Molo walking on his hands on the lawn outside the kitchen window. He took his coffee outside in the garden. Molo ignored him.

'Oi,' said Joe.

Molo took no notice. The upside-down body, amazing, all muscle, continued its upside-down progression across the lawn, step after step, like a ship negotiating waves, steadying after each one, the thick black hair hanging down in a curtain, the broad feet, almost together, outlined against the blank blue sky.

Joe stopped trying to attract his attention and watched. Then he noticed something the other boy couldn't see. 'Molly!' Joe called, then panicked, he hadn't meant to use the nickname, 'Sorry, Molo, watch out, danger ahead!' He was about to catch his strong legs on Belinda's washing-line.

Calmly, hardly wavering on his strong, dark-fuzzed arms, Molo swung one leg, then the other, to the ground.

Joe was watching in frank admiration. 'Show me how you do that,' he said, and to make it plainer, threw down his own hands and made a little bunny-hop.

Ten minutes later, when Joe had discovered how hard it was to walk on your hands, they were starting to be friends. Molo never said very much, but Joe understood the simple thing he was saying. 'I like to see the world the other way up.'

Liam felt horribly betrayed.

27

'I'm thinking about Religious Knowledge,' said Ms Potter to Winston, running into him and the Professor after school, walking companionably in the direction of a beer. Winston was usually pleased to see her, but at this precise moment not so much.

'Oh, why?'

'I hope it's okay to ask,' she said, smiling anxiously towards the Professor. 'Your children, your lovely children, Professor – aren't they, well, Muslims?'

'In a sense,' said the Professor, smiling encouragingly. He had found that phrase useful all his life.

'Are we reflecting that enough in our teaching?'

She was in charge of Religious Knowledge, so 'I think so,' was clearly the right answer.

'But they aren't attending the lessons anymore, are they, Professor, they got an exemption because of, you know, laughing.' There was just a hint of distress in her voice.

'A good solution,' the Professor said, in a consolatory yet final way. Winston, he sensed, was desperate for his drink.

'So now they are meeting with you in those periods instead,' Ms Potter rushed on, 'and I just wanted to be sure you know … We do teach comparative religion, we do teach morality, we do have Muslims in school. And the Red children are very welcome. We're not – I'm not – I'm a Christian as you know, but I'm not *narrow*. People's faith must be respected. One love, Professor. I mean it.' As soon as she said it, she felt relieved.

'I know,' the Professor replied, with a suitably grateful

smile, 'I am taking a leaf from your book and teaching them comparative religion too.'

Once the two men had sunk into two chairs in the pub and the cold, sweet-salt comfort of their drinks, Winston said, 'Well done with Ms Potter. What do you teach them really?'

Bright-eyed, the Professor explained. He'd been telling them how, when this part of Kent stretched nearly half a mile further out to sea towards Belgium, and people were just starting to forget the Roman invasion of sixty years before, five-year-old Jesus was watching the trail of a snail on the shores of a lake in Galilee. How a few hundred years later, not long after Hengist and Horsa rowed across the sea from the north in horse-headed galleys, a boy called Muhammad was born in Makkah, a valley high above sea-level in Saudi Arabia, as swallows swooped overhead. ('Jesus and Muhammad grew up hearing many of the same teachings,' he told Winston, who was looking dazed.) Muhammad was a youth of twenty-five by the time a middle-aged monk called Augustine in Rome was told to set off for England by the Pope. ('I think we agree, dear fellow, history's all about migrants.') After a two-year journey, Augustine sailed into Pegwell Bay, bringing God with him to Kent. Thirteen years later and four thousand miles away, Muhammad heard the words of God in a cave in Saudi Arabia.

'It's all a matter of perspective, you see,' he concluded.

'That's quite cool, Juan,' said Winston, laughing, as they parted. 'Especially if you're not making it up.'

'Oh, I'm not. But life, you know. Always stranger than fiction, yes? The problem is how to make the fictions strange enough. For example, today. One of mine, as I think of them, Molo, came to me and said he had been talking to a tortoise, and the tortoise had a message for me.'

'He was joking, right?' Winston asked, smiling.

'No more than I am when I tell you about St Augustine and Mohammad being alive at the same time, without knowing it. The point is everything's happening at once, and the voices are all talking at once, the whole universe is a network of messages …'

Winston did not want the Professor, his friend, to sound like his wife when overexcited. 'Okay, what did the tortoise say?' he interrupted.

'He apparently said we must go home,' said the Professor, giving Winston a faintly sad salute as he went on his way.

28

By late April, as the heat built up, the evenings seemed longer and lighter than usual, which made the Red people more visible, in Ramsgate, St Lawrence, Broadstairs.

Suddenly it seemed that they were everywhere, big, friendly, youthful people using bursts of newly-learned English and laughter to ask for jobs on the fishing boats, the seafood stalls, and, as Eileen Killarney was heard to complain, 'even Waitrose!' Others were turning up just before dawn alongside the other foreigners to work at Planet Thanet, but not complaining, like everyone else, about the wages. Hosts were delighted and touched when their guests handed over all the money they earned, though most, embarrassed, refused. We saw their heavily built (to us) but genial figures clearing the tables at Wetherspoons or washing the floors. At weekends and in the evenings they were all round the town, looning on the harbour quay in ungainly, amicable chains, staring and pointing at the masts of the yachts, drinking, though they drank like people who had never drunk before, becoming loud and euphoric after a few sips and then pouring the rest of the drink into the water of the harbour far below. Young men! It's true, we had missed them.

If indeed they were men, which some disputed. 'They're extra-terrestrials,' one of our own lonely young men said, and his mates laughed. There was something not right about them, he insisted, something off, something –

'They're aliens,' Benny Barolo said. 'Could be robots?'

His brother, who was drunk, agreed, but the brother's

girlfriend, a nurse, said, 'Rubbish. They never come in on their own when they hurt themselves. I had to give one a tetanus shot and his mate held his hand and when I did it, the other one winced and you won't believe it, but an actual tear ran down his cheek. They're so ... human.'

The Red people had fallen in love with chalk. Wherever they came from clearly didn't have it in such abundance as Ramsgate, where the sea swelled in great creamy whorls of chalk in summer storms. They loved the beaches, and went to them whenever they weren't in school or working, wading into the sea in their clothes after they got told off for going in naked, making sand-heaps – not sand-castles but almost identical triangular heaps, often with one long, low slope facing a second sharp slope, as vertical as sand would go. They came back from the sea with their pockets bulging with the soft white stones they had collected, big pieces, little pieces, chalk with round holes in it, oval chalk, pointy chalk, chalk.

Very soon the graffiti began; always the same cross-hatched lines, the same mad ladders for a game of noughts and crosses that never began. Mad to us, second nature to them. If you found them doing it, whereas local lads caught doing graffiti looked sheepish or aggressive, the Red folk smiled and looked proud. For a while the local taggers picked up on it and copied the complicated hashtag in paint, but the Red people only used chalk. Still, people didn't like it, even me; it was evidence of a foreign presence; a claim; outsiders had decided to leave their mark on our beautiful harbour. 'At least they don't use yellow paint like the PBF,' I said to calm things down. We didn't understand till much later what they were drawing.

Then Red children were spotted collecting wood. Wooden crates and pallets, from container ships, some broken, some intact, often washed up on the sand, and occasionally bigger things, timber baulks or planks that were being shipped from the north, or the remnants of houses or beach-huts silently lost, like the cliffs and beaches, to the sea.

In fact, they were getting ready to make a raft. In History Club, which Little Eagle attended, Mr Phelpham had talked about ancient peoples crossing from Siberia to America on makeshift rafts. 'They're our friends,' Little Eagle had said, and Twainelle, who had only come because of him and wasn't sure she wanted to be there, giggled, but Mr Phelpham looked at Little Eagle with hooded eyes, folding the information away for later.

The Red children had watched with fascination the other means of transport that soared across the coastal waters, the speed boats, the jet-skis, the lilos. But they had no money, and they didn't see the point of the noise which the jet-skis were famous for, and they liked to make everything themselves. And so, with the aid of a picture in a book from the library, they began to make a raft.

That day I was sitting on the edge of the promenade with a coffee reading a book about cave art but watching from time to time, as were others on the beach – I recognised Ramadan Bakri, in yellow shorts, with pale, curvy Sandra, shy in her bikini.

First they laid out the best straight pieces of wood on the sand in a sort of lattice. Three parallel verticals, three long horizontals, and two short ones which wouldn't quite go across. At that point they all got excited and danced around it – I was bemused, then realised it was the same shape they drew everywhere, the hashtag they loved. But maybe they were just happy, because they started adding more pieces and I realised: it's going to be a raft.

The Red people had always liked string. It was one of the things they brought with them, and one of the only things which the older ones, with their first earnings, bought for themselves. Now they lashed their construction together and carried it down to the sea, triumphant when it floated. But before it had gone ten metres it started to come apart. Cries of dismay, and they all splashed in to save the wood.

Ramadan and two other Sea Cadets ran down to join them. 'Diagonals,' Ramadan was shouting. 'I'm going to be a sailor – maybe,' he added out of honesty. 'Me and my mate Freddy. So we know about it. You need bits that run corner to corner, to brace. It's something called 'Hull integrity'. We've been learning it for Seamanship. Come with us. We'll show you.' Sandra, left alone on their striped beach towel, looked cross, and I suddenly saw that one day she would look like her mother.

What happened, I found out later, when the aspens whispered it to me, was that the Sea Cadets took the others along to the Park, and after discussion, cut two of the strong young aspen saplings which grew too thickly and needed coppicing. The modified raft was a lot stronger, though that too was destroyed in one of the early summer storms that blew up.

But the friendship between the Sea Cadets and the Red people lasted. On summer evenings, you would see Freddy and some of the older Sea Cadets teaching their Red friends to row, in the harbour. They were naturals, with their muscular build and strong arms. One day this talent would stand them in good stead.

29

Mr Phelpham, the best sort of teacher, a learner, was trying to teach the Red children things that might interest them. But about them he still had little information, just his own observations, his love of history, his memory, retentive and profound, and his restless mind, still flexible though his sixty-year-old knees and shoulders were stiff. It had only grown more restless as he aged and stayed, the better to raise his many school-age children, for yet another decade in Ramsgate.

His online searches first led him to the Neander valley in Germany, after which the Neanderthal people had been named. Aha. Germany. And the photographic reconstruction of a face – yes. Yes! Yet the Red children's language, so far as he and Anna Segovia had been able to tell, was a mixture of Spanish and Arabic with bits of Italian and English thrown in – it wasn't Germanic.

Most people would have stopped there, but Tony Phelpham burrowed further. His intentions were only good; how was he to know that his endless festive loops of internet links, skimming round the globe and darting back and forth in time, were only adding to the burning multicoloured chains of searches that might help to make a bonfire of the world?

But the question of who the Red people were was so interesting, so surprising. Onward he must go, always onward on his search through the night, which was too hot, surely, for June. There were Neanderthal remains in Kent. It turned out that Kent had more Neanderthal remains than any other part of England, that Neanderthals had migrated here from Europe when there was still a land bridge between the two: Southfleet, Ebbsfleet, Swalecliffe, Baker's Hole, they had lived here in the distant past when hippos and monkeys and elephants still roamed the land. The ache of time, he thought, stretching in his uncomfortable chair, and seeing with a start how much time on his own tiny scale had passed – it was two in the morning, the shed where he kept his library was cramped and he had to be in the classroom at nine.

But before he went to bed, he tried the Natural History Museum website, where a slightly patronising little film told him that the first adult 'Neanderthal' skull ever found, which the Museum was lucky enough to have in its possession, had in fact been dug up in a quarry in Gibraltar.

30

'It's hard to dislike them,' old Graham cautiously ventured in the pub one night, though he and his PBF cronies had decided from the start that they did dislike them. That day however, one of the Red teenagers had picked up Graham's stick and handed it back to him as he struggled to draw money from a card machine and hold his shopping (fish fingers and a newspaper) and his stick at the same time. Threatened by the big presence behind him, he'd been making a special effort to hide his bank card code, so he felt guilty when the stick was gently replaced in his hand.

'Oh they're *likeable* enough,' said the man sitting next to him, Benny Barolo, the leader of the local branch, as though likeability was something you could take for granted; as though he liked them, or anyone else, himself. 'But why did they have to come to Ramsgate?' Ignorant of the plans for a raft, the PBF had more to talk about now they knew the Red people were collecting wood.

'They'll be going to set fires,' said Hank Stitch. 'Pyromaniacs, probably.' The word had a ring to it, and went well with the threatening Reds of their dreams.

Hank Stitch, who like Liam Birch, Belinda's son, was trying to establish his presence in the group, said, 'Cannibals. Going to have a banquet.'

A burst of approving laughter, and 'Yeahs', but Graham, a pedant, demurred. 'Try and remember, my lad, the PBF is not irrational. We make reasoned complaints. These people seem pleasant enough, but −'

At that moment, a big, genial waiter, smiling and bearing a tray of drinks, which he only slopped slightly as he placed them on the table, arrived, rolling the names of the drinks with elaborate care. Was he …? Yes.

Eyes lowered, the plotters thanked him. 'Cheers mate.'

'Thanks.'

'Nice one.'

He lingered, grinning with pleasure and rubbing his big red hands together.

'That'll be all,' said Graham, but the Red youth just stood there, not understanding.

When he finally left, Graham resumed. 'As we just saw, they're gormless, they smell of seaweed, their English is poor, and yet they're still taking our jobs. And stealing our wood. But eating human flesh? Where's your evidence?'

'They eat a lot of burgers,' said Liam, trying to help. 'Disgusting. I'm a vegetarian.'

The rest of the table stared.

'Vegetarian? That's just weird, mate,' said Benny.

31

After Liam finished his evening run along to Stone Bay and back, he liked to walk around the quayside and harbour arm to cool down and look out, in a not very hopeful way, for some kind of happiness he'd never discovered. It was something to look forward to after his runs on the cliff which he'd started to like less and less.

This spring, however, as he passed the lit bars along the front, he kept noticing silhouettes of serving staff against the light that were bigger than usual, different. *Them*, he was sure of it, more of them had got around the owners and tricked their way into the jobs he would need if he was ever to have a girlfriend or friends like his hateful brother who, though younger, had blagged his way into a weekend gig at the local care home, worrying their mum a lot when the two old fools had died there.

'Can't you get a job for me?' Liam asked Joe as they lay in their narrow beds in the stuffy room they had to share. It was a morning in May when Joe, having worked double shifts the day before, had Sunday off.

'Look ... for a start, you've got no references.'

'I have!'

'No good references. Anyway. I would help, Liam, but the truth is, you hate old people, you always said so, you always said Grandma and Grandpa were disgusting.'

'I didn't!' But Liam's denial was so blatantly untrue that he fell quiet for a moment, then said with a spurt of confidence 'Anyway, they don't know what I said at the Care Home.'

'I do.'

'You won't help me.'

It was said with such despair that a blade of pity twisted Joe's heart. He hated feeling that for the elder brother he wanted to admire. 'It's difficult. I can't ask again.'

'You never asked for a job for me before,' Liam said, indignant.

'No.' Long pause. 'Not for you.' Joe stared at his duvet, miserable.

'Who was it for then? It's for him, isn't it?,' said Liam, rage pushing him out of his bed in a single twist, jaw jutting forward in temper. 'Bloody Molo! Your new *mate*!'

'Not Molo, no. Little Eagle asked me. That one who used to swear. He's really bright and good at numbers, you know. So I gave them his name. They liked him.'

That 'bright and good at numbers' – as if he was not! He, Liam, the son of a physicist, his own brother – half-brother ... Indignation ripped through Liam with terrible heat.

Later that day after school, Monica saw them scuffle in the street after Liam 'jokingly' pulled Joe's backpack off his shoulder and his phone fell out and cracked. Joe punched Liam hard, and Liam ran off.

32

'There's going to be trouble,' said Monica to Ginger that afternoon. They were standing together looking out at their daughter Hecate through the hideous new bifold windows at the back of their house (on which Ginger had insisted, because he 'liked to keep an eye'). She was bouncing, bouncing, bouncing higher and higher on her enormous trampoline, so high that at the top of her arc he could no longer see her, a flashing, titian-haired gymnast flaming up and down in front of the dark yews. 'Did you hear what I said? Real trouble.'

'Mon, I said so from the first,' Ginger turned towards her, surprised. 'You insisted trampolines are safe as houses. Where, if you remember, I reminded you that bad things happen, as we both know.'

'Not *her*,' Monica said. 'Hecate is doing exactly what she wants to –'

'People doing what they want to frequently go wrong –'

'Maybe, but not my daughter. No, Belinda Birch's boys. Bad blood.'

'Belinda's all right,' Ginger said. 'You don't like her politics.'

'Something off between them. Worse than it was.'

'Belinda Birch has everything under control, it seems to me.' Ginger liked Belinda. Fit little woman who was very supportive of police charities and regularly asked him in to talk to the Grammar School kids.

'Too much control. I don't like her,' Monica said, and rested her elbow uncomfortably on top of Ginger's shoulder, so her forearm was pressed against his ear. She was taller than him, as she liked to remind him. He shrugged her off, so she lurched briefly across him, then steadied herself, but a splash of black coffee fell on their bright white table. Both of them stared at it, then each other, with unreadable expressions before Ginger went and got a cloth.

'We both like control, Monica.'

'Yes. But Belinda has favourites. Favourites are bad in families or classes. Joe and that simpering daughter are Belinda's favourites, and Liam knows it.'

'You exaggerate,' said Ginger. 'As always. Your evidence, Mon?'

'Saw them fighting on the front. Never saw that before.'

'Brothers,' said Ginger.

'Yes. But outside the house. Quite vicious. And Liam ran away.'

There was a shout of rage from the garden as Hecate fell off. She lay sprawled for a moment, her hair spread-eagled, a crimson shawl, on the surprisingly short lawn, and both parents waited for a wail, but as usual, it did not come, Mon laid a finger on Ginger's muscular arm to stop him going out to investigate, and Hecate sat up, then with another, louder roar like the roar of a soldier attacking, was on her feet and running at the trampoline, up in a bound.

'My daughter,' said Monica, smiling at Ginger.

'Mine,' said Ginger, not smiling. 'She's not immortal, you know.'

'To get back to these boys. I see blood.'

There was a silence as Hecate's bounces grew bigger until she soared out of their sight.

'Not immediately,' Monica added. 'In time, if no-one watches out.'

My friend Monica knew about families, since hers had been involved in a death which was never classified as a murder, and Ginger, too, knew rather a lot about that.

'You've seen blood before, my love,' Ginger said. And now he smiled.

'Don't smile,' Monica said. 'I don't like it when you smile – like that.'

'It meant, in this instance, "You're a bit of an expert on families, Monica." I'll watch out.'

33

The more Joe and Jude hung out with Molo and the other Red children, the more Liam detested them. Easy-going Joe had made friends among the newcomers even before Molo came to stay. Joe competed with them at carrying heavy objects, and sometimes people, when teachers weren't looking, across the yard. The Red children usually won but that didn't bother Joe. He liked the way they laughed. Joe's favourite girl in the world, beautiful Jude, befriended Roosha, one of only two Red girls in the group – 'I love her,' she said, 'she's so *strong*!'

Jude was a favourite of mine as well. Anyone who taught her remembered her confidence and the way she smiled at a new bit of knowledge, showing perfect white teeth and pink gums. She always sat next to Joe and had been close to him since nursery, apparently, when he punched Anton on her behalf, as I told you earlier, but now she did kick-boxing, had a disturbing grown-up shape and long shiny black hair. Anyone Joe and Jude liked, everyone else liked too.

Liam, though admired by his cohort for his superpower, speed, had never enjoyed the status Joe had, and was now in the uneasy position of the boy who should have graduated with a prize at the end of Year 13 but mysteriously didn't. When he came into school for extra teaching, he looked faintly too old.

The Red children's physical ease: that was what he hated most. Liam, who had always felt spikey and awkward in his own body, ran partly to escape into the bodiless thrill of pure speed. Belinda had never found him easy to feed or cuddle. Brad, Liam's father, who came over to 'try and make a go of it' once he knew he had a son, watched Belinda irritably swing the child from breast to breast, too fast, and thought 'Poor kid! But it's not my fault he exists. Gotta save my own life.' And he did. Liam had grown into a boy in need of a mentor, something to believe in, and a father.

One day in May the Professor noticed a thin youth walking round the school library, picking books off the shelves, reading them for seconds, then replacing them in slightly the wrong place. The Professor talked to him, asked him questions, and generally treated Liam with the respect he craved. Discovering the Professor had several degrees from Cambridge, Liam's breast swelled with pride.

That night in bed he could not resist boasting about his new friend to Joe. 'I was talking to that Professor guy today,' he said. Joe was looking at his phone in the dark.

'Yeah?'

'He thought maybe I should be trying Cambridge.' This was not exactly what the Professor had said, but in Liam's memory he had.

'Yeah? Wow,' said Joe belatedly. 'Cambridge. Well, you should.'

'He's, like, an international professor. Not like the teachers in our school. They don't know anything about university. They never said about Cambridge to me.'

That insistent, complainy note had come into his older brother's voice, the one Joe had only noticed recently. He switched off his phone. 'Yeah, he's great, Juan,' he said with a yawn, turning over to go to sleep.

'What did you call him?' Liam said after a minute.

'Uhnnn ...?' Joe was nearly asleep.

'The Professor. What did you call him?'

'Juan. That's his name. We hang out.'

'Who's we?'

'Mate, I'm trying to go to sleep. Me and Jude and the others.'

With that Joe was dead to the world.

Liam lay there burning in the dark. They 'hung out'. Joe and Jude and 'the others'. They called him 'Juan'.

When he finally slept, a bitter, shrivelled, walnut of opinion had hardened in his mind.

34

'Parcel's come for you,' said Holly one day when the Professor came home from school. 'Marked "FRAGILE".'

'Addressed to me here?' asked Juan, surprised.

'Just says, "The Professor, Ramsgate, UK." It's a benefit of small-town living, word gets around. They found my famous friend Shirley Green with just "Shirley Green, actress and singer, Ramsgate". John is a wonderful postman.'

The parcel was a giant cube, with wrapping paper carefully inscribed in blue ink. The postmark was 'Suva'.

'That's Fiji,' said the Professor, happily unwrapping. 'I made a few friends there. Silversea Cruises used to stop by.'

Inside, a large cardboard box was sheathed like a wasp's nest in layers and layers of waste paper. Holly hovered, fascinated, as the Professor finally prepared to remove the lid.

'Tell me it's not going to be a shrunken head, darling,' she said.

He paused. 'It's a mistake, dear lady, to think that Fijians shrink heads.'

'Weren't they cannibals?'

'People get very excited by cannibals,' he said, throwing the paper into her recycling bin.

'Do you mean me? I think there was one on *Antiques Roadshow*,' she said, to justify herself, 'a shrunken head, not a cannibal.'

'Doubt it,' he said. '*Homo sapiens* historians love the idea of Neanderthals eating each other for breakfast – they secretly hope it's true, to prove modern man has progressed.

Neanderthals did much more interesting things, of course. So did Fijians. There ends my lecture. Let's see what this is.'

'You know so much … Good heavens,' she said. 'Oh and look, how absolutely divine.'

It was a glorious thing, large, lustrous, with a fluted lip and a soft pink interior, the spiral point removed to make a mouthpiece.

'It's a conch shell,' she said. 'But such a beautiful one. Let's put it in the window.'

'It's not just a shell, darling,' he said, thoughtful. 'It's a signal, for my brothers in Fiji. They play it.' He held it in his arms, and gazed at her, then out to sea.

'You've got a brother in Fiji? Oh, you're joking. Play it for me!'

'It's not time, but one day it will be. Yes, all right, we'll put it in your window for now.'

'You aren't cross with me, are you?' asked Holly, running her hand across his broad shoulders. 'I so love having you here with me.'

'How could I be cross with you? You make me happy,' he sighed, and enjoyed the feel of her loving fingers relaxing the tenseness in his back and arms.

Juan didn't want to listen to the messages, yet. Too soon. He wanted more time. He wanted to live. There was love to make.

But next day he ran into Molo in the corridor at school and the boy said, as if their conversation had not been interrupted by thirty-six hours, 'And the swifts at Pegwell told Roosha exactly the same thing, Professor. So it's true. We have to go.'

The Professor's green eyes were opaque. 'Well, swifts never rest. But we're human. We have to.'

35

As spring began to tumble into summer, Ramsgaters kept finding new presences in places where they didn't expect them. Though most of the natives rarely used the beaches except in the height of the season, they liked them to be there, and empty, when they did, as a backdrop for selfies, for example. Now there were always odd shapes in the background when they got home and looked at the photos they'd taken.

'Do you think they'll be here every day?' said Joan Rudd, mildly. She had recently retired from her part-time job in a fruit and vegetable shop, and was hoping to take the dog for more walks with some of her fellow widows – since the virus, there were many widows, old and young.

'They're not doing any harm,' said her friend Belle. She had an icecream, the first of the year, and she didn't want to worry.

'No. Still, it's not what we're used to,' said Joan.

'Broadstairs hasn't got any,' Belle remarked.

'Typical! It's like seaweed. Broadstairs clears it ... How did they manage that?'

'Hang on. They're not *seaweed*,' said Belle, who was fair-minded. Broadstairs not having them was a two-edged sword, she thought. Perhaps, in a way, having Red people was a distinction? 'They won't be here forever,' she said. 'Nor will we.'

'No. I should have had a choc ice like you.'

The Red people loved playing, and once they discovered that behind the Wetherspoons where some of them had jobs, Ramsgate's main beach opened, shining, into sunlight, they were there every day, doing no harm, as Joe pointed out to Liam, but making their characteristic triangular sand-hills or digging, digging, into the earth like dogs. And feathers – there were always seagulls' feathers on the beach, and some big dark ones as well. The bigger the better. The Red children stuck them in their hair, they pushed them through jumpers and tee-shirts, they gave the prettiest ones to girls, they made little toys out of stones and shells that they decorated with feathers and sold for pennies, or more often gave away. They liked to knock flints against each other, which made sounds like unearthly music, tapping them and working them, sometimes, for hours, then, with a single well-placed blow, making thin flakes, sharp as knives, fly off, laughing with triumph as if the stone blades cut through to another world.

Winston, strolling with Ella on the promenade that Sunday, smiled upon the Red children he knew. He loved to see them having fun. But he worried for them, as well. They were visible and audible, that was the trouble. Being visible wasn't a plus to the British of the older type, he knew from his mother's side of the family and their neighbours, quiet white people like his grandparents Albert and May, who suffered and loved and died behind their net curtains. Many of that older generation of Londoners, denizens of rows of identical tiny houses, had ended up in Thanet and passed on their stubborn reserve to their children and grandchildren, who might be loud when drunk but otherwise liked to protect their shyness on the beach behind carefully aligned windbreaks.

Whereas the Red people tumbled about and played and dug and wrestled and showed off their skills with flints right out in the sunlight, in the middle of the sand where everyone could see them.

'We'll cut our feet,' said the PBF, most of whom had never been known to take their shoes off on the sand, or indeed walk on the sand. Wetherspoons's terrace was as far as they went.

Other people marvelled at the elegant stone blades, like slivers of hard light, that the Red Children left behind. Mr Phelpham took the youngest of his large tribe of children to the beach and they collected several.

Afterwards he took some of them into his shed and started tapping on his laptop.

Finding 'The tools of the last Neanderthals: Morpho-technological characterisation of the lithic industry at Level IV of Gorham's Cave, Gibraltar', *Quaternary International*, he read a few pages with a grunt of satisfaction, squinting at the images and then at the tools they had taken from the beach. It was the start of a long night of reading. He was chuckling to himself as he read, making dry happy sounds of self-congratulation – 'I thought so,' 'I knew it!' – sparrows fluttering about in a safe thick tree of delightful, incredible thought.

36

Monica, being enormous and odd, yet in her attitude to life heroic, had great fellow feeling for these genial new children, so free of fuss and pettiness, so prone to inappropriate laughter, as was she. Though she had to tell them to slow down, she enjoyed the way they came barrelling through corridors when late for lessons, the way they broke chairs by sitting on them and sometimes paused as if they had never seen such a thing when they got to the foot of the stairs.

'I never felt like other people,' she'd confided in Ginger. 'My family were weirdos. So I like this lot.'

'Your family were criminals,' Ginger riposted, 'so let's hope the immigrants aren't.'

'I need you on my side on this one.'

'Always. Root and branch,' said Ginger, and it was true.

'How are your nature walks going, Monica?' asked Winston, running into her in a corridor just before a lesson. She was so large, he thought: so very, very large.

'Triumph,' said Monica, briefly.

'Yes, there have been fewer complaints about, you know, restlessness.'

'Course.'

'Where do you go?'

'Pegwell.'

'Do they ask to go anywhere else?'

'Yes, now you mention it. Mad. Gravesend.'

'You could hardly walk to Gravesend!'

'Yeah. No, it's because Amonute is buried there, apparently.'

'Who?'

'That's what *I* said. It's Pocahontas's real name. These kids love American Indians.'

'Tony Phelpham told me that. They're keen on all, you know, indigenous peoples. He's been trying to bring them in to History Club. Bit too much genocide for kids, though. Monica, don't laugh.'

'Pocahontas or whoever died on a ship. Any case I told them, "No, Gravesend is a dump and besides, they've gone and lost her body." Careless.'

'That's very sad.'

But Monica was laughing again. 'Sorry, course it's sad but death makes me nervous.'

He ignored her. 'On the plus side, I think, no more PBF letters in the local paper about "people from outside behaving strangely on the Main Sands".'

'Hahahaha,' said Monica, 'hahaha. Yes, "behaving strangely", I remember that letter. Digging on the beach. As if that was strange. We used to play at burying my father. With a stone to represent my father … That letter must have been written by Belinda's ghastly son. Or Graham. The others can't write.'

Winston looked anxiously behind him. 'Liam is a pupil of this school, though his position, as a Year 13, is a bit anomalous.'

'Anomolous Shanomolous, he's a prat,' Monica said, amiably enough for her. 'Gotta go, Winston.'

'Wait. I've been getting complaints from worried parents – the nice ones, mind you, the hosts, the ones who are really trying to help – that the children are staying out at night.'

'Yeah?'

'The mother who rang me today was the fourth one this

week. Semi-hysterical.'

'Where the fuck do they go, in Ramsgate? How late?'

'In some cases, all night.'

But Monica, never late for her classes, was on her way, calling back over one broad shoulder, 'I'll find out.'

37

That Friday afternoon Monica was due to lead her fifth or sixth Nature Walk, though 'lead' was a misnomer, since the Red children pretty much did what they wanted to once they were off the promenade, falling behind, disappearing, reappearing with mysterious objects, digging, doing headstands and so on until she just shouted 'Freak show!' to no-one in particular, put her head down and walked, striding out along the shore.

They took the route the children liked best, along the beach to Pegwell Bay, the stretch of remote, samphire-rich, bird-rich marsh and sand where the Romans had landed. When they passed the tunnel leading into the cliff the Professor, who was walking beside her — two tall, eccentric figures leading the cavalcade — greeted a fisherman packing up for the day and pointed up at two black shapes making a tuneless racket above them. 'Your Ramsgate ravens. Very intelligent birds,' he told her. 'The male doesn't like me.'

('Doesn't like me,' Roland mimicked high above, but the Princess, who had the benefit of actually understanding human language, said in Ravenese, 'Darling, I'm sure he does.')

'Not *my* ravens,' said Monica, gawking briefly up at the annoyances interrupting her flow — she was telling the Professor what was wrong with the school. 'This is a nature walk in name only. I don't do nature, Professor, I have enough trouble with my own, hahaha.'

'I will take care of that side of things, dear lady,' the Professor assured her.

'Hahahaha, you'll have to. By the way, *I* like you.'

'Ha-ha-ha, ha-ha-ha,' mimicked Roland above her. 'Ha-ha-ha-AARK.'

'That woman's not a lady,' said the Princess Ra, shivering her feathers with distaste.

Then the party of humans all climbed over the railings and were down on the brilliant white shore, where the tide was out. The Red children rampaged over the slippery rocks, laughing, climbing, hugging, digging and picking up bunches of seaweed and seagull feathers as if they were giant two-year-olds. Not only the Red children came by now, young Red adults, too old for school, joined in the walk, staying back, a little shyly, as if they feared she would send them away, but 'The more the merrier,' she had shouted back at them, 'You're all right, just help me not to lose any of the other idiots.'

It was the caves that they loved, she realised, as they straggled happily behind her – how many of them, including the adults, sixty, seventy, more than a hundred? – and the sound of their shrieks and laughter, which had grown louder and louder as they hurried along the promenade running east and down on to the shell-crunched sand that led past the cliffs, diminished to almost nothing after the sixth or seventh cave-mouth they passed in the chalk, and when she looked round, two thirds of them had simply disappeared.

Yes, they were going into the caves. Big and small, deep and narrow, opening on to the sand at beach-level or glimpsed five feet up like the hole of an especially large owl, that stretch of beach was a honeycomb of caves, famed for its smugglers and renegades. That was why she always got back to Ramsgate with fewer Red people than she had led out, and sometimes, she would almost swear it, different ones, young adults who had come out of the caves.

At the weekend she went down on her own early in the morning to check. The sun was very bright, the tide was low, the bare chalk where the sand had been washed away from the foreshore was slippery as glass, but she paused outside the mouths of two or three of the larger caves, where the sea only rarely entered, and looked in, but saw nothing, and listened, and then she heard it: a shuffling, something falling, very faint laughter, and someone shushing.

Her hunch was confirmed.

'Kids are kipping in the caves,' she told Winston. 'Together with some of the adults. So long as they don't drown, they'll be all right. It's not exactly clubbing.'

38

Roland the Raven had been in a bad mood all weekend. He had flown with the Princess, who earlier, sleepy, had rejected his advances, in the teeth of a strong warm wind and unfed, from their blue-black pine-tree to breakfast at Holly's. Surely that would put his beloved in a better mood? But there was nothing on the windowsill. Nothing. No meat, no fruit, nothing, not even water. They were forgotten!

It was that man. The intruder, the giant red-haired fraud. 'He's not a real professor, my dear,' the Princess Ra said, to comfort him. 'They rarely have hair. This one has lots. And he's burly. Real professors are stoop-y and feeble, with spectacles. But I see why she likes him, Roland. I like him, he is quite handsome.'

Females. How could males trust them?

Roland rapped on the window with his beak, furious. Inside he made out people talking. Probably love-talk. He picked up a phrase: Holly was laughing – and groaning – with pleasure – that beast of a man! – till she positively sang out '… never, ever go home!'

'GO HOME,' Roland mimicked loudly, twice, with venom, and the Princess, to give him moral support, joined in, though later pretended she hadn't. 'Go home, go home!'

Which would not have mattered if both of the humans inside, having just made love, had not fallen into a happy doze, so the Professor received it as a shimmering message in the shafts of sunlight, words on the early summer air, *go home*.

Which would not have mattered either, were it not that the day before, on his way back from the nature walk, the Professor had seen written in enormous, wavering letters in yellow paint on one of the red Victorian arches: 'GO hOMe!!'. No-one was specified, but it meant him, he realised with sadness; it meant them.

Messages from the universe were arriving. If so, he must listen. All night he had vivid dreams: of drumming, of singing, of thousands of hands reaching out towards him.

His doze becomes wakeful, the bliss of his great body stretched across sunlit white linen ruffled by questions, memories, unease. What had told them to leave on their epic journey? Heat. The hot breath of the universe on his cheek. The little *tarentola* geckos active too early in the morning, the yellow-green tree-frog's hacksaw call out of season, escaped pet tortoises with their warning red stripe driving out the native tortoises his people liked to play with, bake and eat …

It was why they had joined the wave of peoples just starting to swell through the oceans of the world … Hundreds of thousands of matchstick figures on a shining wall of water, fleeing heat, drought, floods. As he and his people had come northwards, always northwards, to find safety. And for him, after so long, happiness.

Stretching out his toes, luxuriant, against the soft sheets, then relaxing, snoring gently, slipping away, it is all he knows. Happy. With Holly. Here, cupped in the moment, and yet –

'Go home!' Roland *cra-arks* one last time, and the rough sound shakes Juan out of the last of his dream of comfort. Something is burning, he's back in a line of people who stretch back in an unbroken chain for hundreds of thousands of years, and his task, his duty is …

Roland and the Princess give up. Off to eat worms.

Now Juan is awake. Sunday, and the smell of coffee in the

air. She brings it to him in bed on that day, unlike the rest of the week, when she can't even open one eye without her Lapsang. From such gifts, such exchanges, such regularities, come the happiness of couples.

And the fear. *Go Home*, he remembers. Of course, it's the PBF who have painted the slogan on the wall. With coffee in his system, he's rational. How can they leave, when they've barely arrived? After so many people have been so kind? Besides, with the bulldozers rolling into Gibraltar, how can they ever go home? How can he leave Holly? Never.

Still, the logical, professorial part of him picks up her Sunday newspaper, later. Instead of turning to the frankly crazy woman columnist whose frenzy of opinion usually makes them both laugh in comfortable disapproval, he looks at world news.

There it is: the name of Gibraltar, little Gibraltar calling to him from an article on global warming. A sharp jolt of worry. He reads that digital servers and searches will soon cause 5% of carbon emissions – far more than flying, says the writer. Digital servers which crouch at the heart of *Paradise Now*, the hellish project that's driven them out of their homes.

Something else makes him sit up on his low cane chair with a whistle of surprise. Demonstrations and protests have broken out across Gibraltar, normally a calm and orderly place. Statements of support from 'indigenous peoples' are arriving from all over the world. From Canada's First Nations, from the Inuit, from the Marshall Islands; from Nicaragua, Honduras, Panama. The names of the peoples aren't there, but he knows them: the Yatama of Nicaragua, the Masta of Honduras, the Guna of Panama, the Kogi of Colombia.

Even the uncontacted brothers and sisters are coming out of the shadows. Yes, that's new.

PART THREE

39

And so, one evening at the very end of May, as the small harbour town grew hotter – as the days grew long and the tamarisk bloomed pink and expansive on the sky and the carved Victorian brick of the harbour marina and the arches of Military Road stood intensely red in the heat, as more and more swimmers plunged into the sea and ran back to their piles of clothing, after, shouting and laughing, as the short-staying swifts dipped their dark sickles over Pegwell Bay and the few surviving swallows curvetted high, high above them after insects, on intense silver wires of sound – as Holly and the Professor sat, content, on her balcony, watching it all, he said to her, 'Holly, we ought to do something for the town.'

'You and I? How alarming!' she laughed.

'No, indeed. By "we", I mean, my people. We have been welcomed, mostly. We're grateful. Yet there are some – '

'Indeed,' she nodded. 'Always. I've told you to ignore them.'

'You have. But I'm thinking of a party. Some kind of party, or occasion. I don't know, Holly, it's not really my field. We must say thank you. In case – I don't know, in case we have to leave.'

'Are you telling me you're leaving me?' Her voice stayed light.

'Not leaving you, ever. But sometimes, the world ... In any case, let's forget about that. Yes, a party – dancing? – have you any ideas?' They had danced on the deck, so many years ago, before they had even grown into themselves, but his heart and his feet remembered, and hers must too.

Holly's eyes widened with pleasure and narrowed again in a smile. She delicately rang the rim of her glass against his, a crystal bell.

'Thousands. Now, let's think. Something outdoors,' said Holly. 'They're happiest outdoors?'

'Well – yes.' The Professor did not say what he wanted to, 'or underground', because Holly's silken sense of tact had stopped her intruding with questions on a life which she knew had been so much rougher than her own, and he, fearing rejection, hadn't told her at the start that his people were cave people. Had been forced to be, really, for a dozen centuries. It had been that way ever since the Moroccan commander Tariq and seven thousand Berber and Arab soldiers landed on their own beloved and remote sunbaked southern tip of Europe, on the great triangular rock pushing up out of the sea which had been his people's *Jannah*, their first heaven, the garden where they had survived the ice after their first great pilgrimage southwards, southwards, one lifetime after another until they reached the edge of dry land and saw, across a mile of sand and tough grass and the shapes of great animals moving, a narrow stretch of blue water – not ice, but water – and beyond it, the blue-grey shadow of Africa.

For thousands of years the Rock of Gibraltar had been somewhere they came and went as sea-levels rose and fell, but then the day of shouts and flashing blades had come and they were not ready, as no-one's ever ready, and could only hide, for they knew the Rock was riddled with caves. Over the centuries they had hidden deeper and longer while Barbary pirates, French, Spanish, British and Dutch fought over the land above their heads. Great sieges, great generals: the Muslims driven out, leaving their language and their genes; Gibraltar lost its firewood. And then soldiers, more soldiers, more fortifications, parades, the encrustations of empire.

And no-one except Señor Goya, coming down south to meet with radicals during the terrible wars of freedom against the Spanish king, really knew that the Professor's people were there – they were shadows on the margins, heavy shapes escaping by night, just enough of them coming into low-paid service of the masters, just enough snatched matings, and Goya's brilliant paintings. Brilliant and black, for like the radicals, the inbred creatures of the *pinturas negras* had been forced down into darkness, beings who weren't really there, to be forgotten, like a guilty conscience, something disappearing into the shadows, a movement at the corner of your eye, like, later, anything the rich guests at the Rock Hotel didn't want to see – the macaque monkeys waiting on the balcony to steal their sugar, the fact that the best and longest-serving waiters were Moroccans or Red people, hidden in black and white uniform.

None of this was easy to explain without pain when Holly's family had been pillars of the British Empire. So he had never explained; never explained that when sometimes on Friday nights, knowing he could sleep late on Saturday, he burrowed right under the duvet, curved his big body into that dark warmth and slept like the dead, he was slipping back into the past, the past when he came to life under the earth, nested inside it as if it were his mother. After nights like those he didn't wake till midday, magnificently rested. But he hadn't told her early on, and didn't, now. Nor had he encouraged her to follow the clues in the name he had chosen after, as a young waiter, he'd watched the farcically inaccurate shipboard lecture on 'Ancient Man: How He Learned to Walk Upright', 'Juan N. E. A. N. Der Tal', – and simplified it to Juan Der Tal.

'What we need is some marvellous space where we can have food and dancing and music,' she said. 'Darling?' Recalling him to her, for his gold-green eyes had clouded over.

'Sounds just right,' he said, making his voice light, with an effort.

'Who will we invite?'

'Oh, everybody,' said the Professor, who having been excluded himself, had a horror of exclusion.

'That sounds expensive.' About money, Juan was naive, Holly knew. But she was not. The various deficiencies of her husbands Holly had always silently remedied. Arguments were so unnecessary – why did people have them?

So with a secret very slight internal sigh, Holly smiled with great sweetness at her Juan, who was stretched out on one of her enormous armchairs beside her on the balcony drinking her gin and said, 'Never mind. I think I'm about to win a huge commission, and darling, I'm desperate for something to spend it on. I could tweak it a little, see what the sponsors think.'

'Midsummer Day?' he said.

'But that's perfect. You're a genius, darling.'

It was done.

40

Midsummer Day, a small but real mark on the clock of the universe seen from Kent, when our portion of the earth is nearest to the sun, when the light lasts longest. But the Professor and Holly had chosen it, and for us ever after, Midsummer Day meant only one thing.

This is where history, with its dates and events, gets things wrong. History will tell you that 'Summer '68' in Paris was the time of the student revolution, when the people took control of the streets and anarchy and jubilation filled the air. But my mother was there. And in most of the streets of Paris, the patisseries and charcuteries opened as usual, the sparrows pecked at the circular grills round the trees, elegant triangular-headed cats picked their way around Montparnasse while Foujita, the artist who had grown rich drawing them, died of cancer in Zurich. Serious young people looked at mysterious Cy Twombly nests and constellations of lines on the walls of galleries or watched new Italian films in the afternoon near the Trocadero fountains, and love, and pity, and boredom, went on as they always did. Even if vans packed with angry *flics* barrelled round corners into the crowds on the Boulevard St Michel, truth remained quietly manifold.

In the same way, in the first great lockdown of spring and early summer 2020, I remember life could not be locked down. Wild wallflowers along the path to the sea were as golden and citrus-honey-scented as ever, people surprisingly locked up together, tenants in the same house, fell in love, babies were born and alas, alas, a few died, sisters and brothers played imaginary murders and missions and ran and laughed and shouted in the quiet roads though their adults hid inside watching, rainbows of crayon bloomed in windows, people cheered the dustmen when they roared down the road instead of complaining that they dropped things, and the dustmen bowed and flourished imaginary hats and secretly muttered, 'Why don't they throw money?' but went home feeling taller, all the same; people washed their clothes and brushed their teeth and chatted while they cooked dinner with only slightly fewer ingredients than normal.

So if you ask me now, many years later again, what happened that Midsummer Day, I know what tale the history books will tell, and I must tell it. But at the same time I know there were thousands of stories in a town of forty thousand people, I know the mason bees were coming out of their tunnels in the soft chalk and shaking out their wings in the sun, I know a young fox was scooping out their nests at night, I know that the ravens had their own stories, I know that each different blue and purple mussel on the rocks near the tunnel had its own epic tale of tides and winds but also of sun-baked hours and survival. I know the birds and animals talked to the big children from far away, or at any rate, the Red children talked to them, and dogs on the beach went into an ecstasy of excitement when they picked up their scent, rocketing or lolloping towards them, licking and leaping and chasing their tails in rapture, despite nervous owners' shouts of alarm. I know that Belinda's decrepit cat and middle-aged tortoise both talked to Molo. I know a seagull mother was grieving and keening for the very last of her big gooby children, still mottled grey and brown, which half-flew and half-fell off a roof. I know, and the start of it all was Midsummer Day, about being a mother.

We will have our events that mark time, we will live that Midsummer Day and the night that followed. But outside my window a goldfinch perches, precariously happy, on the swaying telephone wire, his tiny red head, sharp beak and gold breast outlined in the sun: blink and he's gone.

41

Two weeks before the party, there was trouble in Winston's home: his wife, who might have taken something, had gone quiet, somewhere out in the evening garden.

There was trouble in Belinda's house, too.

According to her, Molo was a thief, 'that child you put with me' as she phrased it in a furious telephone call at 10pm just as his wife ran out of the house.

'What happened, Belinda?'

'Liam's scrunchies all disappeared.'

'Liam's *scrunchies*?' It was hard to hear. Now Ella was singing Aretha Franklin songs on the lawn.

'He has them so his hair doesn't get wet in the bath. He's very particular about his hair, Liam. Anyway, they're *his*. Worse, Molo stole Liam's whole collection of trolls – you won't remember them, you're too young, but they're funny little figures with masses of red or pink hair and sort of caveman faces, it was a craze when I was a girl, I gave Liam my collection when he was little and of course Molo is sleeping in Liam's room and he found them and –'

'Could you go more slowly, Belinda, there's some noise in the background here.' His wife was now singing JayZ's 'Hard Knock Life' very loudly at him through the glass and knocking on the pane.

'– and he made up these satanic looking little parcels with the scrunchies and feathers and trolls and put them under his bed, and Liam went in to get his scrunchies and went mental when he found they were missing and Molo must have been meaning to sell them, you may not be aware of this but everyone else is, these children are *trading* at lunch-times in strict contravention of school rules!'

'Oh dear,' Winston muttered, to her, to his wife, to life, to his headache.

'Now he lies about it. Tries to pretend they're a present for Liam's birthday.'

'When is Liam's birthday?' His wife had gone worryingly quiet.

'Soon.'

'So could they be, might they be, a present? Should you talk to the Professor?'

'No. I'm talking to you. Winston, you'll have to sort it out, you've landed us with this problem, he'll have to go, it'll all have to stop,' she insisted, 'and it's even worse because now my kids love Molo, the other kids I mean, Joe and Sandra, and Sandra is only sixteen,' and now there were two women in his life who were crying, his own wife more loudly and desperately, so he said 'Tomorrow,' like a promise, to Belinda.

Then tomorrow arrived. After rampaging till two, Ella was like a lamb in the morning, apologetic and sane, and though full of worry, he had left early for school, opening his office door with a sigh of relief; his space. Now he could think.

Three minutes later, thundering feet.

'Midsummer Day,' Monica said, without ceremony. 'The party. Fuck's sake, do we have to have focus meetings?'

'Yes,' he said.

'Arse,' she said. 'I'm not going.'

'We have to have local consultation or there's no hope of getting funding for it. You know that, Monica,' Winston replied, with more asperity than usual. He wished she were not in his office, blocking out the sun.

'There's no hope of getting funding, full stop,' Monica said.

She was probably right, there had been almost no funding for anything from central sources for years, but still they had to keep planning and hoping, and occasionally there was a windfall for something they'd never expected to succeed like the (not very good) statue of the refuse collector and the nurse on the seafront, locally christened 'Beach Binman'.

'Monica, give me a break. I've got Belinda on my back.'

'Oh crap,' Monica said, but her nostrils flared with interest. 'In confidence.'

'Course. Tell me more.'

'No,' said Winston, and he didn't. You couldn't let Monica walk all over you, he had realised, or she would.

Monica left, reluctant.

As soon as her footsteps receded, he went to the low, locked cupboard next door and felt inside for the exciting dull gold bag of Ethiopian coffee. At first he couldn't find it. He scrabbled and his fingers closed on the metal foil. But when he pulled it out, Eileen had put it back empty.

Life, he thought. Was it worth it?

He was still crouched down on his heels, too fed-up for a black second or two to stand up, when the feet came back. Fucking Monica.

But it was the Professor, all smiles. '*L'Archivio* was open so I took the liberty of bringing you a latte,' he said. 'Two shots, not much foam, I believe?'

'Professor, I love you,' said Winston. 'But I haven't had a moment to come up with concrete ideas for the party.'

The two men settled, as they often did, to talk. 'Funding's the issue,' Winston apologised. 'We have to consult, we have to do the paperwork and I'm not hopeful. If all else fails we'll do something small here at school, crisps and sandwiches, possibly a student-led disco, but we can't invite the town.'

'Dear fellow, do as you think, consultations and so on, but the funding is settled.'

'You mean?'

'Holly has settled the funding.'

'You're joking.' Winston looked up, his brow relaxing, then gathering again. 'You may not understand the scale of the possible cost, we'd need thousands.'

'Of course. Holly's got a new client, an international museum, they're commissioning a piece to celebrate "new beginnings", revival, how nature rebounds if we let it. She wants to put a spin on it so it links in to our arrival, they seem delighted.'

'Tell me more.'

'It's a sort of golden collar.'

'For a dog?' asked Winston, surprised.

'No, not for a dog. It's a name for an elaborate necklace. She's planning a piece embellished with the flowers that grow here in your home and in Jebel Tarek. She's already designed it. It's magnificent. Sprays of, I think you call it, fennel flowers. Palms. Candytuft. Small gold shells. Maybe two ravens' heads at the front, for we too have ravens, you know. And some other motifs.' He smiled, thinking of the symbols she was incising on every other link which meant so much to him and his people, the geometric sign that linked them with golden lines to their ancient home, to the ancestors, the vertical parallels that stretched from the future to the past, the horizontals that would reach round the earth, and join.

'I am speechless,' said Winston. 'But what would they pay her, hundreds?'

'She works only in 22-carat gold and by hand – though she uses a blow-torch,' the Professor explained. 'It's a very delicate process. Very time-consuming. You look incredulous?'

'It's just that she's such a lady,' said Winston, who hardly knew Holly. 'Hard to imagine her with a blow-torch.'

'And welder's goggles,' said Juan, with a smile. 'It's very exacting work. Decisions must be made and acted on in fractions of a second while the gold is hot. They will have to pay for her skill – she's the best goldsmith in the business – and her long hours. Confirmation next week, but it looks as though they'll pay £25,000. Fifteen of that's earmarked for us.'

Winston drank deep of his latte. Caffeine ran like liquid gold through his veins. How he liked the Professor, in that second, just what he needed, a problem-solver not a problem, and someone who saw that he, Winston, was human too, and had human needs.

'Ravens,' he said. 'That's a stroke of genius. Nina told me "Ramsgate" was originally called "Hraefnesgate," which means "Ravensgate". They're the town birds.'

'Do you know they visit Holly?' The Professor asked. 'A pair of them. When she opens the curtains in the morning, they're there. If we're late, they peck at the glass. It's rather loud.' He'd got used to the idea of Holly leaving apple segments on the balcony, and sometimes, as a treat, chicken livers. 'Brilliant mimics. Sometimes they sound so human they startle us. The male isn't keen on me.'

'Really? Must be jealous. Something else, while you're here.'

'Belinda?' said the Professor. 'Yes, she rang me this morning.'

'Ahh ... It's pathetic, a nineteen-year-old getting upset about scrunchies, but Belinda is one of my best teachers and I would prefer not to have her upset.'

The Professor began. 'Molo is an interesting boy, quite unique in some ways, but …' Long and short of it, Molo had form. Back home he was a scavenger by training from a boy, then a trader. Not all the things which came back with him to the caves had been freely laid down by their owners. He had used great ingenuity liberating handbags from parked cars – the local colony of macaques had often been blamed for Molo's adventures. 'He saw it as helping his people,' the Professor said. 'But the boy has other qualities. He loves making things. He's strong. He's very inventive.'

'He claims he was making presents for Liam's birthday. But the scrunchies belonged to Liam in the first place.'

'Well, that is inventive,' said the Professor. The two men exchanged rueful smiles.

'But what are we to do?'

'I'll talk to Holly. Maybe Molo could spend some time in her workshop, give Belinda a break.'

42

Focus group reports on 'Venue':

School Hall. Seated 200, standing 300. ('A bit dull').

Town Hall. Seated 50, standing 75. ('Dark and small'. 'I resent that,' said the Mayor.)

Harbour Quayside. Seated 0, Standing 1,000, but risk of falling in. ('You know Ramsgate. They will.')

Beach at Low Tide. (Hundreds, viewed as 'exciting'. But 'Negative fatality factor due to oncoming High Tide.')

East Cliff Bandstand and Wellington Crescent Lawns (100 seated, 750 standing. 'In some ways ideal but strongly opposed by minority of East Cliff residents and all residents of the West Cliff.')

West Cliff Marina and Lawns (100 + seated, 850 standing. 'In some ways ideal but strongly opposed by a minority of West Cliff residents and all residents of the East Cliff.')

And so on.

'Do we have to take any notice of these, what do you call them, focus groups?' The Professor finally asked, laying the print-off down on Holly's black glass table, on which shiny flower-flags of scarlet peace lilies flamed and shone in their vase as if cut that morning from garnet. Winston was here for breakfast, this time with Ella.

'Of course not, darling,' said Holly briskly, with the faintest tang of scorn in her beautiful voice.

'So – why do people have focus groups?' The Professor turned to Winston.

'We have to have consultation so people can express their opinions.'

'But then we ignore them?'

'Yes.' Winston bit into his buttery croissant with a small sigh of delight. 'As Holly says, we, in this case you, decide the venue.'

'I bet Holly will sort out the rest,' said Ella, who had a sure instinct already of the likely balance of power in the room.

When they left, Holly pressed Ella's hand. 'So delightful to meet you.' And after they had gone, she said to the Professor 'It's hard to believe that there's trouble there. Such a lovely girl. And seemed so sane.'

'He's hoping there'll be more good days. Says she's working again. She's a brilliant artist. It all started with their second miscarriage, he told me. He said, "A white doctor got her hooked on pills because he couldn't be bothered to listen to her." Is that really how your doctors behave? I never had occasion to use one ... In any case, maybe the sorrow is slipping into the past.'

'Ahh. Ah well, if these things are meant to be ...' Then a graceful shrug, a gesture of hers he loved, and saw often: ringed hands freeing a bird. For her, and for Juan, it hadn't happened. But Holly never 'dwelled'. Life, while it lasted, was moving forward; if her genes were not meant to join the long dance, she would have fun moving life forward for others.

The Professor was sent away to sort it out with his people.

In this case, consultation was swift and informal. Molo, Little Eagle and Roosha would do it. But Little Eagle said he had to ask Twainelle. Then the four of them went for a walk.

43

'It's a walk with a purpose,' said Little Eagle strictly. They had decided to 'follow their noses' and see where they ended up, but it was no surprise to anyone when the Red children turned like one body towards Pegwell, and Twainelle followed.

Little Eagle's chest was hurting with pride at the trust he had been given and he strode out as if he were not two years younger than Molo the athlete. The tide was low, the moon had been a new silver sliver last night so the rocks and the beach shone bare in the sunlight as the little group walked at the foot of the cliffs toward Pegwell, past the mouths of the caves.

'Shit, you go fast,' said Twainelle, panting as she tried to keep up. Little Eagle reached back and took her hand. But where were Roosha and Molo?

In his most responsible voice, sounding very English, his pronunciation modelled, as always, on the Professor's, he said, 'Those clowns have disappeared. I knew they would!'

Indeed, Molo and Roosha had, as they passed the first caves.

'Well, it's down to us then,' said Twainelle, smiling her beautiful smile which showed a slight gap between large white teeth. 'You an' me, that means we decide.'

'Something to do with history, it should be,' Little Eagle said.

'You only say that because you're so good at history, brainbox.' She dropped his hand and hit him lightly on the arm. It was true, Little Eagle had only been at the Grammar School two months when he started coming top in the subject.

Whereas she had had no interest in history or geography at all till the Red children came.

'Well, it's life, isn't it, history,' he said. 'It's everything except the future, and you can't learn that.'

'Do you want a Monster Munch?' she said. It wasn't a real question, she knew he adored them, and every other kind of salty snack, and he dug his brown hand deep into the bag.

'Mmm, mmm, thanks.' They walked for a bit in silence, except for the crunch of shells underfoot and sugar and salt in their mouths.

'Have your lot got a history?' Twainelle asked. 'Mum is quite proud of ours, I don't know that much about it but it's Romans and Vikings and Second World War ... We did well in the Second World War in Ramsgate. Or maybe the first.'

'We've got lots too.' They had rounded another cliff and the green curve of Spartina grass that marked Pegwell Bay came into sight.

'Go on then?'

'Ours is not written down, it's so old.'

Twainelle thought about that. 'How do you know it's there if it's not written down? I'm not dissing your culture ...' They had been taught from an early age at school that you mustn't disrespect anything other people said about their culture. When Twainelle went home, aged seven, and asked her mum, who was white, what their culture was, she had said, 'Normal people don't have culture, it's only Hindus and Muslims who have to worry about that.' But now Twainelle had her own ideas.

Little Eagle replied, 'We're older than history, the Professor says.'

'Wow,' said Twainelle. 'Ooh look, there's a dead bird.'

It was a seagull, massive, its great wings sprawled, lopsided, half on a rock, the red spot on its beak as bright as blood. Round its head there bobbed the first flies. Behind it, a black hole into the cliffs.

'The Professor loves those two caves,' Little Eagle told her. They stopped and looked. 'Our lot, we go in there, but it's a secret, you mustn't tell or I'll kill you.' Their faces were immensely serious at that moment, and he no longer sounded like the Professor, he sounded what he was, only fifteen, like her. 'They look like our sacred caves at home.'

'So your caves are sacred?' she asked. Together, they stared into the darkness. Caves were the mouths of another world, Twainelle thought. Speaking secrets.

'So, is it just that your people were alive before anyone could write?' she inquired, turning her back on the dark.

But Little Eagle had crouched down, taken chalk, which he always carried, from his pocket, and started drawing on a large grey rock that pattern the Red children always drew, the bold downstrokes, the parallel horizontal lines, the final cross-hatching strokes at the base — the sign that meant everything to them, the child of their ancestors' brain.

'Maybe we did writing and drawing before anyone else. But other people came later and did it different, and then they didn't know how to read ours.'

'I love the way you know things,' she said, shyly. 'What is that mark? You do it everywhere, you lot.'

'That's what you would call our culture,' he said. 'The first kind of writing. My people did it. It's just that your people can't read it. It's carved into rock in Jebel Tarek. It's so special even we can't get near that place, because it has to be protected. It's important for the whole world, the Professor says. So we only see it if we climb down in secret, at night.'

'Wow,' she said again. They walked in contented silence for a bit. Then she said, 'Someone says you come from India, is that right? Is that where Jebel Tariq is?' She felt safe to ask him things, now he was telling her things. 'But under the ground?' She could still hardly believe it, under the ground in India must be hot and dirty and dark, but life was surprising, she knew that. And Little Eagle was the most surprising boy she had ever known.

'India?' he said. 'Where did they get *that* from? Unless they meant, like American Indians. The Professor says we're part of the First Peoples of the World. So American Indians are our brothers.'

Twainelle looked puzzled and stopped dead to think better. 'No,' she said. 'Not them. I know about American Indians, they wear feathers don't they, which is like you lot, come to think of it, but I mean, Pakistan India. It was Pakistan people say you came from. Cos your country is Jebel Tariq, and Tariq's a Pakistani name. Are Pakistanis old as well?'

'We're not Pakistani. Give me another Monster Munch.'

'Say "*please*" ... You don't have to take them all! Have you ever met a, you know, Native American?' It was hard to talk about things when you didn't know the right words, and were talking to someone as clever as him. 'I'd like to.'

'No. Because the ones who are our brothers are the ones who live in the jungle and hardly ever come out and no-one even knows if they're there. That's like us. No-one even knew we were still alive, but we were. Mostly under the ground. In caves. Most people think we're extinct. We're supposed to have died out thousands of years ago.'

Their feet slip-slapping on the chalk suddenly sounded so light and small, like a tiny butterfly flapping its wings. The hairs on Twainelle's arms stood on end, though it was warm, very warm, in the sun. 'How many thousands of years?' she asked.

'About forty thousand years.'

'Fourteen thousand years … wow.'

'No, fort-*Y*.'

'That's unbelievable. I mean, it's so cool,' said Twainelle.

'But people like American Indians and maybe Tibetans and people from Alaska and people from tiny islands which are disappearing under the sea, that's the Marshallese, they've got maps of the stars, all know about us, thanks to the Professor. They know we went on living under the ground in Jebel Tarek. Because it was our home. Just like other peoples, our brothers and sisters, go on living in the forests of Brazil, only they're burning down, and … other places, I can't remember all of it. And nobody knows about all of the people like us because some of them are so secret that no-one else has even seen them *ever*.'

'*Wow*,' she said again. She was staring into a small rock pool as she listened and suddenly noticed that tiny shrimps, almost invisible, were swarming about, silver-grey, under the silver-grey surface of the water. It was too much to take in. The world had levels, and then other levels, and then there was time, and star-maps, and islands disappearing, and thousands of years, and … She felt dazed, and sat down and took her trainers off, and dabbled her toes in the pool. 'My family only came from Ramsgate,' she said.

'I don't think so,' he said. 'People's families come from everywhere.'

'You think you know everything,' she said, annoyed. 'No wonder people called you a bighead.' Then she thought about it and clapped her hand to the springy curls on her head. 'But oh yeah, it's true, I forgot, my grandpa and my uncle came from Jamaica, which is kind of linked to Africa. But a long time ago.'

'Er … I don't think Jamaica is Africa,' he said again, but this time she wasn't listening, she was lost in happy thought, in the moment, in the light which poured down upon them. She was on her feet again, dancing around on the sand ten feet away from him, then paused and breathed and dug her toes into the cool pleasure of the sand-grains. 'That's why I'm black and that's cool, too,' she said, 'and I like it and not many people *are*, around here,' and she stood up straighter and breathed deep and felt life, her own life, surge through her.

Looking out to sea, beyond the Sandwich peninsula, right out to where the edge of the water against the sky shone and trembled, Twainelle knew the world was so much bigger than she had ever realised, and astonishing – and oh, she was part of it and could not wait to see more of it, though once she had wanted to live in Ramsgate for ever.

Further away from her now, he followed her gaze. 'That's where the Romans and the Vikings came from,' he said. 'Us too. We came from there.' At the same moment two big black birds swooped towards them, flying fast along the shoreline.

'They're big, those crows,' she called into the breeze. 'Do you want another Monster Munch?'

44

'Crows! She thinks we're crows.' The Princess overheard and, amused, translated for Roland as the pair made their way back from a little spin through the air to Deal.

'Crows!' said Roland with fury, 'do they teach them nothing at school?' Then, wheeling above the offending teens, he tried to assuage his hurt feelings by despising Twainelle. 'It's just instinct, of course. They're not capable of thinking. That frizzy-haired half-grown female probably calls all flying creatures crows.'

Not being indignant, the Princess Ra had time to notice more things. That the pretty young girl had dropped several small golden pieces of food as her hand touched the boy's. And that the boy was one of the new kind of Youmen, newly arrived in Ramsgate – who in fact, as the system of messages that ran all round the globe between ravens had by now convinced her, were a very old kind of Youmen indeed.

'Crows are fine in their way,' she reminded Roland as they soared above the beach, waiting for the humans to pass. 'You like to play with them sometimes.'

'Oh, play with them, yes,' he spluttered. 'But the idea of being one! A mere crow! I've just spotted a snack for you, my dear,' and he arrowed down and landed with great precision near the Monster Munches, gobbled four of them, and generously left her two.

The Princess Ra did not much like the look of the bag from which the golden things had come, so she stayed airborne for a minute or two, watching the boy and girl walk away.

'I like to see the young ones,' she said, finally landing. 'They're holding hands. Not shy about their stumpies, tangling their fingers and stroking and so on. Two different kinds of Youmen. But in love.'

'It means babies,' he said. 'That's all it means. Look, I left you some.' In fact, the foodstuffs were disgusting, all sugar and salt and something that fizzed against his tongue, so it wasn't hard not to eat the remaining two pieces, but he still felt virtuous.

'No babies, they're too young for them,' she said, watching his great powerful beak masticate the last of his food, and his handsome, beloved, head. 'And, Roland, I'm too old.'

He turned his head sharply away, then went silent, and she wondered if for the first time he had accepted it: no more eggs. Males, she thought: no realism. The two slim Youmen diminished in the distance, still twining their fingers and laughing. They looked so happy.

'Still, I'd like you to look for mites in my feathers,' she said. 'I haven't got any. But I like you to touch me.'

And one thing led to another, in a nearby cave: so four living beings were happy.

45

Twainelle and Little Eagle walked along the foot of the cliffs until the sand opened up and on the left, wide green beds of Spartina grass and samphire began: the Bay proper. 'So this is where the Romans actually landed,' she said.

'Yes, and all sorts of others as well. Mr Phelpham knows it all.'

She looked into the distance, now, out to sea where the waves turned into one endless glitter on the horizon, where Little Eagle had told her the Romans and Vikings had come from. She imagined small ships, as small as the birds who were swooping like tiny rockets over the nearest waves, appearing just on the edge of vision and slowly coming towards her, growing bigger and darker until you heard shouts, and saw strangers, but not their faces. 'What must it have felt like, being invaded?' she said, off like a bird after another thought.

'Frightening, I expect,' he said. 'And the old Britons fought them off.'

'They were right to do that. Like us and the Germans.'

'Yes ... but all the same, it always happens. Just because you live somewhere first,' he said. 'Other people always come after. Other people came and lived where we wanted to live in Jebel Tarek. Which is why we had to hide. We've been hiding for thousands of years. Which is one reason why it's good being here.'

Up the precipitous path from the beach they went nimble and light-footed as foxes, clawing themselves up in the steepest bits by tufts of tough grass.

Now they were in another kind of history, the wide stretch of concrete, interrupted by bursts of wild buddleia almost coming into bloom, wild budding roses, wild fennel as high as their heads, of the abandoned Hoverport of the 1970s, the dream of the last century, the hovercraft that had made travel to Europe as easy and fast as flying, if somewhat more queasy, according to Twainelle's grandma, who went and was violently sick.

'Here,' said Twainelle. 'There's room for everybody. Here's where we should have the party.'

'Maybe,' said Little Eagle. They were standing on the edge of the concrete where it sloped down, smooth and easy, to the shallow sea, the launch point for the craft of the past, and now a place where small boats landed people, sometimes, it was whispered, by night and in secret.

'Did you lot invade us?' said Twainelle, suddenly stepping sideways and slightly away as the thought struck her. She didn't want to think it, but she just couldn't push it aside.

He didn't answer but he suddenly turned his whole body and very gently looked into her face. Then he put his arms around her. He wasn't yet his full height, so his eyes could look deep into hers. He pulled her closer. It was, despite what everyone thought, their first actual embrace. 'It's not like that,' he said, once they moved apart. 'We were just running away. We might have died if we'd stayed in Jebel Tarek. The tunnels and caves where we lived might have crumbled with us inside.'

Death seemed a terrible thing to imagine. She had felt his heart beating as they hugged, and her heart had beat in time. Death was grey and flat, like the concrete. 'Not here, for the party. It's not right,' she said.

'No, it feels a bit sad. Like everyone's already been lost.'

They walked higher up the cliff, and then they found it. Behind the Hoverport, up through the cool woods – a strange tangle of self-sown sycamores and ashes, Kentish apple-trees run wild with tiny hard green fruit, dog-roses hanging in rare sunny islands in the close semidark – it suddenly opened before them and they had to close their lids against it, light – a wide ribbon of rolling, sunlit green stretching on for maybe a mile or more by the road, making Little Eagle blink and frown. For what else was he seeing? A marvel.

'Look,' said Twainelle, proud. Right in front of them, dragon-headed and fierce and odd, floating on concrete balusters above the greensward, a Viking ship; one of Ramsgate's landmarks: full-size, surreal, glorious.

'This is the place,' said Twainelle, and Little Eagle agreed. 'Look, it's even got a café.'

'A small one,' said Twainelle, squinting at the kiosk on the edge of the green.

But 'it won't be about the food', both of them agreed. 'It's about music. And … all of us. Everyone can come. And dancing.'

46

'Everyone?' said kind Ms Potter, for once sounding disgruntled. It was too hot: too hot for England. A heat wave before June was well underway was all wrong. It would be followed, sure as fate, by a storm. Her head ached. 'We don't want the Put Britain First lot, do we.'

'It's a public place,' said Winston. 'No choice.' Somehow the meeting had slipped into a discussion of a guest list. He didn't want a guest list. He wanted Open House.

'The idea is to reach out,' said Anna Segovia. That morning, she and Pamela (Ms Potter in her school incarnation) had quarrelled, unusually, and the meeting had been scratchier because of suppressed tensions between them.

'Yes,' said Winston, revived by Anna's support, 'we want to bring people into friendly contact with the Red children who normally just see them as – well, we know all too well how they see them.'

'They'll just come and get pissed though Winston, to be fair,' said Monica, who was standing by the open window trying to breathe in the heat and pulling hideous faces at Roland the raven who sat, head cocked, on a branch of the lime tree not six feet away, stretching up and down on his perch and staring at her.

'Piss-SSed,' the raven says, quite distinctly, but Monica's sure she imagined it. 'I'm not bothered', she adds over her shoulder to the meeting, 'I will help Security if needed, I have form as a boxer, remember.'

No-one had forgotten, but again, out of the green rustling

of the leaves where the bloody bird sits she hears a distinct hoarse cry of 'Remember, remember'.

'Go away!' she shouts, and everyone stops and stares. 'Just talking to a raven,' she explains, and flops down on to a chair. 'Did you notice I didn't say "'Fuck off"'?'

'I don't actually think we'll have Security,' said Winston after a pause. 'I think we all know that the police have had to concentrate on Margate in recent years.'

'Not that night they won't,' said Monica. 'Ginger'll see to that.'

The silence round the table gained a more critical quality. Most of them (not Belinda) had grown fond of Monica, and respected the work she did with the children who had social or family problems, of whom the Grammar School had a surprising number, but her husband Ginger was another matter; he had a local reputation for corruption, and possibly worse. Ginger, people privately agreed, was, well, sinister.

Monica, though unempathic in meetings, felt the chill. 'Okay, I myself could lead a force of, we could call it, "Wardens",' she said. 'With arm-bands. I would be Chief Warden. We could patrol. I'd quite enjoy that.'

Another charged silence.

'Do you think it's a good idea, Monica?' said Winston bravely.

'Why the fuck not?'

'Because you get over-enthusiastic,' said Belinda with a cutting little smile in which her two pointy incisors briefly flickered. 'Also, the swearing.'

'Let's move on to refreshments,' said Winston with haste.

'What's the fucking Action Point from that discussion then Winston?' asked Monica, looming forward oppressively in her seat so her elbows, framing her tremendous bosom, seemed to cover a third of the table round which the Summer Festival Committee were seated.

Winston knew Monica made random use of points of procedure, while herself entirely disregarding it. 'Monica, I'm moving on to refreshments. I am chairing the meeting, so I will decide the action point and you can disagree with it later,' he said, and turned to look Monica full in the face. Friendship depended on honesty, he thought. 'Also, please sit down. And try not to swear.'

'Keep your hair on, Winston,' said Monica, but she sat down.

Refreshments. 'So that jeweller woman wants to pay for it all?' asked Ms Potter, who was definitely not in a good mood today. 'I've never met her. Shouldn't we know a bit about the donor? Anna, you know her, don't you?'

Anna, as it happened, was wearing a thin gold chain round her neck that Holly had made, a simple but beautiful thing with tiny cascading gold seeds – Holly had given her a discount because they both sponsored the Ramsgate Sea Cadets. But because Anna and Pamela's semi-quarrel had been about which of them was more of a socialist, she didn't want to highlight her interest in jewellery, and just stared at the floor.

'Anyone?' Winston said, looking at the Professor.

'Yes of course. But I must declare an interest. I'm currently living at Holly Palermo's home,' the Professor said. 'Holly Palermo is a wonderful woman, a woman of means, and my very good friend. Friendship, she's doing it for friendship, just that.'

'She's very rich then is she?' Belinda asked, for she needed to replace her windows, and despite her good salary, now there were five mouths to feed in the house, she'd had to postpone it.

'Not rich compared to some of the people I've known,' he replied.

'What's in it for her then?' said Belinda, rudely. 'Sorry.'

Then the Professor explained Holly's commission: the wonderful golden necklet she was making: its value, its astonishing beauty. 'Probably best not to say too much about it outside this room,' he added. 'In case we get burgled.' And he laughed; but still, they all nodded, and relaxed, and everyone but Belinda felt happy that the festival was being sponsored by that rare thing, clean money.

'Very nice,' said Belinda, who had always loved, though not owned, good jewellery. 'But it's a pity we can't use the money to update the older class-rooms.' (Where, as it happened, she taught.)

All would have gone well after that if Sandra had not been tearful that night, because she was breaking up with Ramadan, and wanted her mother to sit with her to help her go to sleep. Tired though she was by the early meeting and a day of juggling the needs of the mathematically gifted Red children and the others, Belinda agreed.

'Maybe you and Ram were too different,' she suggested.

'What do you mean?'

'Well – your backgrounds,' she said. There was a pause while Sandra stared at her accusingly. 'Though I liked him very much, you know I did.'

'You mean he's Pakistani, it's nothing to do with that,' Sandra sniffed.

'No I didn't mean that. I meant, you know, culture. Identity, whatever.'

'Mum! You mean, he's Pakistani! You've got it all wrong, that didn't matter.'

Yet Sandra was too sad to be angry, and besides, she knew Belinda had, genuinely, liked him, and had been wondering whether she ought to introduce herself to Ramadan's mother, who had a clothes stall in the market.

'There's someone else,' Sandra said. 'It's –'

'Don't tell me.' Trouble was, Belinda already half-knew, couldn't bear to know, who it was. Her fault. Her fault! She had brought Molo under their roof.

She racked her brains. Sandra was a child who, like her mother, had always loved pretty things. 'Let's sort your jewellery box,' she suggested to her daughter, and sat on her bed as together they untangled and sorted and discarded, and remarked on the cuteness of certain well-loved pieces, though too often Belinda heard her daughter say, 'But don't you think it's a bit babyish, now?'

Belinda found she was telling her daughter about Holly Palermo, the real live goldsmith she'd learned today was living in Ramsgate, and before she knew she was doing it, she had begun describing what she remembered about the 22-carat necklace, 'it's worth £25,000!', and naturally the girl loved hearing about it and soon started rubbing her eyes and getting ready to sleep.

Which was all very well until Sandra talked to her brothers, and Molo too, because she really liked him.

47

But no-one had time to bother about a few shared confidences
or their consequences, because as June continued to blaze, as
the surviving young seagulls, now a happy gaggle of zooming
and plunging adolescents, flaunted their dappled brown wings
over the low waves lapping on the beach, as Liam, sitting on
the PBF table again, got a laugh for the first time and a few
affirming nods when he said in a voice that was louder than
his natural one that the low pyramids of sand the Red people
built 'made it look like fucking Egypt around here' – as the
cones of buddleia pushed up and their darkness turned purple
and white all along the cliffs from Sandwich to Margate, and
as each floret, baring its tiny red-and-gold perfumed heart,
drew hot coveys of hungry bees – as seaweed greened the
beaches but was neatly cleaned up in Broadstairs – Ramsgate
was suddenly full of music and honeysuckle, pink and red
scrambling rambling roses ramping over careful front gardens,
golden honeysuckle sweetening wild back gardens, music
from windows, summer-scented honeysuckle and roses round
windows, scent blowing with the music, every window that
would open thrown wide to let in the warm sweet air; music
from balconies, from the Bandstand, from the beach, even
from the cliffs, where a lone jazz trumpeter played for his dead
friend and the nearby buddleias' fingers trembled with life in
the sound: everywhere, as the sunlight strengthened, music and
a sense of gathering motion, soon to be headlong, Midsummer
Day rushed towards us and everyone, everyone was going.

The local jazz-bands were in their element: Robbie Ross,

Phil Hunt and Pete Cull on bass formed a trio and Robbie's honeyed chords and rapid finger-plucking vibrated the air every evening, and Lianne Carroll, that glorious contralto, drove over from Hastings to sing with them. 'We'll only need the one rehearsal, boys, I'm a pro.' She was going to perform for free on the big day! Maybe she would do a duet with Shirley Green, our beloved soprano? On the West Cliff, clever adolescents' saxophone and clarinet wove torch songs that trembled with love and longing from open Georgian windows, and at last, at last they saw the point of practising, it wasn't just for marks and exams, they were going to *play*, and they played their hearts out, the mixture of pain and beauty in the music stopping Red children in the street as they passed to listen, because despite, or maybe because of, a few blurred notes, it spoke to them of home, and they knew it was for them that the whole town was being transformed by a great wave of welcome which would lift them all up to the peak of Midsummer Day.

48

'It's going so well,' Holly breathed on the pillow to the Professor as the first sun slipped through their blinds on the Sunday before the party. 'Six days left until D-Day … though what does the D stand for exactly?

'I don't know,' said the Professor. 'Though I know what it was. Second World War. The final assault.'

'Is it Dunkirk?' she said. 'No of course not, it can't be.'

'Dunkirk was a defeat,' said the Professor, and somewhere on his skin he felt a tiny cool breath of unease.

'*Reculer pour mieux sauter*,' said Holly, stroking his red hair, still so youthful, she thought, though we're no spring chickens. But we're right for each other. She gave his warm cheek the lightest kiss. 'Retreat to advance. It was a feat of organisation, like this. And Ramsgate played a great role. In the long run, thousands of people were saved.'

'Yes.'

'Coffee, my darling?

'Yes.' The summer sea air blew in through the window she got up and opened, letting the blinds spring up with a happy little 'click'. He lay there on his own for a few minutes watching the sun playing through the white voile of the thin curtains inside the blinds, ribbons of light and shade running fluid as water across the wall, thinking, 'I am here, in the moment. After so much darkness. I choose to be here, in this happiness. This.'

She came back in, and the sweet strong baked-nut smell of roast coffee with her, and something else: music.

'It's early for music.' They often woke early, Holly and Juan;

just as on their very first evening they needed to sleep because they had missed so many nights of dreaming together; in the morning there is no time when they can be alive together in the sunlight to lose.

'It's the band,' said Holly. 'Let's get up and go and watch them. I do love military bands.'

'Military?' he protested lightly.

'Who do you think protects our freedoms, darling? In any case, it's not really military, it's just a name – Sally Army.'

'A woman?'

Sometimes he did sound foreign, Holly thought, as she lovingly poured him coffee, the dark liquid twisting in a carved rope against the white porcelain on the cup, and as she stretched it towards him, the sunlight touched its gold lip and lit them both up, her white hand, the cup.

'Salvation,' she said. 'Sally Army, short for Salvation.'

'They save people? What could be better?'

'From drink, when they started. Now they just save us from inertia. Military music, I love it, it's rather me. My great-grandfather the Governor of Gibraltar, and so on. Part of me. The part of me that gets things done. I don't know if you like that part of me,' she said, her big, lambent blue eyes finding his then dropping in a moment of helpless appeal that was only half-dramatised, though she was also an actress, and knew it.

'I like every part of you,' said the Professor, and meant it. But her great-grandfather, yes: the great silencer. He took his first deep drink of the coffee. 'This is bliss.' A thought struck him. 'Holly, will you take a photo of me?'

'Of course,' she said, surprised, 'nothing nicer. I suggest the blue shirt on the balcony later this morning, perhaps?'

'No, now.'

'Not for the programme?' she said. 'Not half-naked, surely.'

'It's not for the programme, there isn't a programme, as such.'

'What for then?'

'For me. Us. To keep.'

There was something in his voice; she gazed at him, eyes full of light as the sun fell across them, picked up her phone in that second, framed him in time.

This photograph is what, many months later, Holly printed and held in her hand. Professor Juan Der Tal resting back like a pasha on a great sunlit nest of white pillows, his massive torso and shoulders only half-hidden by the spotless white of the sheet, sun dancing on the red-gold calligraphy of curls on his chest, one big arm stretched to the right over her pillow, his broad hand and fingers open, waiting for her to return, and the sun pours on through the blowing voile and dissolves him in moving, running patterns of watered silk, the isthmus of wrinkles that spreads across his temples, deep inlets of smile-lines round his mouth, everything is liquid.

In that three-hundredth of a second when the camera blinks open and shut, the light holds him smiling at her for ever.

She's gazing, transfixed with delight.

'This is perfect. Do you want to see?'

'No.'

'Why not?'

'I know what I'm feeling, darling.'

Their hands briefly touched in the faint sun-warmth on the duvet. Almost too much for them both, the love in that moment. It was a relief when the music suddenly blared louder outside in the harbour.

'People with hangovers won't like that,' he said, and she laughed.

'When the saints,' she said, 'come marching in, it's one of their favourites. Love it. "Oh when the saints…",' and she trilled a few bars in her still girlish, lilting, boarding-school accented voice, and beat gentle time with her spoon.

But he raised one eyebrow. 'I don't know about saints. Where I come from, they were terrible, the religious. Señor Goya showed it. The suffering. The deaths.'

'Yes. But saints … sometimes, we do need people to be heroic,' she said.

'And suffer?' he said. 'Isn't that what saints do?'

'I don't believe in suffering, but I suppose so, my love. Yes.'

49

The weather in the week before the party was spectacular. As the old Harbour Master said to his assistant, 'It's set in fair,' and for the first few days they both enjoyed the way the little office filled with sunlight in the morning. 'Not good for the yachties, though,' they agreed, for there wasn't a breath of wind, and after two days, the heat began to build up.

At school, the new windows installed too cheaply but good to keep the winds out in winter, didn't open, and the boys let their shirts gape apart and fall out of their trousers, and the white easy-launder fabric was transparent with sweat. The Red children didn't seem to suffer so much, but then, they were not complainers. 'Hotter where we come from,' they said, and took their shirts off in class once again, and were sent outside, after which they stood in the shade in the playground, quite happy, and laughed, though they were discussing, with enormous energy and delight, a maths problem:

'For some integer n, a set of n^2 magical chess pieces arrange themselves on a square $n^2 \times n^2$ chessboard composed of n^4 unit squares. At a signal, the chess pieces all teleport to another square of the chessboard such that the distance between the centres of their old and new squares is … For which values of n can the chess pieces win?'

'But there's no solution!' one of them shouted. 'No, there's something missing from the question,' Little Eagle insisted. 'Something like "The chess pieces win if …" I'm going to ask the Professor.' But for once, the Professor did not know how they could win.

In Belinda's house on the Friday before the Sunday that would be Midsummer Day, Liam and Joe, still having to share the hot attic bedroom because Belinda had had no time to turn out the junk room for Molo, were at each other's throats.

'You fancy him, you fancy him, you do, you fancy that weird little twocker Molo!,' and the tenth time he said it Joe finally got fed-up and shouted 'You're gay yourself, you've never had a proper girlfriend,' then saw the misery on his brother's face and said, 'I don't mean it for fuck's sake, I know you're not, but leave it, okay? Molo's not like us, he doesn't get it, and any way, he gave your shit back.'

'See, you're gay for him,' Liam prodded again and Joe punched the wall and went out.

He walked to school early with his mother and tried to talk to her.

'Liam's driving me nuts,' he said.

'I know, Joe, I'm sorry, I should never have done it, I should never have taken Molo in. I just can't do anything about it at the moment.'

'You told me you'd got to like him.'

'I do! You can't dislike him, he's a sweetie. But he's not – they're just not like us.'

'Don't give me that Put Britain First rubbish, *please*.'

'PBF? I left them years ago. They were mostly losers. Benny Barolo, he's Italian, in any case. That idiot from Broadstairs, Dirk White, who couldn't spell. Don't blame them for my opinions. I think for myself.'

'Well, Liam doesn't. He's got hundreds of their leaflets stored in the attic, did you know that?'

Belinda stopped dead, her mouth a small, shocked 'o' of surprise. She did *not* know that.

'I thought it was just someone to hang out with,' she said. 'It's hard for him now his year group's all moved on.'

'Yeah. Hard for him? Hard for *me*, sharing a room with a fascist idiot,' said Joe. 'He's always quoting them.'

'Is he?'

'Yes. And Mum, the fact you were a member encourages him.'

She braked too suddenly and parked in a series of jerks in the road outside the school. 'That's right' – (jerk) – 'give your mum the blame' – (jerk) – 'you're just like Brad.'

'Thanks. Look, you were telling the whole lot of us in assembly the other day to "own our mistakes". Well, wasn't the PBF a mistake?' He didn't expect his mother, who was obstinate, to answer, but as they walked in different directions she said urgently over her shoulder 'Joe! Fair enough, when I've got a bit more time I'll talk to Liam.'

But in fact, there was no time.

No time for the Professor's kindly idea to get Molo out of the house more, either. As always, Holly had wanted to help, and asked Molo round 'for a chat'. She liked him on sight, his frank blue eyes and athletic, symmetrical body, the way he inspected everything in her workshop with real interest, the way he saw the beauty in the golden necklace, which she'd placed casually, for her pleasure, on a milliner's bust of a girl, and most of all 'your English', as she told him, 'which is simply splendid. Your accent is so much easier on the ear than most of the Ramsgate natives.'

'It's not my accent,' he protested, 'I just copy the Professor's. We all do. We share his English. We share nearly everything, at home.'

'How delightful,' she said, pleased. 'In a way, I applaud your philosophy. My work,' – she indicated the golden necklet, glittering like the distant sea in the sun – 'is for everyone. My gift to the world.'

'Is it?' he said. His eyes were an intense dark blue, his face very serious.

The beauty of youth. She smiled at him. 'Of course. If you look at my necklace with love, you own it in that moment.'

'Do I?'

'Yes, well. It's more of a loan. Now, I gather you like to make things?'

'Yes! The Professor said I could be your apprentice.'

'Why not?' She likes keenness, and he's certainly keen.

'How long would it take me to learn to make a necklace?' he said. 'For a girl.'

'Are you in love?' she said, lightly, 'So sweet. And if you love her, give her everything. But it would take you about a year, working full-time, to learn to make the simplest thing in gold. There are all sorts of jobs you could do for me. In exchange, I would give you skills.'

'A year?' he said, surprised. 'Before I made anything? But I'm a quick learner, Miss.'

'Well. Something very simple, a few months.'

'Oh no,' he said, 'you see, I've got to leave. We've got to go home.'

But he gazes with love and awe on the necklace. It was a loan.

50

The London caterers, paid liberally by Holly to do something local firms could have done for a third the price, had worked all week sourcing bulk orders of ingredients. They had assembled regiments of empty containers and a fleet of refrigerator vans, pored over schedules and staffing levels, stirred and spiced the last ragouts and risottos, roasted the salmon till the skin was crispy while leaving the beef and venison pink and rare ('though people will complain we haven't cooked it, they always do'), and were now completing their last venue checks on the green above Pegwell Bay in stunning, unseasonal heat.

'Not a lot of shade,' said Donatella to her cousin Alfredo. Donatella had been put in charge of this very lucrative project because she was known to be gifted and the client was 'rich, fussy and artistic' (Holly, though no-one had actually met her).'We have to bear in mind the two-hour window the food can be left out will be shortened by the heat.'

'*Non preoccuparti*, it's England, it'll probably be raining by then,' said Alfredo. 'We'll move the whole thing under the awnings.'

It was 36 degrees, that Friday, and the short green turf was starting to swim slightly in the heat, and the frailer butterflies, dehydrating, were tacking raggedly across on the thermals to flag in safety in the warm shade of the buddleia trees on the slope that fell away steeply, out of sight, down to the former Hoverport and the sea.

'Amazing venue though,' said Donatella. 'Hugin Green, they call it.'

'Spelled?'

'H-u-g-i-n. *Come* "hug". *Ma si pronuncia* "Hyoo-gin". It's the name of that fabulous ship. Means "Raven", I think, in some Viking language.'

'*Daverro?*' said Alfredo, who prefers to look things up on Wikipedia, and had come on board this project halfway through. '*Comunque*, what is the occasion for the feast?'

'Welcoming some migrants, in a nutshell,' said Donatella. 'And they are welcoming the local inhabitants back.'

'*Un po' sfacciato*, welcoming people who already live here,' said Alfredo. 'Cheeky!'

'Why? It's just friendly,' said Donatella. 'If you come and live here and love it, in my book you can be English too. After all, thanks to our parents coming here from Italy, that's us.'

'I'm Italian,' he objected.

'I don't know what this lot are, frankly. This is all in their honour, though. I met two of them. Sounded as English as anything but – *be', no. Molto simpatici* but a teeny bit … extra-terrestrial.' She didn't want to say 'alien', but thought it.

'Not our business. Let's get back to London. The logistics are fine here, but Christ, it's hot. Clouds building up, though, look,' said Alfredo. 'Out to sea. What did I tell you?'

The thunder and lightning started that Friday night at half past eight, when they were just coming back through Peckham. Donatella parked the jeep in the office car-park with a sigh of relief. They had been having a low-key row because she refused to use the car's aircon. 'Bad for global warming,' she informed her cousin, opening the windows.

'Who cares?' he snapped back. '*Che importa?*'

'*Non ti importa dei tuoi figli?*' she asked.

'My kids can look after themselves,' he said, but didn't mean it, and soon he was agreeing that the breeze from the windows, though warm, was pleasant enough.

As she entered the kitchens, however, the whole steely room flickered an electric blue-white, as if some great switch in the sky had briefly turned on. 'One. Two. Three. Four. Five,' she managed, before the thunder rolled in like the building collapsing.

Down in Ramsgate, Joe was teaching Molo to count to find out how near the storm was. But already the storm was on top of them, almost directly overhead, a wide curtain of mad blue light replacing the sky over the sea, and Joe only got to 'Three' before the first ear-splitting drum-roll of sound shook Belinda's windows, and both boys ran downstairs.

51

The Professor was out on a sweaty walk with Winston to discuss their respective welcome speeches at the party when two things happened. First, the rumbles of thunder over the sea grew more ominous, and the sky darker. 'Perhaps we should go back?' Winston said.

'Too hot for a coat,' Juan replied.

Then the message from Jebel Tarek pinged on to his phone, and he stopped by the cliff path and stood frowning at the screen. 'Message from home,' he explained, reading.

'Holly?'

'No, *home* home.'

And read it again, thinking hard. *'Read Gibraltar story in Times today. Come home.'*

'Everything okay?' asked Winston, seeing his face.

'I don't know. Do you take the *Times*?'

'Yes.'

'Let's get back.'

Winston's house felt smothering after outside. Thinking of his guest, he went to open the windows, then changed his mind, because by that time, the storm was nearly there.

In any case Juan did not even sit down as he read the paper. After he finished, he said with decision 'This changes our plans.'

'Not for Sunday, please God?'

'Not for the party. But it gives me things to arrange. As for our speeches – whatever you say will be fine. Not important.'

'No no, the party is important. A wonderful idea.'

'*Non importa.*'

'Juan, are you alright?'

'Life and death are important.'

A pause. The paper was open in front of the Professor, and Winston was dying to have a look, but something about the Professor's whole mien — tense, energised, inward — stopped him asking.

'Can I help?'

'Maybe. Not now.' Juan's voice and face were returning to normal, but Winston could almost feel the effort involved. 'Dear fellow, I'll have to leave you. I'll be in touch before Sunday. As for speeches — we'll cover for each other. Whatever I don't say, you say.'

'And vice versa.'

No response. 'May I take this?' said Juan, waving the paper.

'I'll just scan it for you,' said Winston, who wanted to keep the original so he would know what was up.

He started reading the story as the machine did its work, and then handed the print to Juan with a question. 'Gibraltar?'

But without a further word, not even 'Thank you', the Professor, normally so courteous, was gone.

52

'Gibraltar,' Winston muttered as he read, the second after the door closed behind the Professor. 'Gibraltar. They come from Gibraltar.'

RADICAL CATALAN-STYLE POPULAR VOTE ROCKS GIBRALTAR

An unauthorised 'Universal Poll' challenging a major new development of Gibraltar's South End is set to take place in a week's time, following months of public unrest in the usually stable British Overseas Territory. The proposed site, where units of luxury accommodation are priced at £3 million and above, borders the unspoiled Upper Rock Nature Reserve and Neanderthal World Heritage Site. The *Gibraltar Chronicle* reports that posters advertising the poll – slogan 'Vote with your feet' – have appeared throughout the territory. The Royal Gibraltar Police said they had no information polling booths would be open. Chief Minister Fabien Picardo said he could not comment on the poll but 'always welcomed public engagement in the future of Gibraltar'.

The *Paradise Now* consortium plans to build more than 1,000 units of high-end accommodation, additional headquarters for global remote gambling operations and 'extensive leisure facilities', but the major purpose of the underground works is thought to be the creation of data centres. Requests for an interview were refused but a spokesperson issued this statement. 'The so-called "Universal Poll" is a publicity stunt organised by foreign activists. *Paradise Now* gained a 97% approval rating in our fully transparent consultation process for the project. We will generate employment and other economic benefits whilst aspiring to be the greenest development in Gibraltar, with most of its footprint underground'.

Winston went to his laptop and started researching Gibraltar, in which he had never really had any interest, despite, or perhaps because of, a shopping holiday his mother had insisted on taking him on as a boy. He soon found that its first name, after the Berber conquest in 711 CE, was 'Jabal-al-Tariq', Tariq's Mountain.

Of course. Of course! 'Jebble Tariq'. Ms Potter had assumed it was the family name of the first two Red children to arrive. He was always in a hurry, always firefighting, he'd never had time to think –

The light in the room seemed to flicker, and he blinked. Then it flickered again, and he realised it was the lightning outside the window. Inside, it was unnaturally dark. There was a crash, then another. The Professor would get wet. Winston sighed and read on.

In 2016 Gibraltar had been granted World Heritage Site status because of its Neanderthal caves. In one of them, an elaborate but enigmatic carving of parallel lines in the rock had been taken as proof of symbolic thought, and nicknamed the 'Neanderthal hashtag'. The Upper Rock had vegetation almost unchanged since the days when Neanderthals used Gibraltar as their last refuge against the coming of the cold. Living on in a place that still had summer as the weather of the world grew cooler, a dwindling band of humans – were Neanderthals counted as humans? – on the move. Surviving in the warm south, 40,000 years ago, in caves on the shore of the tip of Europe.

53

'They survived,' said Winston to himself in the hall mirror, which he was just passing. He was suddenly laughing with joy. 'How bloody marvellous! It's them! Must be! The Neanderthal line survived! They're with us!' Then he thought again, of his deep friendship with the Professor, of the way the Red children had fitted in, after the first rough patches, at school, the way they were liked and accepted.

'No, they are us,' he whispered to himself, with wonder, to his human face in the mirror in the storm-darkened hallway, staring into his own eyes, no longer laughing, every hair on his arms prickling. 'We're ... all one. The Neanderthals are us.'

PART FOUR

54

The edge of England has known storms ever since the ice receded and the waves flooded in and a coastline very roughly like today's stood here staring across at Europe: in the narrow channel, huge winds funnel and roar and are magnified by confinement and whip up the water and break against the cliffs. Only a few of them, happening since humans have had pens and written history, have become famous: the 'Great Storm' of November 1703, for example, where between eight and fifteen thousand are thought to have drowned at sea, 1500 of them members of the Royal Navy, not to mention fishermen, trawlermen, and the usual landlubbing gawkers who came out, awed and quaking, to watch, went too near the edge in excitement and were snatched and sucked down like so many tiny, transparent, uncountable water-fleas, just as the wooden ships had been, suddenly toys, those masterworks of human construction, corks bobbing in the raging power of the sea. After that storm, horror at the loss of life led to the building of our harbour, so vessels had somewhere to shelter, the only Royal Harbour in the kingdom, by decree of George IV.

In that epic rollcall of storms, the storm of the Friday night before Midsummer Day holds its place in history.

People who had never feared lightning before sat silent after the first big thunderclap, put off the lights, unplugged their devices with numb hasty fingers and sat there awed in hot summer half-dark rooms as one huge shock of blue light was followed in one split second by another great rush of sound like the earth collapsing and another white flash, or were they all happening at once, all burning and grinding up land and sky together, it felt as though their houses shook, as though the light and the noise would blind and deafen tiny humans covering their ears with their hands in tight rows of trembling, thin-skinned buildings.

Only the teenagers were wildly excited, and even those stayed in, ricocheting off walls, cheering and screaming and dancing. And some were terrified: Liam, up in the attic, alone, though it was the most dangerous part of the house, but he just couldn't bear to go down and sit in the small front room with the others.

'All right Liam?' Belinda shouted upstairs. The third time she called against the noise of the storm, there was some kind of answering grunt, so she went and sat back down next to Sandra on the sofa. Between Joe, Sandra, Molo and her there were two torches. Everyone was tapping away at their phones, trying to find out what was happening and when the storm was predicted to end. The light was a bit like a painting, she thought, though which one, she wasn't sure. Every so often the kids got up and danced around the room, and she laughed until she was tired of laughing, and they too flopped exhausted, then screamed at the next flash.

Was it the end of the world?

'Liam is brave to stay up in the roof,' said Molo, who was sprawled on the rug by the fake fireplace, every so often turning over and doing a press-up, which Sandra silently admired. 'Have you got a place downstairs, what do you call it, an underground?'

'A cellar,' said Belinda, always the teacher. 'That's c-e-l-l-a-r. No, that's just the eighteenth- and nineteenth-century houses. This one is modern.'

'I would like to live in an eighteenth- and nineteenth-century house,' Molo said.

Belinda looked at him rather hard and veered the torch round so it went in his eyes. 'Sorry, I'm sure.'

'Liam's not brave,' said Sandra. 'He's actually a coward.'

'Don't say cruel things about your brother,' Belinda said, and gave her a little slap on the hand.

'That's child abuse,' Sandra said half-heartedly, and then, 'Liam's frightened of *us*.'

(But then the temperature suddenly dropped, there was a momentary pause in the battering salvos of sound, and they heard: first, Liam's feet pounding downstairs and the back-door being unlocked – 'Where are you GOING, Liam?' screamed his mother, 'You'll get SOAKED!' – and then, in the cold gust of wind that came in through the door, a rapid metallic drumbeat. The back door slammed but the sound went on, growing heavier now, like a fusillade of small rocks against the windowpane, were they being attacked? And they looked from one to another in the ghastly light of the torches, whose wavering made them look one minute radiant, the next monstrous, aged, horrific.

'It's over,' said Belinda. 'Rain's started. Phew.' Yet it sounded too heavy for rain.

'Señor Goya,' said Molo at the same time. 'Like his paintings. Our ... master.'

But no-one heard him, or understood, because at that moment the noise of gunshots got louder as the back door opened again, crashed shut and feet ran into the house.

Liam burst through the front room doorway and the torches all turned on him, almost unrecognisable, blonde hair drenched dark, covered in mud, panting, his face patchy red and white. 'None of you thought about Taughtus,' he shouted, triumphant. 'I did! I just went and found him in the dark, he was under the lavender bushes, I put him back safe in his house. I got hit on the head! Several times! The hail stones are enormous! Like cricket-balls! He could have been killed! So could I! I could have been struck by lightning! I saved him. Mum gave him to you, Sandra, but it was me, your brother, who saved him!'

'You're my hero,' said Sandra, regretting what she said before, and 'You're a good boy,' said Belinda, who was actually very fond of Taughtus, and sometimes wished to be him, slow and steady, not fast and anxious, a being without worries or duties, padding slowly over warm grass-blades.

The release of good feeling in the room, the relief at knowing the military noise had only been hail, made them all relax: they were safe: the crisis was over. Sandra raised her phone to take a picture of this new, drenched, panting, heroic brother, framed in the doorway, transformed.

As she did so, the world disappeared in a giant, heart-stopping, bone-shaking, bolt of white light that jolted, and photographed, hundreds of miles of the coast, and in the same instant, a noise like the whole countryside cracking in two, rolling on for minutes, only half-drowning thousands of human and animal screams.

When it finally died away, every electrical connection was out. A new deep darkness.

55

When the next day dawned, in Thanet, our magical semi-island on the edge of England, on Coll in the Hebrides, with its tall, white Caribbean dunes appearing like ghosts as the light came up, on Lundy, off Devon, where the wet sheep drifted into being like huddled clouds; in a hundred marginal places, a patchy network of power came back, but the internet stayed out.

'Mum! Dad!' screamed Arash's kids on Saturday morning. 'My phone's not working! Give us yours!'

'None of the phones are working,' said their mother.

'How can I talk to my friends?' said her pretty daughter, only slightly consoled when she found she had enough battery to keep taking selfies.

'Must be to do with this house,' said his older son, accusingly, to Arash. 'Mum said you had to rewire it.'

'Don't blame your father,' his mother said, although she had already done so at 5am when she got up to soak the lentils. 'Aunty came round. Her phone's not working either.'

These conversations were happening in every house (not mine, because then I lived alone). Children too young to know what the internet was were equally unhappy. 'Daddy, my phone won't talk to me tudday,' said three and a half-year-old Layla Muggeridge, the caretaker's daughter, who knew her dad could mend anything, and make everything in the world better.

'Sorry, Layla darling, Daddy's phone won't talk to him either,' said the caretaker, who was putting his tracksuit jacket on to go out and check the school burglar alarms.

'Daddy has to go out, as soon as I can get hold of Aunty Jill.'

Layla burst into tears. 'Daddy NOT go out. *Hate* Aunty Jill.'

'You don't,' he said, hopelessly. Nothing had gone right since Layla's mother had left. 'Tell you what, let's both go out. In the garden. You and me.'

This never happened in the morning, when she sat on the sofa and watched cartoons.

Hand in hand, they walked into the garden. 'Daddy, I got the wrong shoes on.'

'Don't tell Mummy when you see her. They'll dry out.'

'When am I gunnasee Mummy again?'

'I don't know yet.'

The air was drenched and fresh, washed clean. The sky was blue, so blue. Next door's horse-chestnut was still in bloom and on their own small lawn, which seemed to have grown in the night, there were clouds of daisies he hadn't had time to notice before.

Layla enjoyed breathing in and out. Something cold and lovely came into the middle of her, and she noticed each blade of grass on the lawn held a tiny bright ball of water.

She forgot about her phone. 'Butterfly,' she suddenly shouted, triumphant.

And there was one. Together, they tiptoed across the wet grass and watched it, a tiny one, really, though big to Layla, silvery pale blue, floating in the sunlight over the red and pink ragged silk of the self-sown giant poppies. Now he was pleased that he hadn't, in the end, dug them out.

At 11am Winston banged on the door of Holly's house rather harder than he needed to. She came serenely downstairs and opened the door. 'No need to do that, the doorbell's on a battery, darling.'

The Professor and Winston had a tense conversation – tense on Winston's side, that is. No, he wouldn't bother with coffee.

'Are you all right, dear fellow?' Juan asked. Winston seemed to be looking at him in a new way, consideringly, glancing away for a second then staring as they settled in armchairs in Holly's library.

'Are *you* all right, Juan?' He asked after a pause. 'That story in the *Times*.'

'Oh yes, that. I had to take some decisions, but yes. Was Ella all right last night?'

Juan sounded so calm and looked so, well, normal that Winston for a second doubted everything he had concluded on the night of the storm. 'Yes. No. She's all right, but the storm ... we didn't get to sleep at all. Never mind that. I've come to talk about the, about the –' He suddenly couldn't remember what it was called.

'Our Midsummer Festival.'

'What are we to do, if the internet stays down, do we postpone?'

'Not at all,' said Juan. 'The real world is not the child of the virtual. It will still be Midsummer Day. That paper - *Kent Central*? – ran its two-page spread about the party last week. We talked to that manic yellow-haired woman who kept saying "feel-good". People will come ...'

'But you need breakfast,' Holly interrupted. 'Follow me into the kitchen. The Aga is working because it always does. Also our land-line.'

'You still have a land-line? My God!'

'Coffee and toast?'

Within half an hour, Winston's tired body was feeling a lot better. He had confirmed, via the magical landline, that the caterers would go ahead. Then the task became how to get the news out.

Accordingly, the three adults were soon on their knees on Holly's floor, which she had covered with an old silk curtain, writing in capital letters on countless sheets of A4 paper 'MIDSUMMER FESTIVAL GOES AHEAD, ALL WELCOME!' Winston then took the flyers away and, with the help of some Year 13s, was soon sticking them in every possible place around the town, Meanwhile, back in Holly's house, the Professor was enjoying massaging Holly's sore knees, and somehow, on the silk curtain on the floor in the sun, one nice thing led to another.

'Sir? Isn't this fly-posting?' asked Liam, trying to impress. They were sticking posters on the red brick of the arches by the harbour; Liam had keenly volunteered when Winston came to the house. Cafés and shops along the quay had been flooded as rainwater poured down from the road above, and one of the Sea Cadets, who were helping mop up, passed on the news that the tunnel through the cliff had collapsed. Liam wasn't listening – he just wanted Winston to know he wouldn't like to break the law.

'You're doing a great job, Liam,' said Winston, trying to absorb the news about the tunnel, which he would pass on to the Professor later. 'Strictly speaking you're right, fly-posting is illegal. But in this life, best not to be rigid. There are always surprises.'

56

And now it is Sunday: the day!

And they are coming towards the wet sunlit green slopes of Pegwell from everywhere, from Ramsgate, yes, but also from miles around, surely, for it turns out that word of mouth, actual human mouths, and leg-work, and knocking on doors, works surprisingly well – a steady trickle, at first, of human beings.

Quiet, the first ones, who have duties: erecting tables, poles for bunting, folding chairs for the old, designated parking zones on the road.

Noisy, the next arrival: Monica, plus some of her wardens. She has chosen the strongest girls in the hockey team, plus the only two boys among the Red children who have shown any propensity to violence (against each other, fighting over a red plastic bag on the beach that both wanted to incorporate into a beach-comber necklace for his beloved) plus three of her children with disabilities, Ida (13), Danish, keen but deaf, which gives Monica an excuse to shout, Javid (17), very bright, with cerebral palsy, and Frank (15) who everyone but Monica agrees should never have got into the Grammar School, who's always falling over ('dyspraxic, they call it', says Monica, with a sniff) and not good at anything much so far as anyone else has noticed, but Monica's noticed him listening to music with a rapt expression on his face, and drumming with his great bony hands.

She is flanked by Ginger who has been instructed by his wife to 'Look after Hecate, remember you're off duty, lots of people don't like you so keep quiet.' He is wearing an alarming 'off-duty' uniform of ironed orange tracksuit top over neatly tucked-in short-sleeved shirt and tie and pressed grey 'smart casual' trousers, and somewhere he has bought a brand-new scarlet baseball cap.

'I'll just make one comment, I have no idea why you've chosen some of this lot as wardens,' he remarks in her ear with a provoking smile as she starts distributing yellow-edged tabards and arm bands. 'They're patently a liability if there's trouble.'

'They're happy. They like their arm-bands. They're my kids, I chose them. If there's any trouble, I'll fix it.'

'Yawwright Miss? Yawwright? What shall we do? Can I have something to eat?' asks Frank, looking wistfully at the long tables in the shade where the caterers are laying out the 'Welcoming coffee, *millefeuilles, eclairs* and *langues de chat*', as requested by Holly.

'Not yet. There'll be lots to do soon. In the meanwhile … WARDENS!!!' Monica thunders and her arm-banded troops look up. 'Go search every inch of this grass for broken glass.'

'Health and safety, Monica!' hisses Ginger reprovingly.

'Nah, me and Anna Segovia and a few others already searched it earlier this morning, it's just to keep them quiet,' says Monica. The yellow flashes on their tabards spread out like buttercups over hundreds of metres of grass, which have started to steam in the heat. 'Hecate, come with Mummy and Daddy and we'll eat some of those cakes.'

Hand in hand, the three of them make their way. 'IDA!' shouts Monica in the direction of her nearest wardens, Ida and Francis, who are doing something under a tree. 'Don't let Francis kiss you now, you're working. FRANK! Stop that!' They separate, abashed. 'That Danish girl is all heart,' she explains to Hecate. 'Francis is slobbery. Girls have to learn to push boys like that over.'

'I know how,' says Hecate. 'I'd just do my karate. You can kill people.'

Monica laughed like a seal, then said, 'Don't.'

'Murder. Against the law,' says Ginger, sombre, but impressed.

'Daddy,' says Hecate, alternating between hanging like a heavy baby between her burly parents and swinging their arms up and down like pistons, 'I love you.' She is staring up into his eyes.

'Thank you, Hecate,' says Ginger.

'But I want to say …' She stops, uncharacteristically shy.

'Go on,' says her adoring father.

'Mummy is more funny.'

He doesn't answer, but gazes at the table of delicate pastries, his eyes slate-grey and blank. 'No sausage-rolls,' he says. 'You know I like sausage rolls, Monica.'

Soon more people, all ages and sizes, are walking in a moving frieze along the cliff-tops or down the Pegwell Road, until it turns into a flood. They've been asked to walk from Ramsgate 'if possible' because the Sandwich Road beyond Cliffsend is blocked for re-tarmacking and besides, 'our new friends', as Winston had called them, after wrestling with the phrase, in his Wednesday announcement to the school, 'do not like cars. Any way, walking is a pleasure.' Cue incredulous adolescent side-eyes.

But look, they are larking around in the sunlight, the young ones, groups of three or four, groups of nine or ten, arms around shoulders, pushing and laughing, as if there had never been any such thing as a virus, and for now, indeed, they are roughly right, those tiny particles of non-life are fast asleep, not ready to wake in the humans, while life with legs, fully realised life, hopeful and in a hurry, is heading towards the party, diving through the warm June air, still fresh and clean from the torrents of rain, coming to the Festival, coming for Midsummer, coming to be happy.

It's Sunday, rest day. Arash would normally be fishing but his wife insisted that everyone's going, so they should too ('Why?' 'To prove we are British' – 'We're not!' – 'Idiot, I know!' – 'You said you didn't like the Red people, and the party's for them!' – 'All the teachers are going, put your jacket on' – 'But it's hot!' – 'The Head will have his jacket on') – and although they have been bickering, they are walking along, now, quite contented, hand in hand, proud of their daughter who, under protest, is wearing her Afghan dress, a tiny bit hot for the weather but flaring pink and green as the fuchsia that flowered in their garden this spring and sewn all over with tiny mirrors that show up her golden skin to advantage, but equally proud of the two shiny-haired boys in miniature shirts and ties ('British!', their mother thinks) who are running along the path ahead of them.

Mrs Jackee West has taken communion early and is hurrying along with some of her fellow Christians to see if they can help out; 'I was the one who first met them,' she reminds them, 'and we did our duty, for those first few weeks in January, we let them sleep in our church.' (She doesn't remind them how much most of the congregation had complained at the mess, the seaweed, the trails of sand near the altar, the purple-blue empty mussel-shells crunching under their feet, the smells of fish … but once the Red children, safely rehoused, were no longer a drain on Church resources, some of them shyly came back to say thank you, adding considerably to the minute congregation of the Sailors' Church every Sunday, giving out hymn books and service sheets beforehand, even though they couldn't sit still.)

The parade has to pass the foot of the tall blue Scots pine on the cliff where the ravens have their nest, but this year, no eggs. As yet the Princess has only opened one eye, although it is late in the morning. Roland has been to Holly's on a recce: nothing on the windowsill. For three days now there has been no breakfast, and Roland's rivalrous feelings about the Professor incline him to blame the big stranger. Worse, rumours reached them only the evening before from raven cousins in Europe that the red-headed Youmen ancestors made capes from bird feathers and even, horror, carved patterns on ravens' bones. At that last his hackles reared up in a great ruff of black rage, but the Princess only jumped delicately sideways, away, churring, as if she guessed he was jealous, 'That's all in the past.'

'It's our ancestors' bones,' he had snapped, performing an indignant percussion with his beak, 'and he's stealing our breakfast.'

'Juan's too intellectual to do anything peculiar with old bones. He writes down his thoughts very neatly on paper.' And she had made gentle knocking noises in her beautiful throat like plucked bass piano strings to calm him down.

This morning, Roland is glad to be distracted by what's going on down below. Youmen of all kinds crowd the path and he's comforted, looking down on their vulnerable heads, tiny as peas and as easily squashed in his beak if he wanted to.

'Lots and lots of them,' says Roland. 'They are all annoyed with their phones.' He has noticed them tapping and tutting then throwing the things into bags, with shrugs and sighs.

'Where are they going?'

'They're excited,' says Roland. 'To a party?'

'Shall we drop in?'

'Later,' Roland replies, and flies off to fetch his beloved a mouse.

Here's Ramadan Bakri and the Sea Cadets, in uniform because they had been drilling for a visiting Area Officer, very smart, but after the first hundred metres, quite hot. 'Do you think we should march?' asks one, but 'Got to be joking,' says Ramadan, a little lonely since Sandra and he broke up, glimpsing a crowd of girls, their hair shaking and gleaming in the sunlight, just coming into focus on the path ahead, but in any case, as he guesses beforehand with a sinking of his heart, the girls let the cohort of blushing uniformed Cadets walk past them as if they don't exist. They're just babies, Ramadan tells his hurt ego. Much too young.

It is, in fact, Twainelle and her friends from Year 9, a summer butterfly-cloud of jostling, dancing girls, only a few of them complaining new shoes are hurting their feet, unused as they are to walking. Since she started dating Little Eagle, there's a fashion for dating the Red boys, and now quite a lot of the set she runs with have washed their hair and manicured their nails with special care because they are meeting the Red boys later, and they keep waving their fingers in the sunlight as they skank and boogie past the pink mallow on the cliff path and the tall yellow fennel flowers, and there's something special they've all got, it seems, because they keep comparing their nails and admiring each other's, and now they're all clustered in a bunch for a photo which Twainelle is taking, though she frowns at her phone for several minutes first, and the other girls copy her, like clones – yes, it will still take photos, but none of them, not one, can accept that they can't get online, and they keep pulling the tiny things from their pockets and pecking at them like goldfinches after seed, but 'Put them away for the photo!' Twainelle orders, since pictures of people with phones are sad, and here is the image of them all they will treasure when they are old, their fore-arms raised like the front-limbs of meerkats and their hands folded down like paws so the nails shine bright in the sun, and what have they done? – each nail has a design in silver drawn by hand on the base-coat of red, or green, or blue, or pearl, or purple varnish, for all of them are different, but all of them bear the same pattern, the same criss-cross lattice of lines, the complex hash-tag which is the sign of the Red children.

Anna Segovia happens to be walking along not far behind them with her and Joan's daughter, who is ten, and thinks she has come across a band of goddesses. 'Hello girls! Off to the party?' Anna sings out in her lilting voice but her daughter pulls anxiously at her arm, 'Mum! You don't know them!'

It turns out her mother does know them.

'Hello Miss, is that your kid?' asks Twainelle.

Susanna hangs behind her mum's back. Her clothes are wrong because stupid Mummy, or else her other stupid mummy, has washed her cool dress.

'Yes, this is Susy,' says Anna. 'If she doesn't know anyone at the party, could she maybe' (Susanna is furiously blushing now, the cliff might crack open beneath her, what is her mother doing, *what is she saying*? *this is death*) 'hang out, a bit, with you?'

'Course,' says Twainelle, and despite Susy's horror, it's done, and perhaps she will.

And here's Winston, later than he wanted to be because Ella was so eager to find the right outfit, but he's not counting the minutes, she's here, for once, because she slept last night, so they both did, because she woke up well, and when he jerked awake fearful in the morning light to find himself in bed alone, she had merely gone downstairs and put on the table sliced banana, cashew-nuts, milk in a jug, granola, and when he hurried tense and barefoot into the kitchen, not knowing what he might find, she came and put her arms around his neck and said, 'I've got breakfast', as if she always made it. 'What shall I wear?'

'You're coming?' His heart beat fast.

'Yes.' Which has made the day more anxious but also, immeasurably better, because he has loved her ever since he first saw her, because he wants his colleagues to meet her, because when she's happy she's happier than anyone else, because she is the most beautiful woman in the world with her hair in a thick, wild cloud, the ends just tipped with the last of the sunlight she added eight months ago with bleach, half-dancing along the cliff beside him, tall and slender in her clinging yellow silk dress, tight over her strong torso but spinning loose and free away from her hips and long legs which are half-dancing already as they catch the first notes of the music, carried on the light summer breeze that is all that remains of the storm. Most of all, because this morning, after they ate breakfast, for the first time since they lost the baby, Ella said, 'I am going to get better. I found a counsellor in Canterbury. I think we can try again.'

Thirty minutes behind him, and sweating, it's Neil, the former headteacher, who's decided, like Winston's wife, that he must go out, but who's brought a neatly packed lunch in a plastic box in case he 'needs to get away', which means 'in case Monica sees me'.

They're all on their way; the little family from Sunrise Fish and Chips, hand in hand with Kuzey, their sturdy son, many other Turks who have come over the decades to love and live in Ramsgate, taxi drivers, fishermen, software engineers, restaurateurs, teachers, all of them different but all of them carrying memories of the great city full of water and domes and prayer-calls where travel on ferries was easy but life became hard, all of them half-wishing they too in their time had been welcomed to England, or had a chance to welcome others, with a big celebration like this, 'But the food will be rubbish, because English food is rubbish,' one Turkish grandfather hopefully opines, but his grandson, who's a chef, laughs and puts his arm around the old man and says 'Not any more, *dede.*'

Layla and her dad, 'Mr Muggeridge', as all the students and staff respectfully call him, because he's the only one who knows what actually makes the school work, the ancient boiler with its weirdly right-angled pipes and mysterious gamut of straining and easing noises, the combination locks on doors and the security system that locks people out at random unless he's to hand, immensely tall Mr Muggeridge, too tall to be cheeked and with furrows of everyday worry on his high forehead. Today is a holiday from worry, he tells himself, and 10 per cent of his forehead un-creases. The security system is, irrevocably, down, since Friday night. But when he rang Winston this morning to see if he should stay on guard, Winston sounded different from usual, more light-hearted, and said, 'I think we'll just trust, for once, in the Lord. Everyone should be at the party. It's for all of us. Bring Layla.'

And half of Winston, this morning, believes it. It's a day of the world washed clean; a day of sunlight and trees, a day of hopeful beginnings, a day of fresh breezes entering small, locked places; a day when minds might swing open like casement windows over a wide bright common, when love and liking might bud, understanding might blossom …

Although, straggling behind the others, two or three hours late –

– long after the fabulous lunch has been spread on the tables and half of it eaten by happy gannets, long after the dancing has started in earnest, long after Holly, magnificent in peacock blue voile with an almost transparent, light-as-air cape of finest blue mulberry silk, has arrived in a white limousine from the Luxatax firm by the harbour, rising above her faint worry about the Professor, who had not reappeared to collect her, rising above her awareness that one window has been broken, at home, by a bouncing hail-stone in the great storm, and the burglar alarm, which is linked to a Margate police station, is down; long after Nina Sharon and Eileen Killarney got here, the latter on protest after Nina said, 'They're honestly lovely, Eileen, and so are you,' which made Eileen want to be lovely instead of bitter and spiteful; and long after Mr Phelpham the history teacher, who's teaching Anarcho-syndicalism to the Year 11s, including Molo – 'Property is theft' – long after Tony Phelpham has proudly led his seven children and half a dozen grandchildren to the table; long after Sam the blonde reporter from *Kent Central*, happy to see Arash, tottered over in heels and greeted him with her usual meaningless hug, leaving him with a lot to explain to his wife …

– long after all that, Liam and about fifteen of the members of Put Britain First are arriving.

They're late because they weren't sure they were included in the universal welcome, not sure they were coming at all, and a strangled form of shyness – what if people stared at them? What if people knew the things they'd said? But on the other hand why shouldn't they go to the party like everyone else? – has sent them into Spoons in advance for two or three beers, and there they've made a plan, a sort of plan, to do something important. Maybe in the caves? Which have become infested, they know, with – 'They're like rats,' said Hank Stitch as he finished his second beer and got ready for his third. 'They brought plague. They have to be got rid of. The Red Rats.' Liam had listened, part of him shocked, most of him thrilled. A silence. He gulped and filled it, his voice sounding weird.

'So we get down there, right, and drive them out.'

Such a great feeling. For once, they'd all started nodding and looking at him with respect, though he didn't have a clue, still hasn't, how they'll do it.

Who isn't here yet?

The Professor.

Oh yes, and Molo.

No: here he is, running, with something in his hand, looking happy!

57

Finally Winston can't wait any longer for the Professor. Holly says, 'Go ahead and make the speech. They're all getting drunk, and Juan won't mind.'

'But Juan is so vital to everything that's happened,' says Winston, almost a wail, though the day is going well, so well, he and Ella have danced with the others, everyone loves the food, the venue, the music (live music from Robbie and his traditional jazz band, Lianne Carroll arriving later), and maybe he's just a tad wistful for the days when Ella would have taken the mike, with a sweet smile that half-averted the anxiety of the performers, and sung like a syncopated skylark; but still, this week's been so much better than any week since the horrors began that he's scarcely noticed the Professor's welcome speech is over an hour late.

'He'll be helping someone, somewhere,' says Holly, who knows her man. 'And of course without phones, he can't tell us.'

'As long as he's all right?' says Winston, who because of his past and his present, is always 5 per cent anxious that life might go wrong. He's left Ella sitting out a dance in the shade with an iced lemonade, laughing with pleasure at Twainelle and her girls, who are throwing incredible shapes on the grass. Is it going too well? Holly opens her hands as if she is releasing a dove, with a smile both resigned and mysterious. 'Everything will be all right.'

Winston thought for the first time how beautiful this woman in her seventies was, with her all-seeing blue eyes and kind lines. 'How did you get to be so calm?' he asks.

'I lost so many people,' she says. 'Two husbands. Worse, I lost Juan for so long.'

'Yes, but ...' It wasn't an explanation, he thought. His twin brother Franklin, who he could hardly remember, just someone who hugged him and fought, chubby arms, perhaps, someone who lived with him in a womb; gone. His murdered uncle. His mother Shirley, who now has some fault with her heart and who took their miscarriages so hard, his father Elroy who longs for grandchildren, his own fears for Ella – but no, he suddenly thinks. She's going to get better. We'll be all right.

'Nothing is gone,' said Holly, suddenly, laying her hand with its magical golden rings on his arm. 'Nothing ever goes. While we're alive and remember, everything ... *is*. I can't explain it, I'm not a philosopher, Winston.' But she lays her other hand on her heart, and for now, it's enough.

As he starts to walk away in the direction of the podium that's been put up for the speeches, she calls, over the heads of the dancing crowd, 'It doesn't protect you from grief, Winston. Nothing protects you from that.' But he doesn't hear her, he presses forward, looking round one last time for his friend the Professor as he gears up for his speech. It's almost seven o'clock. He can give it another ten minutes.

58

A lot can happen in ten minutes. Holly, shimmering calmly through the crowd, suddenly stops dead in surprise. It's Belinda Birch's daughter Sandra, flashing sunlight-bright, like a newly hatched Brimstone butterfly marked with radial veins of bright gold, through a clump of yellow-tabarded wardens, and the wardens, clumsier, shorter than her, reach out longing hands to touch her, but she's flown.

'Sandra Birch! Stop right there!' Holly's voice is surprisingly piercing. Sandra falters in flight.

'Yes?'

'*What are you wearing?*'

Holly knows. She's wearing £25,000. How...? What...? The elaborate golden collar whose every spoke is a delicate 22-carat gold stem with a leaf or flower. Holly has crafted it, lived with it, caressed it daily with her eyes, her heart stops to see it walk past her, but her inner eye can't help seeing how lovely it looks, under a loose golden knot of thick hair, on Sandra's pale neck.

'Oh yes,' says Sandra, and she colours like a pink blush rose, her hand flying to her throat. 'It's perfectly safe, it's a loan.'

'From *whom*,' Holly booms in a terrifying voice, 'did you obtain it? *Was it* from the woman who owns it?' (Yet she's thinking: such a beautiful thief, from a flower-piece by Fantin-Latour.)

'I'm ever so sorry, I thought it was wrong, but Molo promised you said he could have it, just as a loan, and he gave it to me.' Tears start to run down her round red cheeks. 'And it seemed such a waste not to wear it, and I didn't think you would see –'

'You mean you thought you'd get away with it!'

Now Sandra's blue innocent eyes start to well up in earnest. 'It's Molo's fault,' she sobs. 'he wouldn't understand why you're cross, he just wouldn't get it! They're not like us, none of them are! It's all their fault!' She was actually sobbing now. 'He really likes me, though.' She was trying, ineptly, to take the necklace off, but the catch Holly had crafted was too cunning.

'Do you like him?'

'Yes.' (sob) 'So.' (sob) 'Much.'

'Oh dear. Do stop blaming him then. And stop crying.'

'Why should I?'

'Because I want to take a picture of you.'

'What?' Her pretty mouth fell open.

'The necklace looks exquisite on you. The sponsors will love it. Dry your tears. Before the speeches start, do five minutes' modelling for me.'

'That's my dream, to be a model, but Mum says –'

'And then *give it back*.'

59

The Professor, three hundred feet below them, is poised for magic, for virtual worlds. The floods have blocked the tunnel through which he emerged with his troupe that first bright January morning, but no matter, the sea way will take them, he knows, the line of the sun over the sea down which the first four arrivals came. Did they say thank you? Of course. He has always taught them, be grateful for life, and to life. Thank you that we did not die in the dark, *Alhamdulillah*; they did not drown ...

Now he will lead them all on into the future again. He is on the sand just outside their cave. Inside its mouth are stacked their tiny parcels of possessions, done up with string: a t-shirt someone gave to a Red child with a hand-inked hashtag, some seeds of the plants that don't grow at home, pieces of jewellery they've made with black and white crow and gull feathers, though most have been given away, an old-style map which shows sea-currents, another he'd found in a second-hand bookshop that marks places in Kent where their forebears once cut up mammoths with flints.

On the beach, white and stark, written in chalk, their hashtag signals to the sun on the sea, to the golden line of belief down which they must travel: *take us, we're ready*. The time's right: Midsummer Day, before sunset.

They'd got here early. Molo, Little Eagle and Roosha had organised the others to come down in small groups with the last of their possessions to stow in the cave, then helped the Professor gather shells and stones. On the shore, the four of them, working together, aligned hundreds of smaller white ones, tunnelled with holes, to map out their people's symbol, the hashtag, the intricate parallel and converging lines that encode their past and their future.

The first stages of the plan had gone fast, because cliff-falls following the storm had already scattered small pieces of chalk across the sand. Molo, Little Eagle and Roosha left after the first two hours. Little Eagle was meeting Twainelle, Roosha had an assignation with Jude, Molo wouldn't say why. 'I can manage perfectly without you now,' Juan told them.

It was time for him to assume the burden of the leader: steady, he thinks, steady, *mantener la calma, siempre tranquilo, ailtizam alhudu* – be calm and cheerful in this great hour, like Hector of Troy, his classical hero, resolved on peace but steady in war.

Yet the magic of weightless, simultaneous travel only happens, he knows, by drawing vast quanta of energy out of him. Not by being heroic, but forgetting who you are, losing what you have (yet how could they go home bringing nothing? The little parcels, surely, would not weigh heavy).

He must lose his identity as one, become part of the everything.

He has worries no bigger than the tiny good weather clouds that curl like ferns or feathers, streaming up, dissolving, fainting, in the blazing sky. Instead of looking outwards over the sea, he thinks about their store, their tiny hoard of treasures. All over the tightly bound parcels, there are showers of white dirt, and more stones, freshly fallen: the cliff, drenched after drought by the storm, has been stretching and heaving, alive, throwing out, through new fissures, tiny bones. Little Eagle and Molo, stacking the parcels, had to avoid great puddles. New leaks have been spreading, even since then, dripping over what Juan, in love with the Latin he learned on the cruise-ship's 'Latin for Leisure, Roam with the Romans' course, thinks of as '*indumentaria*': possessions of the warrior. Also, food parcels. Nuts, early strawberries, and someone has added five family packets of Monster Munches, despite Molo's protests. And knives. So useful, and here so easy to find. Not all the knives, let's admit it, came from a shop, many have slipped away, over months, from drawers and pockets and gardens here. Something for years to come when they'll shape and cut and remember, back in the hot dark of home.

Home. It's a hum of longing in Juan's heart, the old hive humming, a thrum of heat.

In his canvas bag is the heavy, beautiful conch shell, which will be the signal. When he practiced it with Holly, she covered her ears. 'It sounds like the harbour siren,' she said. 'Not in the house, my love. My ear-rings are quivering.'

'Okay, it won't be in the house.'

It's in his rough bag, on the warm sand, now. Like him, it's ready for use.

But he's been here, now, for five hours. This trick should be simple, yet ... A query eats at the corner of his mind like a tiny termite, an ant-bite echo of the problem that weeks ago puzzled his children, and him, in the playground.

For some integer n, a set of n^2 magical chess pieces arrange themselves on a square $n^2 \times n^2$ chessboard composed of n^4 unit squares. At a signal, the chess pieces all teleport to another square of the chessboard such that the distance between the centres of their old and new squares is n. The chess pieces win if, both before and after the signal, there are no two chess pieces in the same row or column. For which values of n can the chess pieces win?

The Professor can't solve it. In his tall man's view of the human board, the black and white chess pieces are moving ever closer together. Little Eagle to Twainelle; he to Holly; Jude to Roosha; even Molo, so brave but so lacking in understanding, edging closer to Belinda's daughter Sandra. The odd and the even, he thinks, the like and unlike, they're all paired – ?

But it won't work like that. Odd or even, he's almost there, the answer is just at the edge of his mind …

How can they win if, both before and after the signal, no two chess pieces are together? How can they win by all teleporting away?

60

Up above, on the edge of the crowd, Joe's watching the girls in his year group, Jude and Marisa included, teaching some Red children – Molo, Roosha, a few others – to dance. Jude's got her scarlet bandeau top on which shows off her six pack and, he can't help seeing, her small, apple breasts. She's a brilliant gymnast like him, with lithe muscular limbs, and her blonde hair whirls across her biceps. He had meant to dance with her tonight, he'd put on his tight blue t-shirt which shows off his eyes and washed his hair and borrowed Liam's new *Homme* cologne. All pointless. Tonight is the Red people's night. The red bandeau twists and torments him as Jude dances with Roosha and Molo, and Molo is laughing, showing white teeth, and Joe looks away and jabs in despair at his phone. Nothing. And when he looks up, she's gone, Jude's actually gone off with the others and Molo, who's supposed to be his mate.

Then someone puts her arms round his shoulders from behind! *It's Jude*, he thinks, *she's seen what I'm feeling.*

But it's only his mother.

'Where's Liam?' Belinda asks, shouting shrilly over the music. 'Where's he gone?'

Joe shrugs, sullen with disappointment. He really likes Jude, and now she's not here, he wonders, with a gulp, if he actually loves her. Is love this pain? Where has Jude gone, what's she doing? Teaching that … *ape* Molo to dance, with his stupid muscles? What's wrong with him, Joe? Her best friend since nursery? What's wrong with … *our boys?* he finds himself thinking? What's wrong with us? Now his mother's on at him again.

'Why don't you ask Liam!' he says. 'Ask *him* where he is.'

'How can I!'

'Oh yeah, no phones. Why do you want him?'

'Tony Phelpham saw him down in the pub with the PBF lot. I don't want him doing something daft.'

'Mum! Mr Phelpham is just an old woman, ignore him. I've got things to do. I don't have to look after Liam!'

'Well sometimes he can't look after himself, we both know that.'

They gaze at each other. It's the first time his mum has admitted that Liam is weak, and half of Joe's pleased, though another part's hurt – this is Liam, his big brother.

'Ask around, will you, Joe? Please? I just don't want either of my sons in trouble. Oh. And by the way, where's Sandra?'

'Mum!' Joe breaks away, rolling his eyes.

'Any case, Winston is about to start his speech. Got to go.'

But speeches are boring to Joe, and his mother's infected him with worry. Where *is* Liam? Up to something stupid?

Joe gets on the case, pushing on through the crowd, but he's also looking for that flash of scarlet, Jude's bandeau. Then two over-excited class-mates garble a truth. Liam's up to bad shit. A raid on the Red people's caves, maybe started already?

'Yeah, and Jude, mate. I saw her with that Red bloke that's lodging at yours,' says Finbar. 'Lessava drink.'

He's a loser Joe usually genially ignores, but suddenly wanting oblivion, he follows the pair to the bar.

61

Down on the beach, the sun, burning heart of the mystery, still blinds Juan at well after seven, too bright for him to look at head-on.

Our star, he thinks. *Be my friend.*

But it feels like a great staring furnace, unshaded, out of control.

Time presses on. The sand, and his ringing head, hold the heat of the day. His eyes, when he tries to close them, are scarred by a dazzle of blind white writing from staring at the sun as it swings with calm terrible power like a ball and chain across the sea, moving westward, ever westward, and now bouncing like a boat (or he is, going up and down the beach from the cave, checking their possessions, then back on the sand, bending down to arrange the stones yet again, then peering with half-closed eyes at the sun as it crosses the border between sea and land to his right, going down, almost imperceptibly at first, reddening, yes, going down).

We're your children, children of the universe. Stardust. See us, help us, he prays.

Because when the universe finally tells him it's right, when he feels the great thrill that he felt before in his bones and can pick up his conch and give the signal, his people will join him on the beach. It must be before sunset, he knows. *It will happen.*

And if he gets precisely the right second, if at that moment in Jebel-Al-Tarek their brothers and sisters, climbing up out of the tunnels, stare with desire at the same sun – one sea, one sun, 'one love', as Ms Potter taught him – if the palms are the same, and the caves, and the chalk, and the ravens, the fennel, the yearning – if all is well between his people and the planet, and if all of them, in that magical, virtual moment, soar like eagles on the great likeness that links all of being, they will go home.

Then the solution of the maths problem comes, in a flash. Alas, it can only work if 'n' is an odd number. It's the one way it can come out right. What he will do, he accepts, he must do alone.

62

Winston's finally into his speech. But where's Ella? Oh yes, a flash of her there, standing next to a man with white hair. Oh God. Graham. One of the fascists. And the mic's picking up every wobble or waver in Winston's voice. If only he knew what he was talking about, but he's stuck here, in front of hundreds of people, maybe a thousand, including most of his school, and clueless, because the history bit was meant to be done by the Professor. *Deep breath.* The mic picks it up as a roar of repressed fear. '... Pegwell, a very special place ...'

Of course he's had no time to learn the history! He had to get to know the staff, and paint out racist graffiti on the wall of the playground, and cope with Monica, and Mr Muggeridge smoking in the boiler-room, and Belinda (who he doesn't realise is actually listening, like the rest of the staff, scattered through the crowd, full of hope and, in fact, willing him on, for they like him far more than he knows).

'... That amazing ship,' he continues, hapless, gesturing in the direction of the Viking galley, sailing high behind the audience, high above the green on its concrete blocks, the coiled tongue of its dragon head licking the red beginning of the sunset, '... amazing, I think we all agree! An amazing Viking ship! Which, er, refers to nearby Viking Bay, in Broadstairs ...' This has to be right, though oh God, old Graham, next to Ella, is shaking his head and gesticulating, but Winston's got the mic, he has to go on, 'which reminds us how many different peoples have sailed here to Britain to join us, and now tonight, we are welcomed by our new visitors, the Jebble Tariqs!' (He's been warned, not by them, against calling them the Red people, for are they, really, 'Red', and should people be defined by their colour? This item had taken up most of the space at the last Festival Committee meeting, though the Professor said he didn't care. Later Ms Potter reminded Winston that the first two arrivals said their name was 'Jebble Tariq', which did sound – *authentic* and best of all, *unquestionable*, because obviously, any name these days might be questioned, and 'We have to respect their identity,' she said) '… led by the remarkable Juan Der Tal, who came up with the idea for this wonderful party, generously funded by a donor who's asked to be anonymous …' (but his eyes swoop over the crowd and rest on Holly in the half-distance, glistening blue and gold like a mermaid and smiling kindly on him, though he's making rather a mess of things) '… let us raise our glasses, in this very special place' (God, he used the exact same words before) 'this *historic* place' (if only he knew why it was historic) 'to the Jebble Tariqs! Juan Der Tal! And us!'

The echo of the toast is weak and puzzled, something like 'The Giblets'. Many of the listeners are silent, worried, because is the head saying there's another lot of new arrivals coming now, not just the Red children, who they're getting quite fond of, but these Giblet people as well? Others clearly heard him say 'Neanderthal'.

'Now we've got Neanderthals coming, have we?' Hank Stitch asks Liam. 'Fucking Neanderthals, I ask you!' 'I think they're dead,' says Liam. 'I think he said "Tariqs". That's Pakistanis. Muslims,' he explains, with the push of distaste on the first syllable he's learned to use among these new friends. Jackee West just whispers, 'Oh dear! I thought it was just our Red people we'd come to support, who are lovely, of course.'

Now Winston sees people forging their way towards him

through the crowd, oh shit, Ella's one of them, leading by the hand white-haired Graham, talking fiercely.

But the person who gets there first, the giant who is cutting through the puzzled crowd like a hot thick blade through warm butter, is Monica, and help, she's already heaved herself on to the podium, which tips, precarious, as her huge weight bounces on board, and she's grinning at him with bright eyes and alarmingly big teeth as she pushes in front of the mic. And she shouts, her voice a magnificent un-miked foghorn that rolls across the greensward, over the scarlet and yellow ship and over the trees to the sunset, 'So here's to the Red people! Our Red people! And the Red children in school! And their boss the Professor! PROFESSOR, we need you! Get your arse over here and make your speech, Juan! THE RED PEOPLE!'

And this time it works, for everyone knows Monica, she's nuts but she once put her life on the line for their children, and thank God it seems they're only welcoming the Reds, after all – from Cliffsend Green across to Sandwich and echoing back again to Ramsgate, hundreds of voices, hundreds of glasses, together raise a great toast: 'THE RED PEOPLE!'

63

Juan hears an indistinct roar and feels more alone. Everyone's above, at the party, everyone but Juan and two black birds who are pecking nearby. *Cr-a-a-ark.*

Behind him, although he daren't turn to look, a line of shadow creeps down the beach, bringing a faint shiver to the back of his great bull-neck. Late. He's late.

Cr-a-a-ark. The Professor has known since he first crawled from the cave into the light that the universe is alive, but as the little chill of evening creeps closer, his sense of the great oneness falters.

You can be abandoned, he remembers. His mother ... his father ...

No, believe. Wait for the call.

But if half the beach is in shadow ...

Ahead of him also the sand's disappearing, the red-tinged water's lapping closer, slipping inside the sea-grass and the samphire, creeping in glittering runnels and rivulets up to the edge of the great white hash-tag he's made, the sign of power.

He'd started to focus in fear on the two black birds, who are staring at him, heads cocked, charking and chattering. Raven or crows, wings half-furled as they hop and hover, birds of omen ... ravens back home were reputed to live off corpses, mothers called their children closer if one landed near ...

Holly's two ravens, though, were tamed by her goodness, he hungers for her and for them, for the mornings of safety and ease, faint pepper-and-liquorice-and-smoke scents of Lapsang Souchong on porcelain, light on her face as she stretched out her white rounded arm and put the birds' treats on the windowsill, *sapiens* richness and softness folding Juan in with them.

Holly had loved him, believed in him

But she never knew who I was, or where we came from …

Take this cruel, impossible cup away   I will fail them

Juan is alone and the universe no longer sees him.

64

Actually, Roland and the Princess inspect him in gaps between snacks on unripe fruit from the apple-tree grown from a bird-dropped pip near the foot of the cliff.

'Gone mad,' snickers Roland to the Princess, buoyant, for the human giant's talking to himself and now groaning as he drags a notebook from his trousers, tearing the cloth.

'He's a scholar,' says the Princess. 'See, he's got a pen. They're different to us. And he's charming-looking, even now, to me, with that nice red crest. Scholars were highly valued in the Tower, we saved all the writings in a library.'

This has always been a point of contention between them, for the Princess, despite all Roland's sensible protests, insists on believing that the sounds humans make have meaning, indeed are a form of language like that of ravens or crows or dogs or bees. Pretty head turned by her time in the Tower of London, she insists on believing the sounds humans make are a form of language like that of ravens or dogs or bees. Even more fancifully, she pretends that meanings are hidden in the dull, mechanical patterns of marks they leave everywhere, which (it's obvious to Roland) are just a compulsion – in the case of the Professor, maybe a mating display. Females! So easy to fool!

Roland thinks, *I will hate him for ever*. 'Scratching with a stick,' he snipes. 'I can do that.' And to prove it, he snatches up a twig.

'You may think it's the same, but *their* writing turns into books and learning.'

'They know nothing,' says Roland, looking down his

fabulous, Roman-beaked nose. He's rattled, though. The Princess has been flighty in the past. Time for an offering – females love gifts.

'Clever Youmen need more comfort than the others,' she says, and looks down, her elegant head turned coyly to one side as if she might offer it.

'Don't approach him, madmen are dangerous. I'll return, my Princess,' Roland cries and flies off, up from the beach where a thousand years ago Romans and Britons fought to a standstill, and over the concrete of the abandoned Hoverport, where Youmen sometimes leave interesting things after picnics – cardboard boxes, a wedding ring, chips.

On his second tour, Roland spots movement on a wide strip of concrete almost hidden by three bushes, planted as markers for parking spaces long ago when this place was the future, long since bursting their banks into three intermingling, untamed islands of wild pink roses.

65

It's Molo with Jude and Roosha, though Roland doesn't know their names, dancing fiercely in a slightly awkward threesome. The two girls echo each other's moves, intent, until Molo starts to feel left out. Next moment, he leaves them together and goes up to look for Sandra, but Roland sweeps round on one more circuit. The girls are slow-dancing now, and his sharp eye spots a good find.

As Molo joins the crowd up above, they have just been surprised into silence. The head, after some discussion, has yielded the podium to old Graham, who everyone knows by sight with his white beard and hair and frowning blue eyes and the pinstripe suits he affects even in summer, 'but he's no gent, he's pure Thanet,' as Eileen Killarney informs Neil Purseglove. She's sharing the former head's packed lunch, fearing the buffet's infected by the Reds. 'He drinks in Spoons. Wouldn't have happened on your watch, Mr P.'

'Indeed,' whispers Neil. He's still trembling after seeing his former colleague Monica (nemesis, larger than ever) giving the toast. Has she seen him?

'People can't just push in and take over,' Eileen adds, self-righteous.

'So true,' mouths Neil, watching sadly as Eileen's blunt fingers probe his box for the last of his lettuce and (mild) cheddar sandwiches.

Ella calls out to the crowd, 'This is Graham. He's lived here for ever. He knows the history.' It soon becomes clear that he does.

'We are standing where English history began,' Graham says. His voice strengthens. Soon he's not sounding old and faintly comic, with his strangled imitations of middle-class vowels, he sounds like himself, the son of a Pest Control Inspector who died young and a cleaner, a former merchant sailor (which has gained him a limited voluntary role at the Sea Cadets, though he mostly cleans up and does the refreshments). Now the crowd hears in his growing confidence that Graham is also a historian; an Englishman; a proud old local man who spends time not only in Spoons, but in various libraries.

'The Roman legions landed just below us, here at Pegwell, not further down the coast as was once believed. They had to try three times before they succeeded. Why did they come here? Because it's marvellous!' (Ripples of cheers from the crowd.) 'They were led by Julius Caesar himself, but the Britons fought them off. In the end they stayed, of course. So all of us here have Roman blood.' It was an admission, but as long as people didn't get the Romans confused with Italians – the present-day ones that is, such a nuisance when they used to come every year before the pandemics began, language students trailing on walks in great parties along the beach from Broadstairs – it was rather noble that English people should have Roman blood. '… AD 55 … AD 54 …' He was into his stride. 'Let's look again at the Viking Ship.' And they turned, as one body, to look at its proud silhouette, reddened by the deepening sunset. 'Where did the Vikings land? Like the Romans, they landed in Thanet, and just around the coast from us. Hengist and Horsa. Vikings from Sweden, blond-haired people,' he said with a note of wistful approval, for the truth was the Romans, he knew, were small and dark, 'two brothers who had their struggles, as brothers do, but they were tough and they stayed for years. They rowed here, an incredible feat, from Sweden, up near the ice, which is thousands of miles away They lived on dry bread and they slept on boards!' Which was what Thanet's soft young men, what was left of them since the last waves of virus, needed now, he thought, enjoying himself, and the crowd, the only one he's ever had a chance to address, is rapt and still. 'Men! Those Vikings were men.' Squinting through his out-of-date glasses, he sees some of the young bruisers from the peculiar new Red lot are smiling up at him, which makes them look less ugly.

(It's true, they're smiling, for 'being men' was a conundrum the Red people had found it hard to grapple with since coming here, for always, in the memory of their people, it was Red men and boys who had risked their lives to travel and explore, but how did that fit with what some of the Ramsgate teachers talked about, which was 'gender'? The girls and young women of Kent seemed to welcome their maleness in a teasing, curious way, yet they were indignant to hear only men could travel the world, and often made the boys feel guilty, or stupid, because they didn't understand things or couldn't think like girls, so it was good to hear Graham talk about toughness and courage and men, it helped them make sense of who they were, and what they had done. Standing there in the crowd, which Graham dominates, the Red boys are starting to admire him.)

'That was 449 AD, nearly one thousand six hundred years ago, and their gods were ravens, so Ramsgate was a good place for them, because some say our name, Ramsgate, came from Hrafnesgate, which means Ravensgate in Old English. Ravens were here on the cliffs watching each time more foreigners came – I expect, when they died, they pecked their eyes out!'

Now he's cackling, which puts some of the audience off, but he goes on.

The sun's setting, a glory of red all round them; up here, it's still hot, and his audience stares, half-hypnotised, rapt, as Graham comes up to 1949.

'I was only ten, a small boy, when this very ship, that magnificent red and yellow thing up there, was rowed across the sea – actually rowed, that's right, no engine – across the ocean from Denmark. Great Danish men with beards, tough as nuts, rowing through storms across the sea, and they landed at Broadstairs! I remember the music and the parade with people in helmets and tunics marching in pairs, and the best-known film outfit then, called Pathé News, came and filmed it and Thanet was famous ... and I was just a kid with no father, and one of these huge fair-haired blokes from Denmark smiled at me and I asked him a question about the ship, 'Does it have a motor?', I think I asked him, and he saw I was green as the grass underneath us, just a kid who knew nothing about anything, he took me and showed me the oars and the oar-locks and let me touch them and talked about how they did it, how they rowed over great big swells through the night, hearing nowt but the sea and the sound of their coach, who they called the *hortator*, rhymes with 'potater' I think, it's Latin, folks, wish I spoke it! He had a drum, keeping them in time and keeping them going ... course I was hooked ...' ('Danish like you, Ida,' Monica is saying in sign language to Ida, who's lip-reading, with shining eyes.) Here Graham's voice broke: that had been the best day of his life, the most hopeful, it seemed to him as if a god had come down to earth, a great hulking blond god, a dad, and saw him, and opened up the world, though afterwards when he went home and told Mum the new word, 'hortator', she gave him a clip around the ear for showing off and talking to a foreigner.

'And that's how Viking Bay in Broadstairs got named Viking Bay, Mr Headmaster, and that's how old Graham ended up serving thirty years for his country in the merchant navy! And knowing a thing or two about boats. And this dragon-headed boat, this beauty, ended up here, looking out across the Channel as if it's about to take off again. I've said my piece, so I'll finish!'

Winston pops up on the podium for a moment to thank Graham, who gets the huge cheer he deserves.

Then Winston asks the crowd 'Has anyone seen the Professor? Professor, are you here? If not, let's get the Jebel Tarek Beach Orchestra up! For acoustic reasons, they've got their instruments set up over there on the pavement ...'

No, the Professor's not here.

66

The Professor loves light, but it's not what he knows. Tunnels he knows, all his life he has had to burrow through darkness, he trusts Mother Earth who for thousands of years has kept the Red people safe, but sun and sea he knows less.

He stands here in torment, now, as the band of hope narrows, the swathe of pink light, his arms upraised and outstretched, reaching out to the curves of the bay, to the sky, reaching out with more determination than ever towards the far buildings of Sandwich and Deal in the last of the sun to his right where tiny windows flash for a second like blind sequins as the red rays hit them full on and go out, then scans the horizon, the bays of France, clearly visible, now, on the edge of the sea as the pink paints the cliffs of Cap Gris Nez and even tiny distant French houses, but all he can grasp in his growing fatigue is vast distance, distance, and difference – how far there is to go and how cold it's becoming, unless it is him, and life, the great furnace within him, is slipping away.

He clutches his notebook and pen but writes nothing. *I am the recording angel,* he thinks … and then, *I'm not an angel, I'm a fraud and a liar …*

Why was I afraid to tell Holly I have never been a professor, never been to Cambridge, grew up in a cave, shat in holes in the ground, was filthy. We were scuttling creatures to others, giant insects seen at the corner of an eye creeping away, infectious, maybe, subhuman.

A wave of bitterness fills him for his buried, crippled childhood. *Did we not deserve light like the so-called sapiens, the higher-class humans? Did we not deserve to come out into the day and walk like the others without fear? Was I not a man, yes, and a brother? Was I not human?*

Sapiens contempt had always pierced straight to his great heavy bones and his skull, and yet he was human like them. Human. One of the strange animals who don't only think and communicate, as do all others, but leave their individual mark, record and remember. Who collect, as well. Or try to. Without help he can't even save the (sad, they now seem) small bundles of possessions in the cave from the waves – too many, he needs extra hands to gather them in, he needs friends, but his feet are so heavy, his head, his great head, which he's always trusted, feels blank and depleted. How will he tell them?

Cold strikes the base of his spine as the shadow of the cliff at last creeps over him, and at the same instant, the first stones of his message, the most exposed, the tips of his people's magical symbol, are reached by the red line of foam and glimmer, and move, they are coming alive, they are changing …

And with that, the paralysis of bitterness washes away. He opens his notebook and writes something down – the truth of the moment.

I am trapped. On the beach at Pegwell. The tide is coming in. I am drowning. HELP ME. HELP US.

He stares at the page, at the sea. Then he tears the page out, screws it up, because what is the point? Yet after a second he smooths it out, slips it in his jacket pocket. What can he do but record?

The white stones are losing their shape, he runs down the beach and clutches at them, but the water makes little darts at his feet and they're washed away from his blunt powerful hands, he snatches and loses, loses and snatches, panting, and finally knows that his plan and his pattern are over. Briefly, he closes his eyes.

Then he shuffles away up the beach, pulling his jacket round his powerful torso, unable to see as he turns from the dazzling sunset into shadow. He knows, in another part of his brain, that he has forgotten to give his speech at the party, but that doesn't matter, nothing matters except that he's failed his people. Can save no-one. Has never felt so alone.

Then someone's skidding down the path to the beach towards him, someone muscular, stocky and strong – *if it's Molo, he'll help, may it be Molo!* – slipping on the crumbling chalk, half-falling, coming down far too fast.

67

But it's Joe, he's drunk, and upset, and he's looking for his brother.

And spots the Professor. 'Where's Liam?' he shouts.

'Trouble,' ra-arks Roland to the Princess. (He's back, and the Princess is happy, for what did he bring? A red piece of silk that he found by where Jude and Roosha were dancing, so pretty, a broad shiny ribbony thing, which he's dropped at her feet, with a bow of his head and – too large, but she likes it – aquiline, slightly scarred beak.) She's cached it for later on an apple-tree branch where no-one will see it, for few humans know the steep apple-tree path.

But half an hour later, Joe stumbles past it en route for the beach. And snatches it down with the cry of a very young animal pierced by a thorn. *Jude's.* He imagines her without it, maybe with Molo, half-naked.

'Liam?' the Professor repeats, as if he's never heard the name.

'My brother,' shouts Joe, as if he needs to, as if it isn't quiet on the beach, with only the sound of the waves creeping in and the music, far away up on the cliff, plus another sound he can't quite make out, a subdued muttering, yes they must all be here somewhere, though only two men are to be seen, two muscular shapes, one old and one young, facing up to each other, alone.

Twenty feet away, out of sight now for Joe and the Professor, the ravens watch them and chatter, and Roland starts stretching his wings and ruffling his feathers, wanting to do something to impress the Princess.

'You're upset,' the Professor tells Joe, though he himself is profoundly upset.

'Where are they?' says Joe, for he thinks the birds' chatter is human voices.

'Who?' says the Professor, weary. 'Joe, there's no-one here, you can see.'

But both of them can hear a shuffling sound behind them near the cliff-face. In fact it's just wings and feet and the clearing of a big bird's throat, but to Joe it's the Red boys with Jude and the others, he hears them and maybe Liam in the muffled thunder of the cliff, behind them, shifting and stirring with rain-water, still soaking down from the storm, loosening and licking at the chalk and the flint, pushing them in different directions, urging everything apart, and from the other side the rhythm of the reddened, sullen ocean, coming in more swiftly, now, as it gets towards full, a low roar of the rising sea as it pushes long fingers inwards, a drumming. Everything's alive, but for both men, pulsing with different angers and defeats, midsummer day has gone cross-grained, friendship foiled and frustrated, green hope soured.

And they circle each other on the sand, the thickset, lithe, muscular boy and the massive old man, allies in another life but now transformed into strangers on this shore where hundreds of strangers have met head on, hurt and killed one another.

Juan knows he is older, saner. 'Let's go back,' he says, extending his hand, with an effort, feeling a story that's bigger, more ancient than both of them pulling him in. Trying to make peace, he touches Joe's arm. 'Let's go back up, my friend. You're missing the party, I'm late for my speech.'

'What were you doing down here,' Joe hears himself shouting, 'you and the others?'

'What others?' Juan asks, confused, as Joe yells, louder, 'What have you done to my brother?'

'Brother!' a cry comes back from near the cave, which must be Liam, and it comes again, hoarse, perhaps in trouble, 'Brother!'

The Princess puts her head on one side and tries to convey, like a mother, both admiration for Roland's acting skills and a hint of disapproval, for having grown up in the blood-soaked Tower, she knows about human hatred, and war.

68

Liam, in fact, is still nowhere near the cave. He's been trying and failing to rally his men – for a while in the pub it did feel they were his – for the raid. Back in Spoons they had all agreed. At last he would lead, be a hero. Justice! For the Red people had stolen his brother, his mother, his school, they were doing vile things in the caves, they were burrowing into the cliffs and under the ground, and today they had taken over the town with their stupid party, but he, who saw what was happening, would make a stand. 'It was all agreed!' He keeps saying, 'You all agreed!' but his voice sounds weak, and complainy, and young.

A few hours ago there had been the angry, unifying hope of hatred, but since Graham's speech, everything's changed. The PBF are flushed with possessive pride. Their man Graham is leading some of them, together with three Red boys, *as if they are friends*, across to the Viking ship, pointing upwards and showing them all its features, and why can't he, Liam, be in the party, why have they forgotten him so quickly, how has the tide turned?

Liam's noticed something else. Most of the older Red males are no longer here. 'Where have they sneaked off to?' he asks Hank Stitch. 'They've sneaked off to the fields or else down the caves I expect,' says Hank, who is solid, who hasn't trailed after Graham and Benny to look at the ship. 'Took some of our tarts and bitches with 'em, shouldn't wonder. I know what they're at down there.' And he thrusts the index finger of his left hand through his right hand thumb and finger and wiggles it vigorously in and out.

Liam, who has never had sex, wants to be sick. 'We've got to stop it,' he says. 'Come on Hank. If the others won't, we will.'

'I dunno,' says Hank, uneasy, looking at him cross-eyed. 'Thing is, I've had a few bevvies. Might take a look at that boat. See, Benny's gone too.'

'You chickening out?' Liam turns on him, pink with anger, and sneers, 'You just a wanker too, like the rest?'

There's a long pause. Hank's heavy body sways. 'Hang about,' he says. 'Who're you calling a wanker? You're what, sixteen?'

'Nineteen,' Liam insists, but it comes out feeble, it sounds like a plea.

'Don't you ever call me a wanker, you little snit. No-one's coming with you because no-one likes you,' says Hank, with finality, feeling his way, with the instinct that's got him followers, to the thing that will hurt Liam most, 'You're not one of us. Never will be.'

Liam wants to hit him, but instead he grabs Hank's muscular upper arm, despairing, then as Hank shouts, 'You gay!' breaks away and forces a path through the crowd, running, lurching, eyes smarting with tears and blurred red sunlight as he looks for the path that will take him down to the beach.

69

Joe tries to dodge round the Professor towards the mouth of the cave where Liam once told him the Red boys go to make jewellery, fuck and smoke dope. Jude might be there, her breasts naked, and Liam, who'd been right all along, must be down there sorting things out, but Joe slips on a patch of bare chalk and knows he is drunk, though he feels the raw power of the beer in his surge of courage, his pain-swollen heart, and somehow gets back on his feet.

'No-one's there,' pants the Professor, trying to block Joe's path to the cave and his people's poor little parcels of possessions. 'Joe, stop!' Now they're actually wrestling on the mound of blown sand and stones that protects the mouth of the cave and Juan's trying to hold Joe away so he can look him full in the face.

To the boy, though, the sun in the older man's eyes make his irises red and inhuman, his skin a metallic red armour, his nostrils (in fact, tense with fear of what's started to happen) flaring bestial, enraged, just a monster with bright scarlet mane, and Joe jerks back then darts sideways again and on towards the cave-mouth, shouting back one last time 'Where's my brother?', but his cry is returned once again, *must be* Liam, he thinks, but muffled and strange, 'Brother, brother!'

Joe's here for him now as he should have been earlier, anger and alcohol and shame all driving him on. The Professor, chasing and desperate, grabs at his shirt but Joe lurches straight into the cave, the deep dizzying dark, and 'No, Joe, no,' the Professor shouts as Joe vanishes, trips over the Red people's packages, one foot catching in a tangle of string, and falls, yelling 'He-e-l-p!' as his muscular body rotates like a hammer and thumps his dark head, a dead weight, into the cave wall, and the Professor falls after him, felled by the same *indumentaria*, the tangling weight of even such tiny possessions, he thinks in the long final second as his bull-·like torso tips forward, but at the last moment his muscular arms go out and break his fall.

'He-e-l-p,' shouts out Roland, peering in, caught up in the drama. His wife pecks him hard – her Professor may be hurt! 'Stop fooling around, wicked bird,' she spits out, and hops loyally after her clever human.

'No,' squa-arks Roland, 'Don't go in, it's dangerous!' An order which, like all his others, the Princess ignores.

So the last thing he sees is her beautiful wide black silken wings flaring like eight strong fingers and the diamond of her tail flying in, then she disappears.

Seconds later, there's an earth-shattering thunder of noise, going on and on, a drum-roll of something they've heard a few times in their lives, the cliff falling, its chalk dried out by months of flaming heat, the million grass and tree roots which have held it together shrivelled and weakened, then soaked by the storm and now shaken by vibrations of thousands of feet and radiating rings of sound, for above, as the Stone Orchestra sets up and the hiphop band from Hastings begins, five hundred people are dancing, the magnificent speakers thrillingly vibrating, and each tiny shock, after the briefest electrical delay, shivers onwards and down, and here, on the shore, humans fighting have added the last accidental touches that bring living things to disaster and pain.

Or maybe the last tiny shift of particles came from the echoes of a raven mocking a man.

Roland flies straight up and away out of danger, something he'll later forget entirely, but oh, his mate is not there, fear and guilt bring him hurtling back from the sunset sky, hovering briefly then landing in squawking panic as the white chalk dust starts to settle all round him, making him cough.

Just a rubble of chalk remains where the cave mouth was, with a blind black gap of a metre or so.

Can the Princess have survived in there?

He cocks his chalk-whitened head. Yes, a sound. Something large, but too large for a raven, is scrabbling inside. What if his beloved is dead?

Then a fierce warning squawk, the dear voice of the Princess, alive.

Roland likes heights, not small spaces, and feels like a hero as cautiously, stopping after every two hops, he gets to the top of the mound of white stones, and flurries inside.

Juan dares not move a centimetre. Pain. Why the terrible, crushing pain? The world's fallen in, he is dying. Breathe out, and breath in.

Can't breathe. I can't breathe.

But he isn't alone. Someone else, someone young –

Joe. Angry boy. Yes. The fight. And the ravens.

Joe's underneath him. They're both underground. It starts to come back.

An image, vivid and final: Joe sprawled, groaning, having tripped, my fault, thinks the Professor, I chased him … then a thunder-crack and before the long following rumble had ended, before the Professor, on his knees, could scoop all the stinging stuff from his eyes and nose, Joe was gone, just one hand, broad and young, poking out of the great rough blanket of chalk, and the back of his head, white with dust, with the cave-mouth behind them closed down to a crack of red light.

Juan had scrabbled with bleeding hands, sweating, at the slather of stones over Joe, tore off his jacket, threw it with the strength of ten men into a great black kerfuffle of terror and squawking – seconds later he grasped it's a bird, a raven, his jacket had hit it full-on.

('Have a care! Cra-a-a!' the Princess was squawking in her own language, 'Caww! Care! More will fall!')

The Professor scooped stones from the back of Joe's neck, turned his scratched face so the boy could breathe and frantically worked till Joe's shoulders, his arms, were clear,

ignoring the bird – *Have a CARE!* Cr-a-a-a-h! Cr-a-a-a-h!
– till at last he could hook his raw hands under Joe's armpits
to try and drag his whole body out, yes, nearly got him, but
ohhhh – he had only heaved once, twice before something
enormous behind them came loose with a thunder of drums
as if time was ending, then blackness and weight had covered
him, still bent double over Joe.

Now he's no longer Hector the fighter, just Atlas, dumb,
monumental, the world on his back.

Roland comes skidding inside and thuds into the Princess,
who digs him with her claw in silent protest. 'Shush. Stay still.'

'I am here to save you, beloved.'

'Shhh.'

'He's done for,' says Roland to the Princess, as his eyes get
used to the dark and he makes out the Professor sprawled
under the rock. 'Let's get out.'

'This,' says the Princess very quietly. She's delicately tugging
at something white sticking out of the Professor's jacket pocket.
'Writing. Might be important.'

'Leave it. Nothing to do with us. Tide's coming in.'

'Everything's to do with us,' she sighs and flutters. 'You
don't care about our little ones, either, once they fly the nest.
It's being a male.'

'Quick,' he caws sharply, too loud for her comfort, and she
pecks him to be quiet.

In the crack of light from outside, she's reading the writing,
slow, careful. 'He's asking for help. And we need human friends.
Don't forget the persecution. I have an education, you don't –
thousands of us died.'

(The Princess learned it from lectures at the Tower. Ravens
were trapped, shot, poisoned, driven out of all southern

England, forced up to ice-covered Scotland, and only slowly crept south again, till at last a pair flew, triumphant, back down to the white cliffs of Dover.)

'No-one human likes us,' says Roland, still sulky from that peck. 'Come ON.'

'Holly loves us, and the Professor's her lifemate. Promise to help, or I'll leave you,' she says. 'I can always go back to my Ravenmaster in the Tower. I like humans.' And she hops over to the big man's body, the paper in her beak, bows her head, once, twice, and rubs the sensitive feathers of the top of her head against the Professor's dusty warmth, something she has wanted to do for months, and knowing that Roland is watching, perches there for a long moment before she returns to her mate.

'Let's not quarrel, though, dear.' She starts to preen him, gently, in the dim light of the cave, stroking his large, splendid neck wattles and chuckling in her throat in the way he loves, till she feels his tight muscles relax.

'Do you love me?' he asks, his tone suddenly hopeful, the hope of a very young, not-quite-fledged raven, and she caws, 'Course I do, beautiful bird. You are strong. You fly faster than me.' The opening on the sky behind them is less fiery now, growing dark.

'I will do it!' he says, and he clasps the paper in his beak. 'I will take it to Holly – if you, my love, will come too.'

'I will fly with you, yes, my love.'

And the two huge black birds shot forth from the slit mouth of the cave, skidding on a shower of pebbles outside, just as Liam arrived, thinking he'd heard groans from inside. The two black comets explode into his face and terrified, Liam screams.

72

On the edge of the Pegwell Road, on a stretch that has not yet been tarmac-ed, the Red children have set up rows of flints from the beach, and they're making a range of magical, musical notes by hitting them one against each other, and the people are pushing forward to see. I spot Ella, who I knew slightly from running into her at Holly's, just in front of me and after a brief hesitation, because I am shy, slip forward to touch her arm: 'That man Graham was terrific. Great call, Ella,' and her smile is the start of what's now become a good friendship.

We start watching the Stone Orchestra together. But who is this small shambling figure with a yellow tabard now edging out of the crowd to join them?

'Oh fuck, it's Frank, he's that dim one of mine,' says Monica to Ginger, who's poised to hoick the offender back, but, 'No, let him get on with it, if they do,' says Monica. Tentative at first, but after a quick 'Yawwight?' to the Red children Francis is finding two stones, drops one and picks up another, then quickly getting into the rhythm he feels in his skull and his heart, Frank's starting to drum 'like Phil Collins', as his astonished great-grandma, who watched him, says later. Playing with the others, Frank's finding the strange minor music that hides in the earth's flinty bones, and suddenly knows he is good at this, hearing the solo in every stone, and suddenly Frank, 'little fuckup' as his stepdad calls him at home, is the star of the moment!

Ella and I are both clapping in rhythm and, 'That funny boy is the best,' says Hecate, 'even if he's ugly', and Monica smiles, and Ginger, seeing tears running down his wife's magnificent, meaty cheeks, tenderly traces them with one pink stubby finger.

73

Liam wants to flee. He's alone, and something dreadfully wounded is inside the cave. 'Help us … help us …' he hears. What if it's Reds? Let them die. Yet the pain is so primal, so desperate. Human. Calling to his own pain. Random memory of saving Taughtus, carrying him carefully as an egg out of the rain and hail. Up to him. One more second's hesitation, then using his athlete's muscles he slips through the narrow opening without touching the crumbling sides.

First thing he sees once his eyes can read the half-dark is one thick arm and an inch of red hair. It's him. The Professor. Buried. A rockfall. There's something underneath him. Blue t-shirt. Joe. The man's killed him. Death. All the rest disappears. This is real. Heart thumping, 'Joe, it's Liam,' he says, 'I'm here!'

A hoarse roar, infinitely weary, choked and tearing with effort, the huge man on top of his brother is speaking. 'Go … get help. Tried … to save Joe … holding it off him … tried …. really tried … can't manage … much longer. Tide's coming in. Go.'

In a flash Liam sees it. His chance.

He can run. His last drink was four hours ago. No phones, the road blocked off up above, but the lifeboat station's not far. On your marks. Focus. He can save two lives if he only runs fast enough, runs round the shrinking strip of coast between cliffs and sea, as the pink sky fades and life disappears, to get help for his brother and the great crushed ox who's trying to protect him.

Focus. And run. Pace yourself. Run, do not fall. Do not fail.

Now hold on to everything you know, Liam, about breath, about balance, about how to use speed and the need to stay true and calm and not panic, never let doubt overtake you, don't miss your chance. This time you'll get to the final and win.

And Liam runs, Liam runs. It's a mile, maybe two, to the Lifeboat Station and he is a sprinter, but running is running and now he must use something else which he should have been using to survive as a runner, move up through the distances, run as he ran down the coast until lately, but run to win, and yes, he remembers the feeling of winning and yes, he will do it, he'll do it for Joe and his family, he'll show them all, and he's round the first point, splashing through an inch of water and keeping his footing with a grunt, *get your breath back, go on*, then along round the next stretch of beach which is easier, here it's still sand but he knows he must pace himself, don't burn the strength you will need at the end, *keep breathing, go on*

Far behind him in the cave the Professor also is hearing a few words only, again and again   *keep breathing   endure breathe out   even harder, breathe in*

while Roland the raven is flying, stretching his wings out with all the power that he has, the white scrap in his claws, speeding on

as Liam flies on down the coast, round the second point, now, and the sea's up to his ankles, he has to slow down, and the fear starts to rise in him like cold water, his bowels, his lungs, he's such a poor swimmer, unlike Joe, his brother, must both of them drown, they can't, their poor mother

he runs   the power he had always   *he can run*   he runs on
the last point of land will not come any closer   he's
staggering, now   lungs bursting   he cannot keep going
he's losing   he's hurting   but no   he will not let them
down   will not let himself down   can keep going
can   *yes he can*

Very slowly, the last point creeps closer   if he doesn't reach it,
he drowns   waves lick at his calves   at his knees   drag his
jeans   is he running or walking   go on   and it doesn't feel
cold   the blood surges through him   he's warm   he no
longer feels tired   he can run, he can run   and he finally
rounds the point with a great cry of triumph   and sees the
blunt shape of the end of the promenade   and the tiredness
hits him   he's limping   he crawls, hands and knees, up the
steep slope of stone to the promenade rail   he   pulls himself
up   up   up   jagged breath and a split second pause   *he's
made it*   then sags   sags for a moment   no legs.

   His head lifts. Just one hundred metres, his distance, to go to
the lifeboats. A straight flat track.   *Liam, go!* they had shouted,
his mother, Joe, at that heat. He gets back on his feet. Shakes
off the water. And breathes. *On your marks. Set* – arrowing swift
as Achilles, the hero goes.

74

Many things about Midsummer Night will never be clear. But yes, it changed history.

Why did I start drinking? Winston's speech, which was boring? Or was I just happy? So happy. The party, the sunset, the music, Red people, Ramsgaters, all of us hugging and drinking and dancing ...

When the old and the young had gone home, all the other things happened. In the magical hours before morning the bodies were scattered like drifts of daisies across the warm grass. The moon gleamed from our skin, drained of colour by midsummer night, half-hidden and half-revealed. And the crickets sang and mated. And two ravens flew over, their great wings beating, beating against the dark, their wingtips touching, an errand of love. All of us alike, human, animal, living and dying.

Morning. In the cave, the Professor at last hears voices outside. Hearing, the last sense he'll lose. Very cautiously, slowly, at the final edge of his perception, someone is moving a stone over the mouth of the cave away. And as light comes in, and big helpful people, he can let go, and the light is strengthening, the wonderful light, beyond pain, the light where he's going …

Thanks to the earth which will again release him …

Glory to the universe, glory to the likenesses that bind the world together, glory to the great net of mirrors which reaches out to the constellations, from the scorpions in sand to the far pale Scorpion of stars … glory to the Twins who ride in white flame on the blue sky of his beloved home, yes, they are reaching out their arms towards him, glory to the feelings all living things tremble with, similar, similar, he's smiling and releasing it now, *Alhamdulillah*, his arms, his hands, his long musical fingers, the antennae of his light-rinsed nerves, as they drag Joe from beneath him, as he soars, climbs into brightness, goes home.

These things I know.

That somehow, despite the blackout, the coastguards were alerted, the lifeboat put out, without a fully trained crew, since their electronic contacts weren't working, using volunteers from our town, against all regulations.

That Liam Birch managed to run the strip of coast between Pegwell Bay and the Lifeboat Station, where his arrival was noted at 10.03pm, a distance of several miles, in half-darkness, some of it through water, in 18 minutes three seconds, by his own account, is the stuff of legend, and the time, despite an annual race every Midsummer Day since then, has never been beaten. A mixture of the glory he received in the local media and his mother's praise and pride led him to join a distance running club, and for many years he was back in the national rankings, and later a coach.

That he married Jackee's daughter, who was delighted to think he too was a virgin, and they weren't very happy, but stayed together, and shared a deep love of their boy, who they called Juan, though quite soon it turned into John, and their tortoise, who by now was quite old, a gift from his sister. And they looked after Taughtus very well, and he, in turn, kindly overlooked their inability to understand his language.

That the party went on up above, that it lasted all night, that the bodies were spread like flowers on the grass, as I said, that I was there with many other women, that we were happy, and still trailing sleepily back to our houses as the sky grew red again for dawn and the cormorant shot down the coast with its long black neck outstretched like an arrow, pointing to the cave.

That the half-trained crew were only able to extricate Joe from the cave, that the danger of further cliff-falls meant they had to leave the other man where he lay, almost certainly dead, his massive frame crushed underneath a big rock he had held off the boy until he could no longer do it and his great heart gave out, is recorded in the Coastguard log for that day.

There's another tale involving magical messages which I hesitate to pass on. That when Liam got to the lifeboat station, the call for crew had already gone out. That a raven had brought a piece of paper to the window of Holly Palermo, the goldsmith — as if anyone sane would take any notice of a message from a raven!

Though I should record that the Royal National Lifeboat Institution is a charity, and Holly Palermo is a major donor, and local patron.

She said nothing then, and, always self-effacing, has said nothing since, except, when pressed, that Liam Birch is a fine young man, and a brilliant runner. She doesn't want to talk about that night, which everyone understands, because she's in mourning.

One astonishing fact is that when, quite early next day, the coastguards went back with two policemen to retrieve the Professor, he was not there. The stone had been lifted, they supposed by the sea.

The cave they assumed was his tomb contained no body.

Despondent, they muttered and hawed and hummed, standing in the chill of early morning sunlight. 'I still don't get it,' said one of the policemen, who hadn't enjoyed the ride here because he got seasick, had muck all over his uniform from scrambling into that cave, and dreaded the bumpy ride back. 'First this chap is so stuck they can't shift him, then he disappears, *poof*, just like that.'

'But you're land people,' says one of the coastguards. 'Power of the sea. We see it all the time. Nothing surprises us,' and the other seamen sagely agree.

'Then look at *that*!' says Andy, the younger of the two policemen, who's got sharp eyes and is twenty-three. 'Tell me what the hell is that, over there?'

His tone is so sharp, they all turn.

Is there anything there?

Most of them see nothing except a vague blur of red near the horizon that could be a container ship, moving fast, with the early morning sun on it, but Andy says, 'It's an effing galleon, or something! I can see the oars moving! They're effing rowing!'

Which gives the older men a laugh before they get into their launch, but as he gets in after Andy, the senior coastguard officer says, quite quiet, in his ear, 'Mate, I saw it too.'

Five minutes after their departure, unknown to them, power comes back to the South of England, the internet flashes back up, but they're in the boat, with no signal, so it's not until they're back at base that one of them reads the headline on *Kent News Today*:

MIDSUMMER FESTIVAL MAYHEM – HISTORIC SHIP STOLEN

77

Once electronic life flashed back on in a quicksilver tree of excitement that branched through Ramsgate in an instant, the phone calls began, and the realisation: all the Red people had gone. Before people were up. The crew of the fishing-boats mostly had blinding hangovers, and saw nothing. In the houses that had hosted them, empty beds, windows flung open. Left on chairs, folded, were the clothes they had been given, though some young ones had taken the books they had been using in school.

Some of them left gifts: wreaths of dried fennel, from Pegwell, necklaces of shells, a cape of black and white seagull wing feathers on Holly's doorstep, made by Molo, a beautiful though unhygienic thing. Most left only the familiar tiny shining rivulets of sand on the floors of the rooms that had been theirs.

Rumours spread. The Professor had died saving Liam. No, Liam nearly died saving Joe. No, both boys were alive, but not the Professor, who had died holding up a collapsing cave.

More incredibly, the Viking Ship had been stolen. 'No, who would steal a great thing like that? Must have been moved as part of the roadworks. It'll be back.'

More details, from people who lived near. There had been an orgy. No, party-goers had run amok with the tools and materials of the firm who were replacing the tarmac on the road – there was tarmac all over the green where the ship had once been.

'I have no information,' said Winston next day in assembly.

'But we have sustained a great loss, if we've lost the Professor and so many friends.' The children gazed at him, upset and uncertain. Miss Birch wasn't here, so it might be true something had happened to her boys. Besides, none of them had ever seen a head teacher on the edge of tears.

Ramsgate, which had sometimes longed to be free of the Red people, didn't know what to feel. It was shaken with a flurry of speculation, blame, puzzlement – where had they gone? Why with no warning?

PART FIVE

78

Main Street, Gibraltar. It is always a maze of heat and gossip, the place where people go to show off new clothes and parade new babies, to see who is sitting outside the law-courts, who's eating *churros* in the blaze of midday. Usually some of the older Gibraltarians, understanding the sun, or at work, come out later, walking more slowly, dressed more modestly, from different, narrower, steeper, parts of the town, as the streets empty, as the day, even here, begins to cool down.

But recently days do not cool down, not even as the sun does its usual last-minute black and scarlet plunge into the Strait and the birds at Europa point start their noisy settling to sleep. Recently, all Gibraltarians, Catholics and Moroccans, Indians and Genovese, Maltese and Spanish and ex-pat Brits, swarm like burnt ants in the street. The macaques who have crept down, boldest of the troops, to rob, are amazed at their luck – people keep forgetting to protect a backpack or bag, and so in two seconds the smartest macaques unpack it of crisps and snacks and escape. But why, they think, as they lope back on long flexible limbs to the top of the Rock, are the humans forgetting their obsessions with possessions, and shouting and rushing about?

Posters. Everywhere.

UNIVERSAL POLL. VOTE WITH YOUR FEET! Have your SAY on PARADISE NOW UNDERGROUND DEVELOPMENT!

Wherever there's a poster, people stand and argue. They're right! They're wrong! It's insane! It's essential! Everyone knows about, everyone talks about, the Universal Poll. Nothing will happen, everything will happen. The police will crack down, but the police support it, I know for a fact that the British are behind it. I know for a fact the British will suppress it. Apparently the Chief Minister wants it. Apparently, the Chief Minister will stop it.

Only one thing is certain: if the polling stations open, they'll vote.

79

On the night before the poll, two mariners on HMS *Cutlass II*, the Royal Navy Patrol Boat, had a surprise. The Strait was calm as a sheet of tinfoil. No Spanish infringements in the past week, none expected while talks were in progress, so they were relaxed, having shared a strictly unofficial tot of whisky at eleven.

'Small craft on the radar,' said the officer. Both he and his oppo had started to get sleepy, but instantly both were alert.

'Not expecting anything, are we?' said the other man. 'Fishing boat, it'll be.'

No answer. The officer was staring intently at the plotter. 'Actually there are two. No three. Bloody hell. There are ten, twenty.'

'Declutter – it's just sea clutter, sir – manual up,' said his oppo, who though junior had served ten years longer.

'Can't be. No waves, no rain. Look, it's on calm. I'm still seeing targets. Dozens. Closing … not fast, but fuck of a lot of them!'

'Let's get on deck. Mark One Eyeball!'

In the long night that followed, hundreds of small craft, some little more than rafts, converged on Gibraltar from all over the world, landing at Rosia Bay, Sandy Bay, Catalan Bay. Both the Navy and the Royal Gibraltar Police (who had their own launch, the *Sir Joshua Hassan*) explained afterwards they were 'overwhelmed by the numbers'. An insider claimed that once the Navy realised the first boats they intercepted held neither cocaine nor terrorists, just people coming to vote, there was no attempt to stop them. As for the police, there were rumours that the *Sir Joshua Hassan* began picking people up from flimsy vessels and bringing them over to Gibraltar to join the others. Some even said it did more than one trip to the coast of Morocco, ferrying people across to take part in the Universal Poll.

80

At dawn on polling day, a cleaner, Mrs Julia Gomez, cleaning her bright daughter's classroom at the Loreto Convent School high on the side of Gibraltar early so she could go to the Universal Poll, was looking out of the window as she polished and saw something improbable sailing across the Strait of Gibraltar. Her hand stopped moving, her eyes opened wide. '*Madre de dios!*'

She would have to give up the nightly *Soberano* she had taken to drinking since her daughter hit the difficult part of her teens.

Last night, Ximena had been sobbing and raging about her homework, which involved an essay about the Vikings, who had conquered Sicily but sailed straight past the Rock. 'So why do we have to study them?' she screamed. Then, with an adolescent's stunning unfairness: 'Why don't you know anything about Vikings? Or Phoenicians? Other people's parents do.'

'Other people's parents are teachers or lawyers,' Julia had said. 'Your mother's a cleaner. Don't be a cleaner yourself.'

Which had made Ximena cry and kiss her, and trudge off to bed.

But now, as Julia stared through the freshly-cleaned glass, the sun, which had climbed over the summit of the Rock behind her as she worked, hit something coming across the water, drawing it out of the dark. A boat with a red dragon head and a gleaming row of shields along its sides, and above them, dozens of men rowing – actually rowing – their oars flashing red in the sun, the smooth water rising like fountains of light from their blades. It was something from history, she knew. *Dios mio,* it was the image blue-tacked to the wall in front of her, between the windows.

It was a Viking ship, rowing full tilt towards Gibraltar from the West, and she closed her eyes against the magnificent gold and scarlet glory of her delusion, and prayed.

Still nearly a mile away from their goal, Molo, on the deck of the galley and for only the second time in their journey taking a rest from the oars, having been their *hortator* and captain throughout, called, 'Keep going, men! The Professor would be proud. We'll make it in time for the Poll. I'll guide us in.'

And as they near shore, he raises a heavy pink thing, glistening like a wet rose in the sunlight, mouth of a shell from the other side of the earth, and he blows, he blows, with all the power of his lungs, he raises the conch and he blows: 'Hallooooooooo!'

Awake! Awake, it's time! Awake!

Full-throated, haunting, with all his young heart and spirit, he blows the Professor's conch for the dead and the living, and as the sound echoes around the Rock, the world comes alive.

81

That morning, the whole Rock of Gibraltar seemed to shake and tremble as the sun caught the edges of the waves. The limestone of the Rock, dumb in sleep, was opening into the air, one by one, secret mouths. Unnoticed, unguessed-at caves – two hundred are 'known', but three hundred or more, an infinite number, are there – branching from unnoticed, unguessed at tunnels, not made by humans but thousands-of-years-ago sea wearing notches of tides into the stone, the entrances covered with Jurassic sand-drifts, then five million years ago, as tectonic plates jostled and Africa pressed closer to Europe, raised hundreds of metres up into the air – Gibraltar's most secret caves yielded their creatures that morning, crawling or flying out into the light. Alpine swifts, inky purple Spotless starlings, martins and tiny wrens who used the cave-mouths as roosts swooped out for breakfast as usual, with tiny spiders, some so rare they are still unnamed, scuttling stop-start-cautious below them. But other, stranger movements are afoot, and the pipistrelle bats still straggling in from their night under the stars are beep-beep-beeping and tut-tut-tutting *what's happening?*

Something very big is going on.

Other creatures are emerging. Bigger, heavier, noisier, rubbing at, wrinkling their eyes, their feet drumming on the grass as they start to hurry, hurry to get somewhere.

Tall, broad creatures, half-dressed though they're wearing their best, naked torsos and broad, strong, shoeless feet. Human creatures but different, large-headed, short-limbed, bright-eyed under strong brow-ridges, many red-haired and pale-skinned, some with the marked jaw-lines of Basques or Celts. Some have clean shirts, some patterned trousers.

Not Basques, not Celts. They stay close together as they walk in a line. Some are laughing, others are muttering. Is it a trick? Once they've been seen, can they ever go back?

'We can never go home in any case, if we lose this vote,' says a clever young woman, one of Roosha's cousins. 'So we vote. It's our homes they're destroying. We are Gibraltar. All of us. Actually we are the world. We matter. We vote. We come out.'

And most of Gibraltar's lost people, the Neanderthals, so long mis-named, obscured and traduced, feel alive and triumphant this morning as the light steadies and they march boldly, heavily towards the top of the Rock and start to glimpse others come to join them: other roughly dressed, oddly-dressed, half-dressed people, all shapes and sizes, descended like you and me, reader, from who knows which ancient humans, maybe the 'hobbit people' of Indonesia, maybe Denisovan giants on the steppes, maybe ... or do these names matter at all? Coming across half the world in response to their summons, coming from their boats and rafts on the beaches, all the world's First Peoples, some in smart suits and rope sandals, many talking fast on their mobiles, for even in fairy-tales, someone must tell the media and organise the miracles.

So the Red people are not alone underground any more, they are here with others, they are human, human, one species, as we always were, though lovers of ranks and distinctions slice us into hominin, human, Neanderthal, Sapiens, primitive, modern, richer or poorer, blacker, whiter, redder; standing in the sun, they are here, they are one.

Look, there's a tide now coming from the other direction, coming up from the town via the steep main road where the young men race in their cars to impress their girlfriends, but today the whole width of the road is blocked by walkers, townspeople, smart people, crisp shirts and ties, dresses and t-shirts, young and middle-aged, up early in their eagerness to join the Universal Poll. Last of all come the mythic old, the very last civil rights rebels and survivors from the 1950s and 1960s, some in wheelchairs, some, slow and stiff, supported by others, limping, stopping every few steps to catch deep rasps of breath, but determined, eyes bright, *we'll do it, we did it before*, looking ever upwards. The macaques are around, subdued, puzzled, for when people are walking not driving the macaques can see they are monkeys too, not strange cruel princes. Above the astonishing winding line of human beings stretching along every road that curves up the outside of the mountain, the Rock's ravens cha-aa-ark and chatter and try to mimic the pan pipes of the Colombian Indians, who play as they walk. Semi-naked delegations from half a dozen Uncontacted Tribes in Brazil smile and wave but hang back to avoid infection, while two Batwa from Uganda begin to hunt rabbits because they are hungry, queuing with the others thousands of feet above sea-level on the narrow windy path along the spine of the Rock to vote in a simple body count: pass the Polling Point to one side, it's NO to development: pass to the other, it's YES.

Thronging together, they use little language because all their languages are different. They feel their friendliness, speak with smiles, touch their chests to show that they think with their hearts and live in their bodies as they come together to save the underground homes of the Red people, and also to show, and thus one day maybe save, themselves.

Last of all, hardly able to walk upright after long days and nights of hard rowing, shivering and semi-starving, having slept like the dead for an hour after landing, but now exalted and hopeful, taking up the rear, come the Red people of Ramsgate, there just in time, shattered from rowing all night but coming to the rescue of their home, keeping the Professor's word to his people: and what a welcome, what embraces, what bone-crushing hugs as their families, still dazzled by daylight, see the tired travellers at last and lumber with great cries of welcome towards them.

On the margins, painting the whole in beauty, the butterflies soar up and hover over the people: elegant striped Southern Swallow-tails, eyed Geranium Bronzes, Small Coppers and Holly Blues, Clouded Yellows and orange-blushed Cleopatras, dancing and mating and spinning across towards the pinky-grey promontory of Africa in the distance, and look, a bold, chic red-and black Vanessa lands on a woman's pale hand, and she stops, flattered, and smiles.

But first: should the earth be torn apart?

Vote now. Everyone please, vote now. Vote with your feet, vote with your hearts … Last chance, last chance for the Universal Poll.

82

The result?

The bodies have been counted as they passed along the path, the whole ten-hour sequence has been filmed in case of dispute, but once dark had fallen the footage was checked and the figures recounted, all in the teeth of various officials, in various emergency meetings, declaring that the Poll had no significance: no significance at all. Indeed it told you no more than the Catalan vote of 2017 – did anyone even remember it now? (A rhetorical question, quickly quashed: some people did.) But look where *that* ended up! Had the Catalan vote for independence told the world anything about what the people of Catalonia really wanted, various men sweating in suits loudly demanded? 'Yes,' a stubborn secretary taking notes in the meeting muttered as she tapped, but she was just a woman with a long memory and close family and friends in Catalonia, so no-one listened.

Apparently her boss had heard her, though, because after the meeting he paused briefly by her desk and said, 'Let me see those minutes before they go out.' There was something stubborn in her downcast face that annoyed him, so he insisted, over his shoulder, 'You will learn. Grass-roots movements can never be an instrument for deciding policy.'

'Ah.'

The rumour afoot, based on rough and ready exit polls, was that over 80 percent had voted against the development.

Then it was revised: only 20 percent were against the development.

Paradise Now was on the way, it seemed, the bulldozers and diggers would rumble in after all in October. In the bars downtown, which filled up early, two thirds of the drinkers were in despair. It had been a very long walk up the Rock, in blazing heat, borne up by a conviction of rightness: but all, in the end, for nought.

Or maybe Paradise was already here up above them on the Rock, perhaps all the First Peoples, who had settled in, afterwards, for the day, along with many of the office-workers, who had stayed behind, shedding a neat shirt here and a pair of uncomfortable high heels there, and were making music, dancing and (there was a rumour) at least one or two of them doing other things – a nun claimed, with an innocent smile and a prayer for their forgiveness, that not only the butterflies were mating.

Next morning the flood of incomers had gone, gone like water, leaving virtually no rubbish. Ramsgate's Red people, explorers, navigators, returning heroes, stayed up late to rejoice at surviving their long sea voyage, but now they slept. In the caves and tunnels, home at last, half a hundred people slept after their great adventure, and dreamed.

83

'Did we, actually, dream the whole thing?' the Environment Minister asked the Chief Minister, who had suggested a walk on the Upper Rock before breakfast.

'The *Gibraltar Chronicle* took dozens of pictures,' said the Chief Minister, grinning. 'And look at the headline!'

'I suppose you supplied it?' the Environment Minister said.

'No! I did go for a drink with Brian, though.'

With a flourish, he unfolded the newspaper stuffed in his pocket.

They were two small men, stick figures to Gibraltar's ravens, who had flown over from Europa Point to see what was going on. Though related to Ramsgate's ravens, Roland and the Princess (fifth cousins, twice removed, of Princess Ra, they claimed, though the Princess herself thought it rather more distant), they had not quite believed the messages from Ramsgate: 'The red-headed professor has died. Look out for an ancient ship from the days of the Vikings, the Hugin, named for a raven.' Then the day before they had seen with their own eyes the red and yellow Hugin come surging in, its oars rising and dipping like wings in the sunrise. When the crew disembarked, the red-headed man was not with them, but the young men were carrying something heavy, carefully, reverently, in a long sack.

Now, far below them, the two ant-people, both of whom they knew to be very important in the world of humans, were laughing and clapping each other on the shoulders, as happy as if each had just eaten another bird's egg for breakfast.

Then something even more remarkable. They were grown men, however tiny they looked from above, and not slim, but one had seized the other by the waist, and his friend put a hand on his shoulder, and then they danced: they danced: they danced, though the ravens heard no music, like children.

And the paper blew away, and around the world, and in through thousands of windows, and shivered across the world's internet like an electric pulse of lightning, which might start life, or send it in another direction.

POLL: WHOLE EARTH SAYS NO.

84

Back in Ramsgate, Ramadan Bakri, the Sea Cadet who saw the first Red people naked on Ramsgate Harbour, was missing Sandra Birch, his former girlfriend, and now Molo was gone, she was missing Ramadan, although neither of them wanted to say so.

They felt awkward when they passed each other in the street, and looked in shop windows, or took out a phone, until one day when fate brought them both to the same spot on the baking August quay, Ramadan took his courage in his hands and said, 'Sandra, I know you've seen me.'

'No I didn't,' says Sandra crossly. She's put on a bit of weight, and feels sticky in the heat. Since secretly she still likes Ramadan, she wishes he hadn't seen her.

'I'm sorry,' says Ramadan. 'I am.'

'What for?'

'Dunno, everything,' he says, falling into step beside her, thinking how pretty she is, with her long blonde hair like her mother's, now lying free on her round pale neck and shoulders, which gleam with sweat. 'Whatever I did.'

She walks without protest along the pavement. After a bit she says, 'I did worse. Midsummer night –'

But he doesn't want to hear it, he'd seen her dancing with Molo and guesses what she might say, so interrupts, 'You won't believe what went down that night. But you mustn't ever tell. Not anyone. Not your mum, not your brothers, *no-one*. Right?'

'Promise,' says Sandra, who loves secrets, and best of all, passing them on.

'Also, I think we should get married. I'm going to talk to my mum.'

'What? You joking?'

'Course not.'

'Better ask me first,' she says, but her eyes brighten.

'So a whole crowd of us, Sea Cadets and Red boys, went to look at the Viking Ship 'cos of what Graham said in his speech –'

'But Molo was with me,' Sandra objected.

'We didn't need *him*, did we? … Most of 'em joined in much later … giving us chat about having to go home … it was insane, so we heave the ship off those blocks, all together … bits of it didn't look water-tight, then Graham tells us … caulk it with tarmac and cloth from the, you know, marquee thingies … and we'd done Seamanship at Cadets! We knew about hull integrity, that's making it watertight, to you … it was fantastic, doing it all of us together, it was great! So we got it on our shoulders …'

And the more extraordinary the story became, the more Sandra leaned against him, and looked up into his eyes, and sighed, and breathed, and admired him. He was careful to say a lot about the Sea Cadets, their skills and their strength and how key his own input had been, and to omit all mention of Molo's leading role in the later stages. 'See, it's our mission, Sea Cadets "Empower seafarers", wherever … and you'll never guess what, you know Freddy, he's really good at rowing, he went with them!' In an inspiration, he added, looking in her eyes, 'I wouldn't, though.'

'Why not?'

'Cos for ages I've wanted to get back with you.'

The Red people *were* ungrateful, Ramsgate's older generation decided, around tables outside on the quay in the heat. Though of course the Professor had been a wonderful man, a hero: 'there are always one or two good ones.'

'Really good bloke. And brainy.'

'Have to say he was a hero.'

'Absolute mystery what happened to him.'

'Sea took him, mate. Sea'll take everything in time, my dad used to say.'

'I blame the PBF. Devil-worshippers. Grave-robbers.'

The PBF had lost popularity since Midsummer Day, although Graham had gained it. He was no longer sitting in Wetherspoons in the afternoons; 'writing a history of Ramsgate,' people said.

'Absolute hero, the Professor, is what Joe Birch says, and he should know.'

'No other word for it, mate. Holding up a cave on his shoulders.'

'Professor was a bit of a thinker, as well. Helped my Richard, you know.'

'Pity he had to die then. But some of the others! Filthy habits. We're better off without them.'

'That's harsh.'

'But they weren't like us. They were never, you know, *one of us*.'

'I loved them. They were always round our house, playing music.'

'Where are they now?'

'I told you they'd take advantage.'

'… Now we can be normal again.'

'What's normal?'

'You know. British. Knowing who we are. Each to his own, in the end.'

But somebody whispered, 'Don't you feel – empty?'

'I miss them.'

'They were interesting. They made us special.'

'Leaving like that, though. Leaving us secretly. You know, with nothing.'

Most of them shook their heads and deplored it, but really, the whole town felt sad.

87

July and August were hot and blank. Nothing to feel passionate about or deplore, once we grew bored with deploring the way they'd left us.

No big-boned people playing and calling on the shore, the sun picking out their muscular arms and torsos, running and wrestling like children. No-one making sandcastles, as they had, hunkering down on their strong bare hams. No-one for the dogs to adore. No-one to chase away from the boats on the harbour or walking in long, amiable lines along the quay. And their symbols, the hash-tags of chalk which had bloomed everywhere on promenades, walls, boats, began to fade to white ghosts of spider-webs with the onslaught of wind and rain.

The Public Library was half-empty again. The librarians were saddest of all. They had loved having their beautiful spaces heaving with eager people, loved the Red children's joy in the books, loved helping them read. Now they stuck up a newspaper picture of the Professor on the wall, under a new, beautifully-lettered sign, 'GREAT CITIZENS OF RAMSGATE', next to Sir Moses Montefiore and Lady Janet Wills.

And one of the librarians, a passionate researcher, added a new section to the text under the portrait of Sir Moses Montefiore, an obscure bit of history linking his noble head to the equally noble head of Professor Juan Der Tal, now pinned alongside him.

Way back in the nineteenth century, she had discovered, Sir Moses Montefiore was one of two travellers who carried the first adult 'Neanderthal' skull (a woman's, found in Forbes Quarry, Gibraltar, eight years before the discovery of a similar male skull in Germany's Neander Valley) from obscurity in a dusty drawer in Gibraltar to the British Association for the Advancement of Science in London – too late for Neanderthal Man to be renamed, as he should have been, Gibraltar Woman.

And yes, it's perfectly true, reader. Trust me.

As September came around, then October, the streets away from the centre were too quiet. I missed the way our Red people laughed and made the world larger. Just after sunset, I would walk to the cliff-top and look across the sea, trying to make out Europe in the distance. Could that be France there, those lights? No, just a container ship, covered, mysterious, passing us by.

Till one morning when everything changed.

I had something to celebrate.

88

All inquiries had drawn a blank. People missed the Viking Ship, which *Kent East News* referred to as 'a beloved local landmark', but the signs that it had been half-dragged, half-carried across the Hoverport led nowhere. Only to the end of the concrete ramp, that is, from which long-ago Hovercraft were launched. 'It wasn't sea-worthy. Was it?' people asked, shaking their heads.

All the same, the Red people left the same day that the ship disappeared. And where were they now?

Had they turned up in Gibraltar? A crazy suggestion from Anna Segovia and Pamela Potter. Oddly, Winston passed on the idea to a journalist from *The Times* who came down to Ramsgate asking questions. 'Who were they, really?' the reporter asked. 'Syrians? Iranians? Afghans?'

'Probably Neanderthals,' said Winston, without a smile, but the journalist laughed.

'Very funny.'

'No, really,' said Winston. 'At any rate, their descendants. Look up Neanderthals and Gibraltar.'

Professor Clive Finlayson, Neanderthal expert at the University of Gibraltar and Curator of Gibraltar's National Museum, telephoned by the same journalist, laughed in a different way and said, 'This line of questioning is not really scientific.' Something about the way he said it, though, put the man on the next plane to Gibraltar. There he soon heard gossip that Clive, his wife (the world-famous marine archaeologist and diver, Professor Geraldine Finlayson), their son Stewart and his family were seen on the night after the Universal

Poll making an unusual visit to Gorham's Cave, with torches, heavily loaded. Amar's Bakery said they had ordered a hundred loaves with no explanation.

Holly Palermo was still grieving for the Professor. Neatly folded, left dead centre on her workshop desk, she had found a farewell letter which explained many things, but gave her great pain. 'Why didn't he tell me?' she said to her ravens, who stared, attentive to the new deep tone in her voice. ('Didn't tell me, tell me,' mimicked Roland.) 'I wish he had. It would have made no difference, none,' she continued. 'I loved him so.' The Princess jostled her partner out of the way with a brisk sideways jump. 'Loved him so, loved him so,' she repeated sympathetically. 'You dear birds,' Holly said. 'What would I do without you? And you,' pushing the liver closer to Roland, for it was he who had clasped the message in his great blue-black beak that night, 'you tried to save him. You are my hero.' And the Princess Ra said not a word, though she could have done.

Holly was both glad and sad when she read in *The Times* that Gibraltar's planned excavations for huge new digital servers and the biggest casino in the world, on the brink of going ahead despite the enormous public outcry generated by the Universal Poll, had been stopped after a Neanderthal skull was discovered, complete, with a minor injury, perhaps from violence, the skull of a middle-aged adult male. Preliminary measurements showed his brain size had been enormous, and genetic analysis suggested he had been red-haired.

Her blue eyes filled instantly with tears, but after a few minutes, she started to laugh. 'Professor, I love you,' she said between peals. 'Marvellous. I do, I do.'

The Finlaysons were non-committal in public but smiled in private. Just when it was needed, Gibraltar had a new skull to convince the doubters! The World Heritage Site listing was re-invoked, and the Minister of the Environment made a stern statement which other government ministers quickly supported. All work on the *Paradise Now* complex stopped. 'You don't understand what this means!' the overall manager of the project, furious, shouted at the Chief Minister when they ran into each other on Main Street. 'If popular sentiment and a few dirty old bones are allowed to get in the way of economic growth and development, it's – it's – it's the end of civilisation as we know it!'

The Chief Minister smiled. 'And that's a bad thing?'

Weeks later, an expert from America, working only on photographs and jealous, no doubt, of the find, said Neanderthal morphology was indisputable but dating of the skull 'appeared entirely anomalous'. The Gibraltar National Museum team did not disagree. Two weeks later however, after all the heavy machinery for *Paradise Now* had been taken away, they released a statement saying the dating of the first skull found was indeed anomalous, but irrelevant, as they were now in a position to reveal a cache of hundreds of Neanderthal skulls indisputably dating from 40,000 years ago 'and onwards'.

I had things of my own to celebrate. When I went to buy one of her rings, Holly was delighted for me, and over a glass of wine ('One will do you no harm, my darling, surely?') told me the Gibraltar end of the story. 'My darling Professor would have been so happy, Mary,' she ended.

'Why did he have to die, though?' I said. 'It's cruel.'

'Juan would say everything's part of a pattern. Not until you die is the pattern complete. Sometimes much later.'

'I must be missing something, Holly.'

And so she explained.

89

At long last, in mid-November, when we were all really sick of the heat, it began to get cold again. Some time around then the rumours began.

'What's up?' bellowed Monica, when we met in the street. She had Hecate firmly by the hand.

'I'm fine,' I told her.

'You look fat. Never mind. Better than skinny!'

'Thanks. There's sickness in town, though. Vomiting.'

'I won't catch it, I never get ill. Course, all the kids will barf over me —'

'Yeurchhh,' shouted Hecate, miming repulsion, and her mother cuffed her affectionately, then looked at me in a penetrating way.

' — hmm, weren't you feeling sick, a month or so ago?'

'Yes, but I'm over it now.'

'Hmm,' she said again. 'Kids are great, you should try it some time. Gotta go, Hecate's got a kick-boxing class.'

'I can go on my OWN!' Hecate announced, deafeningly, but Monica held on to her with a wrestler's grip.

'Not till you stop practising on people you meet on the way. Daddy disapproves. Practise on Daddy.'

In the surgery, when I went for my regular appointment, there were a lot of people sitting waiting. Mostly young women, though with my head in a book, as usual, I didn't really take that in till later. In London, life was normal, but in Ramsgate, people started wearing masks again.

Then a curious fact was whispered in my ear at the sports

centre by the physio, who knew everything that happened in the surgery.

'You're not wearing a mask?' I asked him, a little put off.

'No.'

'There's supposed to be another virus about,' I said.

'I wouldn't worry. By the way, you're looking well. Spectacular, in fact.'

'Do you mean I've put on weight?'

'You look radiant.'

'Thanks.'

'Any special reason?' he said. Something in his eyes.

'Not that I'm ready to share just yet.'

'All right, I'll tell you, but it didn't come from me, all right?' He was clearly dying to tell me. 'Go on.'

'Doctor says everyone is pregnant.'

I felt myself blushing. 'What do you mean?'

'All the young women in town.'

'ALL of them? Not literally.'

'Lots of them. Another thing,' the physio added, 'only don't tell anyone this either, all of them have got the same due date.'

My heart was thumping. 'When?'

'March.'

'My God.' A long pause. 'If they're due in spring, they must have got pregnant ...?'

'June,' he said. 'And you are looking very well.'

We stared at each other. Midsummer. The night of the party.

On my way out, freshly showered, my towel flung over my shoulder, my hair still wet, someone hailed me. 'Mary! Is that you?'

'Ella!' She was just going in. 'How are you?'

'Actually, I've never been better. I was going to tell you –

I'm pregnant!'

We stood by the turnstile laughing and hugging like fools till the pressure of the queue behind her made us break apart.

'… and Winston has booked us a holiday in Gibraltar,' she called over her shoulder. 'I thought he'd never take the hint!'

Two days later the local paper had the story. 'Pregnancy epidemic in Redsgate.' Normally no-one bought it, but every copy of this one vanished in seconds. *The Sun* got it next: 'PRAMSGATE!', they bellowed, on page 2.

It wasn't just me then.

So the Reds hadn't gone, entirely. I heard their laughter inside me, but the more virtuous young matrons of the town refuted the rumours with fury.

'I was never out of my husband's sight all that evening.'

'I could never stand those Reds. Animals!'

'It's disgusting what they're saying.'

There were fights between some of the young men, but most people were delighted, particularly those like Ella and Winston, who'd been trying for a long time. The sensible ones just said, 'Wait and see.' And lovely young Sam from the end of our road said, 'So what, in any case? Babies are babies. And we got the jackpot.' After two miscarriages, his wife was expecting twins, he told me, one day on the promenade.

His eyes widened as the wind blew my coat apart. 'You too, Mary?'

'Life going onwards,' I said. 'I'm so happy.'

Sure, there were quarrels, fights, and uncertainty, in our town, and the doctors were all out of appointments – they had to reopen the hospital to cope with expected demand, which was a bonus – but although we were moving into winter as some of us started to expand, although the lifts to the beach were closed and the swifts that dart across the mud-flats at Pegwell had flown far away, life had come back. Young women had taken to walking in twos or threes near the tunnel, even when the tide was high and the waves were shooting up over the promenade and falling like curtains of shattering silver-green glass.

And the ravens hovered above them, watching, waiting. Knowing. They'd seen it all, the comings, the goings, the ebb and flow of invasions.

Ro-aark! Aaark! It was like laughter.

'Babies,' said the Princess.

'Lots of fuss and trouble,' said Roland gruffly, though really, as she knew, he had a soft heart, on and off, and had rebuked a young crow for pecking the eyes out of lambs in the fields near Pegwell. True, having chased it away he summoned the Princess, and after they'd said thank you, a habit she had learned in the Tower where the Keeper and his family said grace, they had a feast. The words were their own, or as near as made no difference: 'They died so we might live.'

March came. Ramsgate's 'Blessing the Sea' ceremony was held early. It was a beautiful afternoon, and although I had only two weeks to go, I thought, 'Yes.' The zigzag path that led down to the beach had a fringe of Erysimum, yellow and purple wild wall-flowers loved by our local bees, and their smell, apricot-sweet, blew on the breeze.

The path ahead of me was crowded with young and not-so-young women, some with their arms around each other, some with toddlers or dogs, all walking down to the sea. All the gulls and bluetits and finches and blackbirds and chattering sparrows in Ramsgate were rehearsing their roosting chorus. This moment will end, I thought. But as we rolled very slowly away from the sun, everything seemed right.

The further I walked down the path, the wider the expanse of water, like woven metal thread.

I walked carefully, heavily down the ramp from the promenade and on to the live sand. It felt like a body, parts of it soft, part bony with stones, parts crunching with long-dead bivalves.

Usually this beach is an almost blank sheet of sand, but today all along the beach there were women. Crowding across in a ragged line, their heads cut out black on the brightness, arms linked. The breeze blew jackets and coats away from a row of water-melon bellies.

In the middle of the pale East Cliff promenade a tight group of dignitaries had gathered – two beauty queens, three priests in their best robes and four mayors of Thanet with their great gilded chains of office, standing up straight like a small dark book of matches flashing fiery gold when struck by the sun. Ramsgate's own mayor, Raushan Ara, re-elected after many years, shone in the light, her dress under the robes like a living orange flame. They were here to thank the sea for bringing St Augustine safe to our shores fifteen hundred years ago; others of us closed our eyes early and silently thanked it for our loves and our friends.

For ten minutes – twenty minutes – more? the upright little group on the promenade intoned their prayers. To the right the dark digit of Deal and Sandwich and Dover marked the end of the bay, but in front of us, the sea blazed. On the horizon, a blur of pink chalk, the French coast, growing pinker now before sunset. *Europe, come back.*

Then a golden-skinned child or five or six clutching a small fierce blaze of flowers appeared from behind the officials and ran the short distance to the edge of the foam, where she bowed her head once, twice, and threw her bunch of red and black anemones on to the bright water. She looked round at us all, then before she skipped back up the beach, made a shy kind of blessing or thank you sign to her gift bobbing out with each brief retreat of the tide, and a great cry or sigh arose from us all, all along the beach, a kind of wordless, communal 'Yes'.

'*Tašakor,*' whispered Arash, her father. And remembering the fish from the sea and the red-haired Professor who'd appeared like an angel before him on the cliff, he said in the language of his boyhood, '*Alhamdulillah.*'

Then the sea caught fire, as the waves reached the steepest part of the sand, and grew bigger, meeting resistance, long rollers of blood. Too bright, so I half-closed my eyes. Something was arrowing towards us, unstoppable, surely, something big –

A boat, human figures shouting with laughter and tiredness, their oars spraying fountains of red and silver, muscular forearms scattering light, light bursting off bright wet scarlet. Was it the fathers, the Viking Ship, soaring back through the sunset?

93

My daughter has many children to play with, on these wide sands. Arrivals, ourselves.

We British, small islanders – Belgians, Romans, Angles, Saxons, Normans, Vikings, Norsemen, Africans, Arabs, Indians, Pakistanis, Caribbeans, Russians, Latvians, Lithuanians, Afghans, Iranians, Syrians – in five or six generations, who will know the difference, or notice?

Fast forward. Fast forward again.

One far away day, the ice will return. The ice-caps will grow, and shrink, and grow again, two white flowers blooming and shrivelling against the blue. Civilisations will fall, but life will go on, as before.

Stretching way back to stromatolites, green on the edge of the sea. Flat carpets of moss, our ancestors. Hidden inside, the first changes, the marriage of strangeness to likeness.

We are alive. One love. Everything that is.

Appendix I
Professor Froy Niemand, 2060

This manuscript, which evidently has fairytale elements, is nevertheless of some scientific interest in the light of Redsgate's preferential rates of survival during the 2035–2040 and 2044–2050 pandemics. A large number of the young people born as a result of the events it narrates proved to be strongly resistant to the novel corona viruses which followed SARS, MERS, Covid-19, PERS, FARS and so on, up to 2060's as yet unnamed respiratory syndrome, either exhibiting no or very mild symptoms and zero fatalities during years when populations in other parts of England, Scotland, Wales and Ireland were severely affected. An initial study in 2020 (H. Zeberg and S. Paabo, *Nature*) suggesting a deleterious effect for Neanderthal genes in infections with Covid-19 was qualified by another in 2021 (PNAS Proceedings) from the same researchers specifying a positive protective effect against severe Covid-19 infections for the haplotype on chromosome 12. The debate continues today.

Contemporary genetic analysis proved that the Redsgate population had fractions of Neanderthal genome as high as 53% or in one case 55%, and it was concluded that some Neanderthal genes did indeed confer immunity to novel corona viruses, as had already been suggested [Stringer, 2010] for influenza. All descendants of the generation who were children during the 2030–2035 pandemic have to date exhibited the same favourable trait. However, this population has strongly resisted attempts by geneticists to isolate specific genes in the genome and transfer it to other infants in utero by gene-splicing, and refused at least one offer believed to be worth several billions from Elon Musk the Third to patent them.

'If you want our genes you'll just have to come and live with us and love us,' the mayor of Redsgate, who said she'd be 'proud to be called a Neanderthal', declared. 'And welcome.'[1]

---

1 Transcript of interview with Rory Nicholas, BBC World Service, 15 June 2059.

Author's Note

You might not guess that this strange fairytale, which in its present form came to me almost as a dream, is inspired by relatively recent scientific research into human origins.

Very long history is always changing as the present throws its wavering light into new corners of deep caves. I still have my childhood *Pictorial Encyclopaedia* (Sampson Low, 1952). It illustrates 'The Advent of Men' with an evolutionary family tree where Neanderthals are on a branch called 'ape-men', some way below two other (clearly separated) branches labelled respectively 'European/Mongoloid' and 'Negroid/Australoid'.

The standard image that shaped my generation's thinking in books, charts and even museums was a simplified 'rising slope' model of evolution, where small hairy creatures raised first their forelimbs, then their foreheads, as they moved towards the right on the page. There *homo sapiens* walked confidently into the future, leaving for dead Neanderthal, Ape, and Monkey. (As recently as 2010, an article about human evolution in the respected *Smithsonian* magazine was still using a version of that graphic.) The Neanderthal, jut-browed, low of forehead and with dangling limbs, was hairier and smaller than the gleaming pale *homo sapiens* – a figure rather like us, the majority British population of the day – who had replaced him. As a skinny British child with round National Health glasses, I was not dissatisfied. It was all of a piece with my contentment when I discovered that most of the world map was coloured pink and that pink meant, once again, 'us'.

But I did grow up. In the 1960s and 1970s, reading about

civil rights struggles and South African Apartheid taught me about injustice. From 1986, when our daughter Rosa was born, I lived in multiracial Brent and became more sharply aware of the blinkers of colour and culture through which humans see each other. The last three novels I wrote there, *The White Family*, *My Cleaner* and *My Driver*, were in part about the tragic and comic consequences of those mis-seeings. Reviewing science books for *The Daily Telegraph* in the 1990s, I was further stirred and shaken by the ideas of Steve Jones (in his books and Reith Lectures) and Marek Kohn (*The Race Gallery*), both showing with wit and logic how scientific attempts to classify different physical racial groups were not only inaccurate but had become overlaid with spurious beliefs that they had different mental abilities.

I do not know exactly when it occurred to me that the graphics of early human evolution I had taken for granted, and the assumptions about 'apemen', Neanderthal and *homo sapiens* underlying it, were another invented hierarchy, another story where the apex of development, the lord of creation, looked suspiciously like 'us'. Could it be that our fondness for classifying and dividing had yet again resulted in mis-seeings? In 2010, the publication of the first Neanderthal genome told us that Neanderthals had interbred with *homo sapiens* and contributed to our DNA. The barriers were breaking down.

So when my husband Nicholas Rankin was commissioned to write a book about Gibraltar, and I discovered to my amazement that the first 'Neanderthal' was not in fact found in Germany's Neander Valley but in Gibraltar's Forbes Quarry, I knew I wanted to write a novel which explored these ideas. In 2014 I was immensely lucky to meet Drs Clive and Geraldine Finlayson – now both Professors – who were working, with their team at the Gibraltar National Museum, on the fossil remains of Neanderthal habitation in the Gorham's Cave Complex, at sea level on the southeast face of the Rock of Gibraltar. (Two years later, in 2016, it became a World Heritage Site.)

Even better, the Finlaysons were accepting and welcoming to an ignorant and endlessly curious stranger. They were ready to share bold and original ideas, some of their long years of knowledge and access to the mysteries of the extraordinary sea-cave via a precipitous path down the cliff face, with a sheer drop on one side. Inside it, revealed only by artificial light, was the matrix of carved lines, intersecting parallels, carefully carved into the rock, which showed that Neanderthals were capable of symbolic thought or elaborate play. Nicknamed the 'Neanderthal hash-tag', this carving appears as a magic graffiti throughout my book.

And I learned. Neanderthal people had survived on earth for 300,000 years or more, far longer than *homo sapiens*. Global cooling around 35–40,000 years ago led to a southward drift in successful Neanderthal breeding populations. Eventually on this southernmost peninsula of Europe a small group may have become isolated. The Neanderthals I started to see in my mind's eye were totally different from the 'primitive man' ideas I had grown up with. The Neanderthals who sometimes lived in Gorham's cave had gathered shellfish, cooked, perhaps made jewellery from shells and used feathers and talons for decoration or clothing. Their brains were if anything larger, not smaller, than ours; they may or may not have had pale skin and red hair; they hunted and had complex relationships with each other and non-human animals.

In the nine years it has taken me to write this book, my idea of the story has changed dramatically. I thought I would set it in deep time and in Gibraltar: but in the end my Red people arrived on the southeast coast of England sometime in the future, very near where Julius Caesar landed in 55 BC. It is from Gibraltar that they have travelled, after thousands of years of preserving their way of life secretly in deep caves and tunnels under the Rock largely unseen (except by painter Francisco Goya, I claim, in the early nineteenth century) as wars were fought over this strategic peninsula by modern humans. At the start of *The Red Children,* first a small advance party of these Neanderthal descendants, then a larger group, decide to come north because of global warming, reversing the drift of their ancestors millennia ago as the climate cooled. In a world of migrations – the world we have always lived in – the heroes of my novel are migrants arriving on our south coast like so many others.

They are, in the end, welcomed. They teach us many new things. And the children they share with us, the 'Red Children' of my title, will become the new us.

Acknowledgements

Thanks to Professor Clive Finlayson and Professor Geraldine Finlayson. Thanks to Bath Spa University, where I teach Creative Writing, for allowing me time to travel for this book and encouraging my research. To the Gibraltarian people who welcomed and surprised us; to the Gibraltar Literary Festival for treating us generously and leaving us with many enduring friendships; to Shireen Cantrell who let us stay in her beautiful waterside flat in Gibraltar; to the Rock Hotel for sunset evenings, and the Caleta Hotel for sunrise mornings. To writers Mark Sanchez and Rebecca Calderon for the laughter, and to Brian Reyes and Alice Mascarenhas at the *Gibraltar Chronicle* for contacts, kindness and support. May more of the world become aware of Gibraltar's rich and complex history and culture and listen to what Gibraltarians themselves are saying.

To Sarah Hosking Hon FRSL and the Hosking Houses Trust for offering me (and many other overburdened writers) weeks of unhampered and idyllic time to write. To John Coldstream, wisest of literary editors, for asking me to review science as well as fiction for the *Daily Telegraph* thirty years ago, where I came across the work of Professor Steve Jones, Dr Marek Kohn and WD Hamilton. To Professor Brian Rotman, who helped with the concept of the maths. The maths problem appearing on pp. 168, 208 and 213 is taken with thanks from the paper set for Round 2 of the tests for the British Mathematical Olympiad, January 2019, by the UK Mathematic's Trust.

To my friends who read early drafts, always so important. Professor Barbara Goodwin; Peter Sheldon Green; Hanife

Melbourne, who read a very early extract; writer and neuro-surgeon Dr Omar Al-Khayatt, who also made a simple suggestion I freely pass on to other writers: get up early and write for several hours before you do anything else – it saved me during lockdown. To writer Amie Ferris-Rotman, founder of *Sahar Speaks*. To Professoressa Selene Genovesi, who lit up lockdown and helped my limping Italian.

To my novelist daughter Rosa Rankin-Gee and Leah Wawro, later-stage readers who kept me up to the mark and up to date, laughing, questioning, encouraging. To Professor Mine Ozyurt Kilic of Social Sciences University, Ankara, for unfailing support. To University College London, Berlin Literaturhaus Climate Fiction Festival, Cappadocia University, Turkey, and the Annual NMLA convention in Pennsylvania USA for their invitations to read extracts from this book and discuss writing about climate change.

To the people of Ramsgate, who have made us as welcome in real life as their fictional counterparts do the Red children in my book. To Polly Gasston, goldsmith and artist, whose great heart and skill inspired my fictional Holly Palermo's. To all my darling friends in this beautiful, historic coastal town and elsewhere, who kept me cheerful, even when we could only shout up and down at each other on lockdown doorsteps or raise glasses on Zoom. To the encouragers: Ivy, Tony and Maureen, Elizabeth, Christabel, POW Thanet. To Sally and the line-dancers. To Lee, Martin and (especially) Steve Cummings who welcomed me to the world of the Sea Cadets. To Shirley Green, Robbie Ross, Annie and Pete Cull and John Ramos, who did not refuse cameo roles in my book.

To Katherine Bright-Holmes, the publishing powerhouse who was brave enough to unleash my character Monica on the world in *Blood* (Fentum, 2019). Monica's back!

To Nicholas Rankin for giving me everything, including hot dinners during lockdown and sensational readings of books by Elizabeth Gaskell, William Thackeray, Anthony Trollope and Catherine Fox, among others.

Lastly, with feeling, thanks to Musa Moris Farhi (1935–2019), our writer friend who introduced me in 2001 to Saqi Books, independent publishers since 1983; to its head, Lynn Gaspard, my publisher, and Elizabeth Briggs, my editor, who have read this story with such sympathy and intelligence. You have given my tale a physical body, so it can go out into the world. Thank you. I stop typing and find my hand is on my heart.